The Master Bedroom

The Master Bedroom

Tessa Hadley

JONATHAN CAPE
LONDON

Published by Jonathan Cape 2007

2 4 6 8 10 9 7 5 3 1

Copyright © Tessa Hadley 2007

Tessa Hadley has asserted her right under the Copyright, Designs
and Patents Act 1988 to be identified as the author of this work

First published in Great Britain in 2007 by
Jonathan Cape
Random House, 20 Vauxhall Bridge Road,
London SW1V 2SA

Random House Australia (Pty) Limited
20 Alfred Street, Milsons Point, Sydney,
New South Wales 2061, Australia

Random House New Zealand Limited
18 Poland Road, Glenfield,
Auckland 10, New Zealand

Random House (Pty) Limited
Isle of Houghton, Corner of Boundary Road & Carse O'Gowrie,
Houghton 2198, South Africa

Random House Publishers India Private Limited
301 World Trade Tower, Hotel Intercontinental Grand Complex,
Barakhamba Lane, New Delhi 110 001, India

The Random House Group Limited Reg. No. 954009
www.randomhouse.co.uk

A CIP catalogue record for this book is available from the British Library

ISBN 9780224078542

Papers used by Random House are natural,
recyclable products made from wood grown in sustainable forests.
The manufacturing processes conform to the environmental
regulations of the country of origin

Typeset by Palimpsest Book Production Limited,
Grangemouth, Stirlingshire

Printed and bound in Great Britain by
CPI Mackays, Chatham ME5 8TD

To Shelagh

One

It was not a sign. Kate refused to let it be a sign.

She hated driving anyway. As soon as she got home, she was going to sell the car; but of course she had needed it to bring all her stuff from London. The back seat was piled up with boxes of books and holdalls stuffed with that miscellany of her possessions which it had seemed impossible to leave behind, so that she couldn't even see out of her rear-view mirror. She always expected when she was driving to die at any moment, and braked and changed lanes with desperate recklessness as if she was gambling; but actually what happened not long after the Brynglas tunnel coming out of Newport wasn't her fault. No one was going very fast. She had meant to time her journey to miss the rush hour, but the minutes and hours of her morning, taken up with dropping off keys, dropping off marked exam scripts at the university, had drifted off evasively as usual. Her life would never fit inside the lucid shapes she planned for it. So here she was in the middle lane in a queue coming out of Newport in dreary winter dusk and rain, shrunken among towering lorries whose wheels fumed with wet, gripping the steering wheel with both hands, longing to smoke but not daring to fumble a cigarette out of her pack on the dashboard. The cat in its basket, strapped into the passenger seat beside her, slunk round in circles with its fur flattened, expressing precisely the mingled unease and ennui that she felt.

Then in the dim light something fell from the sky: at first Kate thought it was a bundle of dirty washing wrapped in a sheet. Even as she took in the catastrophe, the thing bounced against the side of a big container lorry in the slow lane and turned out not to be a bundle that might fly harmlessly apart but a mass flung back by its own weight into the path of a red car ahead of Kate. Which must swerve: what else could it do? The grey formlessness bounced onto the red car's bonnet and then clung blinding across its windscreen, carried forward as the car slewed into the path of the faster traffic in the outside lane; it threw out one long wing, dazzling white feathers ranged in rows of perfect symmetry, lit up by headlights. Then the mess was thrown free onto the road, and swallowed up in the advancing chaos. The red car was hit side-on in the fast lane, and went spinning into the central reservation. Cars waltzed to a halt, finding whatever space. The actual moments of disaster were surprisingly reflective: Kate drove decorously and without fuss into the rear end of a white van, her little Citroën skidded round half a circle and stopped at a right angle across the road. Something hit her then and shoved her forward another few yards. She wasn't hurt, she didn't think she was even jolted. How melodramatic, she thought. What a welcome home. Only the cat wailed an indignant protest.

It was an irony and not a sign.

Astonishingly, no one seemed to be hurt. The woman in the red car climbed out of the driver's seat and walked around it examining the damage. The others moved their vehicles onto the hard shoulder if they could, and waited for the police: Kate's Citroën was badly dented in two places but it started without difficulty. It was unbearable though to sit waiting inside it; Kate left Sim and joined in the improbable sober camaraderie, sharing someone's umbrella. It must have been a swan, everyone thought, brought down by power lines. No one could tell for sure if it was dead already when it hit the first lorry. Or was it only a goose? A swan, confirmed someone who thought they had seen its long neck outstretched. Kate looked where they pointed; the swan was indistinguishable now from the oily dark wet of the road except in its bulk, like a sodden mattress.

The woman from the red car – who had taken on a certain poetic importance, as if the bird had chosen her, and she had escaped it – came and stood among them: a blonde in a white mac that was soon dark with rain. People asked if she was all right and she nodded angrily, staring into the distance as if she was holding back tears and wanted to be left alone. Someone lent her a mobile and she made a call. Then Kate recognised her as a woman she vaguely knew. She couldn't remember her name; she was married to David Roberts, Carol's younger brother. Carol was Kate's best – or at any rate her oldest – friend. Kate had met this woman once or twice a few years ago at Carol's and had thought her a nobody: conventional, a primary school teacher. Now – probably it was the aftershock of the accident and the romance of all their survival distorting her judgement – she thought she could see what might be attractive in the rather raw-boned face and big vulnerable mouth: fiercely shy, as though she might bite if you tried to be kind. You could find that farouche thing sexually interesting; at least for a time. She wasn't the sort of woman who liked Kate, anyway; she would surely take offence at anything she considered intellectual talk. Kate pretended not to know her, thinking she'd probably prefer it. Certainly Kate would.

Kate's mother, Billie, still lived in the same house she had been born in. Kate was born there too; like Billie, in the big master bedroom nobody slept in any more. Billie's father, Sam Lebowicz, who had owned a chain of haberdashery shops in the Welsh valleys, bought the house when he married in 1910; his wife called it Firenze because that was where they had had their honeymoon. It overlooked a boating lake that was the culmination of a long narrow park running up out of the city proper; from the park across the lake you looked into a vista of misty blue and purple hills as if you were at the edge of civilisation, although in fact you could walk round the lake in twenty minutes and the city these days stretched several miles beyond it. Firenze was a gloomy red-brick villa built on a rise beside the lake, with a precipitous front garden whose path wound up in zigzags through a gigantic rockery from the road; there was easier access from a side street. It had a round turret and a long enclosed first-floor veranda, in belated imitation of more lovely Pre-Raphaelite fantasies in the city centre. At the back of Firenze there had once been a broad lawn and shrubberies and beyond those a little wilderness where Kate had had her swing; but Billie had sold off most of this land in the seventies and eighties to developers, and the back windows now overlooked a block of flats and the end house of a small private estate.

Kate had let her London flat and given up her job (or at least taken a year's unpaid leave); she was coming home to look after her mother, who was eighty-three and growing forgetful. Anyway, she was bored with her life teaching in London, she was ready for a change, she didn't want to grow old doing the same thing over and over. She drove in at the gravelled side entrance, turned off the engine, and sat in the silence, letting the howl and roar of the crazy motorway drain away, thinking that at least she would never ever have to drive again. The dents in the Citroën didn't matter; she would just give it away. Expecting Billie to come hurrying down to welcome her, she waited in the car with the door open, smoking the cigarette she had been thirsting for: an intimately known suburban peace sifted down onto her through the dark. The falling rain was blotted up overhead by the tall monkey-puzzle tree or pattered onto the evergreen bushes. Below on the lake an invisible duck blundered splashily. A cold perfume of pines and bitter garden mulch seemed to her like the smell of the past itself. She unfastened the door to Sim's basket and let him come out to claw on her lap and make question marks against her face with his tail. He knew where he was; Kate had always brought him when she came home for weekends. She had only got the car in the first place because it was too complicated to take Sim on the train.

Billie didn't come down. When she had finished her cigarette Kate tucked the cat under her arm and climbed the steps to the front door, which jutted from the side of the house in a long porch with stained-glass windows where once they had grown house plants. She didn't need her key; the door was slightly open, although everything was dark inside. She went through into the hall and put on the light. The hall was wood-panelled and baronial and the one weak light bulb was screwed into a monstrous bronze fitting like an upside-down cauldron with sockets for four, suspended ever since Kate could remember by chains from the ceiling.

—Billie? Kate called. —Where are you? I've come home! I'm home to stay!

She kept Sim under her arm as she looked in all the dark rooms, though he meowed and struggled to go down, kicking with strong back legs. He was a pure black cat with a small hard head that seemed to stand for the particular density of his cat-will.

—Mummy? Where are you?

Hanging on to Sim she climbed up the wide panelled staircase that rose at the back of the hall and was always lit in patches of colour by a street lamp shining through the stained-glass window on the landing: girls balancing water jugs gracefully on their shoulders gossiped around an ancient *shaduf*. Billie had taken recently to sleeping in a different bedroom every night, although she never slept now in the big front one, and she swore that she didn't sleep in Kate's. Kate found her in a little room at the back where they used to store the spare chairs which Billie put out downstairs when she gave one of her concerts. The bed was made up correctly with striped sheets and a pillowcase and blankets, but Billie lay on top under one of the ancient dirty silk eider-downs they hadn't used for years. She was sleeping absolutely tranquilly, not as if she had paused for an afternoon nap but as if it was bedtime; she was in her nightdress, even though it was only six o'clock in the evening, a glass of water and her pot of face cream on the bedside table. Yet Kate had telephoned at lunchtime before she left to remind Billie she was coming. She had expected tea when she arrived, or at least the gas fire and the television on.

She let Sim go and sat for a while with her mother in the dim light from the landing, feeling the cold rise up numbingly through her feet and legs even though she was still wrapped in her thick black-and-white check winter coat. Billie slept like an angel. That was just what Kate thought she looked like, lying there: an old angel, with her pink skin so fine that the perfect shape of her skull showed through, her deep melancholy eye-cavities, the nose that leaped in its lean strong arc from her face (Kate had inherited the nose). Her snow-white hair spread across the pillow, unbound from the neat French pleat she could still make in a few quick motions of her hands; perhaps she would remember how to do that when she had forgotten everything else. She always slept on her back, like nobody else Kate had ever known, like a child; her mouth had sunk open and she dribbled and snored lightly. She didn't have much of a chin; angels might not. Kate was overwhelmed with doubt, finding herself temporarily alone in her new life. She quite liked the idea of tying on an apron and putting everything to rights, making this a home again, cooking little nourishing dishes for her mother, tending new house plants in the porch. But she couldn't genuinely imagine it. She didn't have much of a track record for domesticity. Closing Billie's door behind her and treading quietly so as not to wake her, she went back down into the hall and picked up the phone. It was the same old fat brown dial-phone they had had in the 1970s, before Kate left home to go to university.

—Max? she said.

She really shouldn't be phoning Max. For four years Max had been desperate with love for Kate; when he finally understood that he couldn't possess with certainty even enough of her to preserve his dignity, he had saved himself and found a sweet girl instead to have babies with. All this change was new enough for the babies not to exist yet except as an idea; and Kate hadn't been good at learning to adapt.

—Katie, this really isn't a good time, Max said.

His soft American voice that had sometimes made her sick – too compliant, too delighted – seemed to Kate at that moment to promise everything desirably metropolitan: good wine in big glasses, deep designer sofas, conversations about articles in the *London Review of Books*, expensive gadgets from the right shops.

—I've made a terrible mistake.

—I warned you. Where are you?

—I'm here, I'm home. She's forgotten I was coming, she's just gone to bed, she's fast asleep, she's lost all sense of day and night. Max, what will happen to me if I stay here? You know me; I have enough trouble myself, keeping night apart from day. And she'd left the front door wide open. I'm just going to turn round and head straight back. She'll never even know I've been here, will she? She probably won't even know that I promised to come. Do you think they'll give me my job back at the Department?

—Aren't the tenants moving into your flat tomorrow?

—I'll call for the keys first thing in the morning. I'll compensate them. I'll make a scene. I'll tell them Billie's dead.

—Katie, you can't do that.

She could tell from the way he measured his voice that Sherie was in the room with him; or listening from the kitchen, where she would be cooking up some supper out of the River Cafe recipe book. Max wouldn't ever

9

pretend that he wasn't talking to Kate; but he would want to express at the same time to Sherie his regret, his reservation.

Kate banged the phone down, scornful that he had been so easily trammelled. Trammelled was a word, wasn't it? It ought to be.

She hadn't even told him about the swan.

She studied the hall. It was at least clean, as far as she could see in the weak light; that meant someone from Buckets and Mops was coming in three times a week as arranged. Perhaps the Buckets and Mops lady had made up all the beds, too, for Billie to sleep in. As yet the only sign of Kate's arrival in the house, apart from Sim, was her handbag, which she had put down on the oak chest before she went upstairs: very soft dark brown leather, roomy, Italian, with a tortoiseshell clasp. She felt tenderness towards her sophisticated professional self, who had known how to choose such a fine unconventional bag, how to carry it off strikingly. That self surely couldn't come back and live in this crazy place, this nowhere. Wales, for God's sake. At that moment Sim stalked out from the passage to the kitchen. She scooped him up and snatched the bag and shut the front door behind her and forced Sim back into his travelling basket; he spat in his outrage, and cursed her in cat language. Then she lit another cigarette, climbed into the driving seat and smoked it.

But she could never really have driven all the way back to London. She couldn't have faced the nightmare of traffic again. Also, there was nothing to go back to.

Anyway, now she'd seen her sleeping, she couldn't quite bear to think of Billie waking up alone, to an empty house.

David knew something was wrong as soon as he saw Suzie. He had noticed as he parked on the drive that her car was missing, but he'd only thought she must be running Hannah to ballet class, or to a sleepover, or taking Joel swimming; he didn't always remember the busy running-order of the children's arrangements. He was late, he had left a message on the phone to say he was staying on in the office to finish a paper for a Health Protection Conference the next day. Through the lit window as he came round the side of the house he could see his family in the kitchen eating pizza, and it did occur to him then that it was late for them to be having supper. They didn't see him, in the dark outside. They lived in a raw new estate at the growing tip of the city where it met the motorway that circled the periphery; beyond them there was only a golf course, and then the grounds of an old house which were open to the public, and then fields. David paused before he opened the back door, enjoying being alone in the humming dark that was always nervous with the noise from the motorway: not a roar, but a thin murmur of movement and speed that somehow sucked substance and permanence from everything it reached. David didn't mind this, he even felt it as a kind of lightness.

—Where've you left the car? he asked while he wiped his feet on the doormat.

11

Suzie was putting something in the microwave, she didn't turn round.

—Smashed up, said Hannah relishingly. She was standing up at the table to eat her pizza, and had a piece of tomato on her chin. She liked crisis. Joel, who didn't, sat absorbed in some game with his Beanie Babies.

—You're joking.

—I was involved in an accident, said Suzie calmly. — On my way home from the in-service day at the Gwent teachers' centre. But I'm all right. The car in front of me hit a lorry pulling out. No one was hurt, amazingly enough. But the car's a write-off.

—Good God, said David. —Why didn't you call me?

Suzie shrugged. —I was OK. There was no need.

But he knew as she turned round that she wasn't OK. Usually Suzie was sturdy and steady; she had a wholesome closed muzzle of a face that made him think of a fox, with its sandy colouring and the fine fair down that showed in a certain light. She was tall and lean and big-boned, her broad shoulders set defiantly against challenge; only now something was jangled loose in her as if she'd touched a live wire, and her hair had dried in a dark mat that clung to her head. It frightened him to see her blue eyes startled open.

—Actually, Suzie said, busy cutting up Joel's pizza, —I called Giulia.

Giulia was Suzie's headmistress at Ladysmith School, and her friend.

—It was easier for her to come out from the school and bring me home, once I'd given my statement to the

12

police. Then she insisted on taking me for a check-up at the hospital. Jamie was picking the kids up anyway, because I'd thought I might be late. And I was fine, they said. Just a bit shaken up.

—I wish you'd called me.

She tried to smile at him. When she put Joel's plate down on the table he saw that her hands were shaking.

—Never mind, she said. —It doesn't matter now.

David made her describe to him exactly where the accident took place; he wanted to understand why this lorry had pulled out so carelessly, so outrageously into the traffic. Suzie couldn't remember things precisely. She said it had all happened very fast. He imagined the chaos, the rain, the scorch of horror that had brushed close.

—Where's Jamie? he said angrily. —Why isn't he helping?

Jamie was David's seventeen-year-old son from his first marriage.

—Call him. Ask him if he wants pizza.

—You shouldn't be standing here doing all this. Why don't you go and lie down? I'll take over. I'll bring you a cup of tea, or a drink.

—I'd rather be busy, really.

Jamie was in his bedroom in the attic space. He lay on his back on the bed, smoking, and he didn't even turn his head as David lifted the trapdoor and climbed through; the room was thick with the rank smell of dope. A familiar sensation of impotence seized David; he didn't know how to talk to this boy, or how to know what his thoughts were, or how to forbid what ought to be

13

forbidden him. Jamie didn't rage or fight, he simply ignored whatever they told him: don't pull the ladders up into the attic after you, don't smoke, don't smoke in the house, don't stay out at night without letting us know where you are. When they tried to be outraged he smiled as though he was embarrassed for them. David opened the skylight to let out the smell.

—Suzie asks, do you want pizza?

—Is she OK now? Jamie said. —I'm sorry about the swan.

—What swan?

—Hasn't she told you? The one that came down on her car.

—On her car? What are you talking about?

He thought the boy might be befuddled with dope.

Jamie sat up on his elbow. He was wearing some sort of torn vest; he shook back the thick copper-brown hair that he chopped off with scissors himself at shoulder-length. Something in the wide face, with its faint adolescent rash over the thickening cheekbones, distinctive thick creases under the eyes, and black brows like quick pencil strokes, stirred and pained David, who was not used to thinking of men as beautiful; the boy was like his mother (which was not reassuring). Jamie's brown feet at the end of the bed were bare and huge, with dirty soles and coarse sinewy knobbled toes; they had transformed out of soft child-feet in some instant while David wasn't looking.

—A swan came down and hit her car, made her swerve into the fast lane.

14

—She didn't tell me it was a swan. Perhaps she didn't want to upset the children.

—It must have hit power lines. Then it bounced against the side of a lorry and onto the bonnet of her car.

The picture was vivid to David for a moment: melodramatic, not Suzie's kind of thing at all. —Knowing what Hannah's like, he said. —She'd be more upset about a swan than if people had been hurt.

—They rang home from the hospital. Giulia was with her.

David was flooded with irritation again. Sometimes recently when he and Suzie disagreed – over whether they should consider sending Hannah to Howells, the private girls' school, for instance – Suzie quoted at him Giulia's opinions, Giulia's wisdom; she didn't know she was doing it, or that he minded. Giulia was against private education, she involved herself headlong in all the ragbag of social problems the pupils at her school presented, she paid out of her own pocket the taxi fare for a family of Roma children who travelled to the school every day from across the city. David liked her but he thought she acted impulsively, with a dangerous idealism. Sometimes when he came home he found the house empty and all of them round at Giulia's. Or Giulia and Suzie would be sitting drinking wine at his kitchen table, talking animatedly and rashly, the way women did, so that he felt shut out from their fun.

The children reacted in the aftermath of the accident. Hannah thumped through her keyboard practice with hot cheeks and swelled with surplus emotion, weeping extravagantly when Suzie told her off for tickling Joel, who hated it. Joel lay mute and still in his bath, then shivered in his Spiderman pyjamas and refused to get into bed, because he caught sight of the moon through his bedroom window. He had been afraid of the moon when he was a baby. When David came downstairs after reading their stories he found Suzie standing in the kitchen over a sink full of winter branches she had cut in the garden to take into school for her January table: bedraggled yellow jasmine and gnarled apple tree and silver birch thickening and reddening already with buds. Her hair was wet again and she seemed to give out into the centrally heated air the cold breath of the rain-soaked garden. She pretended to be busy, tying up the branches with twine. Her hands were big and unbeautiful: skilled at cutting out with infant scissors, tying laces, rubbing magic cream into grazed knees.

—You shouldn't be going into school tomorrow.

—I want to, she said heavily without looking at him. —I'm really all right.

—I'll give you a lift in, then.

—There's no need. Menna's picking me up. The new teacher, covering our maternity leave.

He expected her to tell him then what had really happened on the motorway, but she didn't speak. They went to bed after David had watched *Newsnight*; he lay trying to pick up the threads in the article on veterinary medicine he was supposed to be reading, listening to where water was sluicing noisily somewhere outside from

16

a gutter blocked with leaves. Suzie was sorting piles of clean washing and putting them away. She was tidy and house-proud: the children had clean clothes every day, the airing cupboard was piled high with ironed sheets and towels. Even though the house when they bought it four years ago had been newly decorated, Suzie had redone every room since then. Her little touches were everywhere: curtain tie-backs, friezes pasted on the wallpaper, bowls of potpourri, carved acorn light-pulls, dishes of glass pebbles, thriving house plants. The children's toys were tidied away each evening into labelled storage boxes. The only place Suzie hadn't reached was Jamie's attic: Jamie had said calmly once that he would leave home if ever she touched anything in there, and Suzie had agreed that if he wanted to live in a pit then who was she to interfere. All the transactions between these two had used to flare with violence, even though Suzie had looked after Jamie since he was small: things had been better recently. So the attic was bare and painted white without rugs or a blind on the skylight, and Jamie stacked his books in piles against the walls and kept his clothes in heaps and slept in dirty sheets he changed himself every few months.

Suzie finished putting things away and began to undress for her shower; she fumbled out of her clothes with her shoulder blades hunched as if she was uncomfortably aware of being watched. Usually she was blithely indifferent; the readiness with which she stripped had shocked him when they first slept together.

—Why didn't you tell me about the swan? he asked,

looking at her over the top of his reading glasses while she was smothered inside her T-shirt. When she pulled off the shirt, her hair still stiff with rain stuck up in a ruff around her face, as if she was roused against him.

—How did you know?

—You told Jamie.

—Did I? I don't remember.

She sat down in her underwear on the end of the bed, hugging her arms around her chest, her long back bent, her near-nakedness private as a child's.

—I'm sorry, he said. —I don't mean to make you talk about it if it upsets you. All that matters is that you're not hurt.

—You won't like it, Suzie said.

—What won't I like?

—What I felt I saw.

—Tell me. How could I mind?

She lifted her eyes; her face was cloudy with the effort of thought.

—When this thing came hurtling down out of the sky at me I thought it was Francesca.

—Oh, for God's sake.

Francesca was David's first wife, Jamie's mother; Suzie had never known her. She had killed herself by jumping out of a window when Jamie was three, after leaving David and going to live on the ninth floor in a high-rise council block.

—I hadn't been thinking about her. I never think about her. Then: thump, on my bonnet. Intuitively I just knew, it was her.

—That's ridiculous.

—You see: I knew you'd hate it.

David took off his reading glasses and folded them. —I don't feel anything about it except that it doesn't mean anything. The mind throws up all kinds of rubbish when you're in shock.

—She wasn't rubbish.

He was patient, turning his eyes away. —I didn't mean her, needless to say. I just meant, your making any kind of association between that and what happened to you today.

—We never talk about her.

He shrugged. —Why would we? What could there be to say, after all this time?

—You can't imagine the force of the blow when it hit me, how heavily it fell: the whole car leaped, it leaped. Surely too heavy for a swan. And then everything went dark. I hadn't time to think of any rational explanation.

—But now you know what the rational explanation was.

—Yes, I suppose so.

Irritation squeezed David like a fist: he had chosen Suzie just because she was sensible.

—You know so, he said absolutely.

—Yes. Suzie stood up, to go into the bathroom and take her shower.

—Did you talk about any of this stuff to Giulia?

She shook her head. —No, not to anyone.

And then, when she had showered and they had put out the bedside lights, Suzie fell easily asleep in spite of

19

everything: on her side with her back to him and her knees drawn up, breathing lightly through her nose, radiating clean heat scented with whatever shampoo she'd used. David lay aridly awake. Long afterwards he heard Jamie dropping down from his trapdoor like a cat, prowling the house, helping himself to food in the kitchen, letting himself out at the front door with his bike; he cycled for hours at night and then slept half the day, probably missing classes at college. David tried to imagine how it would feel, to sleep and wake when you wanted to, to choose your life without thinking of anybody else, not to be broken in to the hard frame of adult necessity.

David and Suzie had first met in Regent's Park. Neither of them had ever been there before or after that day, so it remained a bright free space in their imagination: sunlit stately walks, vistas down aisles of tall flowers, fountains splashing. David, who was working at that time at Guy's, had had a free morning: he was wheeling Jamie in his pushchair. Suzie was in the second year of her teacher training at Goldsmiths, she was skipping lectures. Jamie was really too old for the pushchair, but he refused to walk anywhere: he would sit in it with his knees up almost to his chin, leaning keenly forward, weaving his old rag of yellow blanket into its ritual knot between his fingers, sucking its corner wrapped around his thumb, frowning out at the world from behind its safety. That morning in the park he hurt himself – probably he trailed his foot and David ran over it, that was always happening.

Suzie was a tall fair girl in a sleeveless flowered dress, passing: David had only resented at first that she was witness to his shame, his helplessness, the screaming child. That year after Francesca's death was the worst year of his life.

Suzie was eating an ice cream. She hesitated and looked at Jamie.

—Would he like some?

David had lifted him out of the pushchair and put him on a park bench to look at his foot (which was only bruised); Suzie sat down on the bench and held the ice-cream cone tentatively out.

—If you want it, she said, —you have to stop crying and come onto my knee.

Jamie had looked at her suspiciously, but then to David's surprise climbed onto her lap; he wasn't a child who cuddled easily, but he allowed himself to be hugged against her chest in return for licks of ice cream; his sobs subsided. Suzie's freckled arms around him were awkward as if she wasn't used to little children.

—I'm afraid he'll make you sticky.

—I don't care. This is only an old thing.

When David said then that her dress was pretty he was only politely anxious for it, he didn't take much notice of women's clothes; but Suzie misinterpreted. She'd only stopped in the first place, she told him after-wards, because she thought he was attractive.

—Where's his mum? she asked, appraising David frankly.

That little scene, the child calmed and surrendered on

her lap, hadn't really been at all representative of what was to follow. Suzie had found mothering Jamie fraught and difficult, Jamie had not easily allowed her close. But in that decisive hour, Suzie's uncomplicated openness had seemed to David like a door out of the dark maze of his troubles.

Two

Carol Roberts called one morning to see how Kate was getting on. She and Kate had been to school together, and then to University College London; that was all long ago. Out of the gang that had been friends together then, perhaps Carol had changed least: she was still shy in personal relations, brusque, graceless, generous; she still had her coarse straw-yellow curls, although they were darkening and silvering, which suited her strong square physique and red complexion better. Carol had been working back in Wales for years, for one of the big housing associations, of which she was now the Director. She would be borrowing the time to see Kate out of her unimaginably busy life, in which she was no doubt resourceful and formidable, and about which she never complained, though occasionally she groaned and lay flat on her back on the floor with sheer weariness, or told hooting outraged stories about Assembly Members, or pleaded for huge slugs of gin in her tonic.

She parked her car by the lake, then walked up the steep zigzag path through the rockery as she always did, for old times' sake, because once she and Kate had played here, pretending to be in the French Resistance, or revolutionaries escaping from the state police. They had not made friends until they were thirteen or fourteen, but Kate was a fantasist, prolonging imaginary games long after they were supposed be left behind. At the top of the zigzag she peered through windows into the empty dining room, then pushed round the side of the house through the overgrown laurels and escallonia, waiting at the front door without ringing the bell; music floated from indoors. Carol was practical but also afflicted with strong sentiment. A violin and a piano were playing something nineteenth century, written to be haunting in its sweet slightness, and to suggest the lost past. Carol had been coming to this house for ever. These last few years Kate had come home often for weekends, and when she did Carol had always visited; she had visited when Billie was alone here, too, insisting that she didn't do it out of kindness but because she genuinely liked her friend's mother. She said she thought of Billie as a character out of the sort of novel she wasn't subtle enough to read (Carol had done Sociology at university; Kate had done Slavic Languages). Kate said the novel was getting to be *Finnegans Wake*.

—God, you're in tears, Kate exclaimed when she opened the door; the music had finished and Carol had pressed the bell, which chimed rustily a long way off (for the attention of the maids there hadn't been for fifty years).

—Aren't I an idiot? Carol said. —It was hearing you play.

—Were we that bad? Billie, do you hear? We were so awful we made Carol cry. You look smart: I suppose those are your work clothes. I'm rather in awe of you in a suit. There's a touch of alderman about it on you, you know. Or dowager. Dowager alderman.

—Are you all right? Is it really the truth that you've given up your job and let your flat? Max phoned me.

—I'll tell you what: I'm almost crying with cold. The central heating's playing up and the man says naturally that we need a new boiler, and I refuse to believe there isn't something he could do to fix this one. So we're at an impasse. Keep your coat on, I would.

Billie was sitting at the baby grand in the drawing room at the back of the house, in a dress patterned with blue cornflowers and a white cardigan. The gas fire was turned up high and the room seemed impossibly hot to Carol.

—Mummy; it's Carol.

—Oh, how nice, said Billie, smiling serenely, turning round from the piano with her hands still poised over the notes; her pink skin hadn't wrinkled but had turned matte and soft with age. She had taught piano to Carol once long ago and very little of it had stayed except that the hands above the keys must be shaped as though holding oranges. —Dear Carol. It's such a long time since we've seen Carol. Isn't it?

Carol kissed Billie, peeled off her mac and her jacket. Her face flared up with heat; she resigned herself to feeling,

25

in the presence of these two diminutive tiny-boned women, as she always had, as if she was made of some coarser grade of flesh than theirs; Kate's face with its shadowed sculpted hollows and long Nefertiti eyes seemed finely complicated where Carol's was straightforward. Kate was dressed in her usual bemusing layers, maroon and green and cream, suggesting the kind of London shops Carol wouldn't dare go into, although she wasn't afraid of any other kind of authority; the cuffs of Kate's black lacy cardigan were pulled over her hands as if she was cold and the tip of her nose was red. Carol dropped onto the chair that was as far from the fire as possible; the panes of the French windows that ran the length of the room were actually steaming up. The winter-dead wisteria that fell like a curtain from the roof of the open veranda at the back of the house blocked out the light, so that they needed the lamps switched on in the middle of the day.

—We're only playing to keep warm, said Kate. —We have to go out soon. Buckets and Mops are coming and if we're lazing around the place doing nothing while they clean our lavatories and wash our floors it might foment revolutionary discontent. We walk in the park and then we drive down to have coffee and do our shopping. I swore I wouldn't ever drive after I came home, so Billie does it for me, it's a treat for her. And when we come back our lavatories are clean, and B and M have taken their money and left us enigmatic little notes. Don't you think it's the life?

—Billie's never passed a test. Does she have a licence? Billie, you mustn't let Kate make you drive.

—Darling, it's easy-peasy, Billie reassured her. —It's great fun. We don't go on any big roads.

—Carol has to fuss. There's a tradition of public service in her family. Don't take any notice. Shall we play it again? Only you're not to criticise. We're both very rusty. Or to cry. That's just as off-putting.

Carol gave herself up to admiration. Her own fingers in the old days of holding oranges over the piano had only ever seemed, for all Billie's patience, too thick and too fumbling. Kate, swaying in time, with her violin tucked under her chin at the music stand, her thick bob of black hair thrown back, was a figure of romantic higher discipline and finer sensibility. And Billie showed no signs yet of forgetting how to play. Carol herself had said to Kate that it must be good for her mother to keep practising the skills she had, stretching to her capacity. The music moved Carol deeply but she didn't discriminate, couldn't remember a tune the minute after it was over, couldn't tell Haydn from Schubert or Mahler from Debussy. In weak moments when she was alone she was likely to find herself humming some awful scrap of a pop song as if it meant everything to her.

When they had finished – glamorous the flourish of accomplishment with which musicians re-entered the lesser atmosphere – Kate took Carol upstairs, to talk to her while she put on her coat.

—Do your wee-wee, Mummy, she called over her shoulder on the way up. —Otherwise you're bound to need one while we're out.

Billie cheerfully agreed.

27

Kate's bedroom was the same long one she had had always; at one end a little panelled bay with a window seat hung over the back garden, and diamond-paned casement windows suggested captive maidens looking out for rescue. The room had last been decorated when Kate was a domineering teenager given a free hand, so the walls were faded purple, scarred with Blu Tak and the shapes of old posters: all around the room, above the picture rail, the ghosts of a nursery frieze showed through the paint, the Pied Piper and Rumpelstiltskin and princes slashing through thickets of thorn. Now it was newly crowded with Kate's accumulations brought from London: books spilling out of the bookshelves and piled against the wall, clothes hanging from the knobs of the wardrobe and on the back of the door, her computer not set up yet on the big ink-stained desk where she had once worked for her A levels, a vast brightly coloured Chinese paper kite, a steel standard lamp with white glass globes. Framed prints from a Paula Rego exhibition and of Kertesz photographs and a Rachel Whiteread house were propped against a wall along with other art Carol recognised from the London flat.

—I'm trying to introduce elements of the twenty-first century, Kate said, —but this house chews up my postmodernisms and spits them out as Burne-Jones and Dante Gabriel Rossetti.

—This isn't half of your stuff. What have you done with it? You haven't just left it for your tenants to destroy?

Putting on red lipstick at the long cheval glass, Kate

blotted her lips together and shook her head. —I loaded everything I could into the car, put the rest in the small spare room, and locked it.

—When we rented that house in Kilburn in our third year, we broke into the locked room. We read their letters and went through their things and invented lives for them and wore their clothes.

—We were awful. I'd never have let my flat to anyone like us. I asked for very boring; judging by our one short meeting, I think I got it.

—What are you going to do all day here? How will you stand it? Have you got a project, something you're working on?

—A project. What an uncharming idea. You sound like my Head of Department. Kate changed her shoes, swapping high heels for very high ones, square-toed, black and green with green leather bows, chosen from jumbled rows of astonishing shoes inside a cupboard. —By the way, I hate your conspiracy with Max. Don't you dare talk to him about me.

Carol took no notice. —This is going to be very hard work, you know. Billie's going to get worse.

—Don't lecture me. There's money. I'll pay for help.

—And you should have stuck with Max. He's such a lovely chap.

—As if you didn't understand that that's precisely why I haven't 'stuck with him'. Stuck with him! Weren't you a feminist once?

—But now you're sorry. Don't try to pretend to me that you're not sometimes panicky, having burned your boats: and all of them. Not only Max, now. The job and the flat and London.

Kate wrapped herself in her big black-and-white coat, which went on like a cape, fastening with huge black buttons diagonally. —It's quite a conflagration, my boats.

—Don't be clever. It's not a metaphor. You talked about having children with him at one point.

—That was rubbish. I was off my head.

—Soon it will be too late.

—Good God, Carol. Are you actually broody on my behalf? How indecent! Have your own bloody babies. Soon it will be too late for you, too.

—Oh, I'm an old workhorse. I'll die in harness.

—Even workhorses have reproductive parts, you know. While we're belabouring these figures of speech.

Carol lay down abruptly on her back on Kate's bed in her smart suit that was already wrinkled; her feet in their flat brown shoes stuck out over the end. The Habitat silky bronze bedcover was double-bed sized; its excess tumbled across the floor.

—And now you're sulking. Kate frowned down at her.

—Truly I'm not. I just suddenly thought how delicious it would be to close my eyes. I'll only be a moment.

Kate moved round the room as quietly as she could in those shoes, picking up her bag, finding her keys, spraying perfume. Carol had always been able to do this. She had fallen asleep often at school, once lying along the wooden lockers where they kept their gym kit; she had slept in a train luggage rack when they were Inter-railing; she had gone out at Kate's dinner parties, or beside her in the theatre. She would only be absent for a few minutes; then her rather pale blue eyes would pop wide open again, and behind them immediately whatever was vigilant and responsible would resume its watch. Freezing even in her thick coat, Kate picked up a corner of the silky bedcover and dropped it tenderly across her friend.

David walked down from where he worked for the Department of Public Health, in Cathays Park, to the Millennium Centre in the Bay; the evening's cold was iron hard, moonless and still. Muffled in his camel over-coat and scarf, he strode out in a tension that was partly protective of his core of heat and partly excited expec-tation of the music he was going to hear: the WNO were doing Handel's *Jephtha*. He only knew it from record-ings; he was looking forward with a leap of pleasure to hearing it in the dignity of live performance. White lights were strung in the tracery of winter trees in front of the museum with its pillared portico; the pale mass of build-ings in the civic centre – museum, law courts, univer-sity, the Welsh Office, the central police station – was the only place that ever made him feel in the least colonised, because he thought that the old administra-tive buildings in Delhi or Ottawa must look like these did at night, dreaming in melancholy hauteur. Beside the long road that linked the city centre and the Bay, not meant for pedestrians, black water winked in Alexandra Dock, so that the city seemed suddenly afloat on a black sea, unmoored from its daytime self. He didn't care what people thought about the new Millennium Centre in the

Bay, all the arguments about its architecture, its curved armadillo-back; he knew he was rather easily impressed visually, not caring enough, impatient to get to what was inside. He imagined his love of music sometimes as caverns underground in him, immense and studded with crystal and inaccessible from the surface.

Suzie was meeting him in the foyer; she was bringing her car – the new one they'd had to buy after her accident – so they could drive back together. He always bought two tickets for the opera or for concerts, but usually he took his mother or his sister; Suzie had never wanted to come before. He stopped inside the doors to look for her in the current of sociability, people coming in from the cold, leaving their things at the cloakroom, buying programmes; he saw her with her back turned, looking for him, her rough honey-blonde hair caught inside the collar of her black coat, her hands pushed down – out of nervousness he guessed, knowing her – into its pockets. When she felt out of place she stood with her shoulders hunched and awkward, and her head tilted defiantly; she challenged the crowd who took no notice of her, flowing around where she waited, or only sending in her direction the ordinary interested glances because she was young and attractive. Catching sight of her, he remembered to wonder why, after all the years of her being cheerfully not in the least interested in his music, Suzie had wanted to come to this. There had been a little distance between them, these past few weeks; perhaps this was her gesture of conciliation.

When he touched her arm from behind Suzie turned

on him in relief and accusation. —It lasts three hours, she exclaimed. —I overheard someone saying so. You didn't warn me.

—You didn't ask.

He kissed her cheek; she had put on make-up, pink stuff on her skin, and perfume.

—This really isn't my kind of thing.

—You haven't heard it yet!

—I mean all this, she said, looking around her, smiling edgily.

David tried to see what Suzie saw in the opera crowd. It was surely all innocently pleasantly provincial enough, the noisy greetings and the stuffy dressing-up; it was hardly Covent Garden. There were funny old wrinkled couples with bags of sweets, and students from the Welsh College of Music and Drama. But Suzie took offence easily, if she ever imagined she scented pretension.

—Let's put our coats in the cloakroom. Then we can go and order drinks for the intervals.

—Three hours! Suzie said. —I'm going to need a drink.

—I'm glad you came, he said encouragingly, in the queue for programmes. —I'm sure you'll enjoy it.

—I thought I ought to see what you got up to. If it's so marvellous.

—It is marvellous.

—I've never been to an opera in my life.

—Strictly speaking, of course, this isn't one. It's an oratorio.

—And what's that when it's at home?

33

All day long David had been aware of Handel waiting for him at the end of it, spacious, public, subtle music; now he began to fear that anxiety over Suzie was going to distract him from his precious opportunity. When they had ordered their drinks for the interval, they stood over a first gin in the bar, behind one of the giant letters cut out of the facade that curved like a ship's prow, spelling on the outside in Welsh and English some lines of poetry he couldn't remember. She was wearing her white trouser suit and a silky blue top; searching for something to talk about, they resorted to the children, rehearsing the parts of a cheerfully married couple for the benefit of anyone watching. Suzie was more animated when she remembered to tell him about the new teacher they had at work, filling in for a maternity leave.

—It's eerie, Suzie said. —She says she has second sight. She was sitting beside me in the staffroom, we were having coffee, she gripped my arm and said, 'I'm sorry but I can just see this so intensely, I have to tell you.' She seemed to know all these things about me that she couldn't possibly have found out. She knew about my mother losing my grandmother's ring in the sand, all those years ago. I've never told anyone about that at school. She knew what my mother was like. She said, 'That's the sort of thing she always does, she's careless with precious things. Careless with you and your sister, too.' I mean, how did she know I had a sister?

—They have tricks, David said. —They draw these things out of you, without you noticing. It's all fakery, of course.

—She knew about that accident. Not exactly. But about me being afraid of something like a white bird, falling.

—You probably talked to Giulia about it. I'm not sure I'd want someone who believed all that stuff teaching my children.

—Oh, don't be so solemn. What harm could it do?

—So what did she see in your future?

She was vague then, as if she didn't want to tell him. —I don't know, the useful stuff. Change.

They quarrelled at the second interval. David found the tray with their numbered ticket on it, two more gins and a bottle of tonic.

—I hate it, Suzie said, loud enough to twitch a few backs nearby. A swell of the crowd coming out from the auditorium washed them too close up against one another. —It's horrible.

He poured out the tonic, distributing it carefully between the two glasses.

—I'm sorry you're not enjoying it.

—It's not the music.

—How can it be 'not the music'? The music is what it is.

—For all I can tell, the music may be very brilliant.

—I'm sorry you can't tell. It really is.

—But you're all sitting there, enjoying yourselves – yes, mmm, very interesting, very nice orchestration there, very effective counterpoint – listening to a man who's taking seriously a God who asks him to kill his daughter. I mean I'm sorry. Am I the only one who thinks this is pretty sick? We have kids coming to school covered with bruises and so on. Isn't it the same thing?

The blue silky stuff of her top settled around her breasts, the light on it changing as she breathed fast; David straightened his back in his determination not to care that everyone around them was listening. If she didn't know the answer, then there was no point.

—And we're supposed to sympathise with his dilemma! 'A father's bleeding heart'! It's disgusting. If this is high civilisation and all that.

She took a gulp of her gin very fast and some of it trickled down her chin.

—You're bringing some very twenty-first-century assumptions to bear on an eighteenth-century work.

—I'm afraid I'm a very twenty-first-century kind of person. Don't think I don't know how it's going to end. I don't even need to look in the programme. He's going to decide to go ahead with the sacrifice and then angels are going to appear from heaven at the last moment and make everything all right.

—That's about the sum of it.

—I don't think I can bear to sit through that. I've had enough.

He was cold with disappointment in her. —OK.

—How will you get home, if I take the car?

—Walk. Or taxi. It isn't a problem.

—Kate Flynn's here, did you see? Carol's friend.

—I didn't see.

—Sitting a few rows ahead of us. She might give you a lift. Or I'll stay if you want me to.

—Absolutely not.

They stood awkwardly while she finished her drink; he fished in his jacket pocket for her cloakroom tag.

—Why did you come? he asked. —What did you want it to be?

She shook her head as if he couldn't understand. — Something else. I really did want to like it, honestly. Something uplifting and different. But I should have known.

He thought he might feel relieved when she was gone; but his heart was dancing with rage, and he only felt conspicuous. He might as well have left too; there was no chance of enjoying the rest of the oratorio after what had happened. He went back before the bell to sit inside. Just before the lights dimmed for the third act he did catch sight of Kate Flynn, in the stalls five or six rows ahead of him, reading her programme. He hadn't seen her for a while – a year or more, perhaps. He was surprised how immediately recognisable she was even from behind, without seeing her face: the head as straight and alert on its long neck as if it was held up by a wire; big earrings dangling from under the short bob of her hair. He remembered that Kate had always, even in her teens, had two pure white locks in her thick black hair, one growing from her temple and one on her nape, she used to be teased for it; he wasn't sure he could see them from this distance. Kate was two or three years older than him: his sister Carol's age.

She seemed to be sitting alone; there was an empty

seat beside her but no one came to fill it. That idea soothed him as the lights went down. It was the best way: it was fallacious to imagine that these experiences could be shared. All through the last act, through Jephtha's visionary aria, 'Waft her, angels', this sense of himself and others in the audience listening together but in their separateness sustained him. Actually it didn't matter that Suzie had gone home, that she didn't care for the things he cared for. It freed him up. It would have been worse, say, if she had enthused over Jephtha and then come back the next week and said she liked *Madame Butterfly* or *La Bohème* just as much. Suzie was wrong, she was surely wrong. The music, pushing open the almost abstract words, did not express the complacency of authority but its effort and its pain.

When it was over and the audience were making their way out, David found himself waiting, while people pushed past, for Kate to catch up with him. Wrapped in some sort of dark shawl embroidered with flowers, thrown back over one shoulder, she was looking carefully for the steps under her feet; but her expression was rapt, she was still absorbed in the music.

—Kate! Kate Flynn!

The urgency with which he hailed her might have surprised her; they had never been intimate, in fact, they'd never in their adult selves completely outgrown that arrangement in which he was her friend's kid brother, to be tolerated. She seemed pleased enough to see him.

—David!

She stopped and put out both her hands, causing a

hiatus in the flow of people; he took them with a warmth he hadn't known he felt. She did still have that white lock, swept back from her narrow intellectual-looking face with its finely emphatic nose and slanting black eyes.

—Are you here with Carol? I know she comes with you.

He shook his head. —Alone.

—Shame. I haven't seen Carol in a while. I'm alone too. I had a ticket for my mother but she changed her mind.

—Perhaps we could have a drink?

She gave him a quickly reassessing look. —Here?

—If you like, here. The bar's open downstairs, isn't it? Or anywhere.

—Why not? We could catch up.

David was all of a sudden reckless, as if Suzie's leaving him scalding with justified indignation had handed him a new freedom to go after what he wanted. He wanted a friend; he was imagining a companionship like cool air, a mingling of intelligences. He had been afraid of Kate's intelligence once. She had seemed sophisticated and sarcastic when he was a studious tongue-tied boy studying sciences at school.

—Why don't you come back to the house? Kate said as they made their way downstairs in the press of people. —I ought really to check on my mother, although I hope she's asleep in bed. I've got a bottle of Glenmorangie that needs drinking.

—The house being?

—The old house. The same old place. I've come back to live: didn't Carol tell you?

—She might have mentioned it: but I didn't take in that it was permanent. I know your mother hasn't been well.

—Her health is fine, only she's losing her marbles. After I'd got her dressed up in all her finery this evening she suddenly made her mind up there was something on the television she had to watch. Something she'd seen the first part of and couldn't bear to miss finding out what happened. I looked in the *Radio Times* and there wasn't anything, of course, but she wouldn't be persuaded.

—I'm sorry, David said. —I always liked your mother.

—You will still like her. She's awfully charming even in her disarray. But she'll be in bed when we get there, I hope.

They shared a taxi to Kate's old home beside the lake. David expected his pleasure in having made his bold gesture of friendship to subside, but it didn't. He had only been to the house a few times, in his youth, but he remembered everything vividly; when Kate opened the door with her key and led him through the imitation-baronial hall into the long drawing room, he saw that it had hardly changed. It had been the grandest house he knew; he had thought of it when he was a boy, with a mixture of awe and unease, almost as a palace, with its tower and its long verandas at front and back, and its stained glass. The decoration in the drawing room had been old-fashioned even in the seventies: some kind of light silvery wallpaper, a chandelier, watercolours and still lifes hanging from the picture rail, a baby grand piano, huge stuffed armchairs, dainty occasional tables. The paper was shabby now, there were brown damp stains in one corner, and the carpet had faded to blankness; the armchairs sagged with broken springs and on their arms the faded silk was worn away, so that their stuffing leaked. But it was all still somehow gracious. A young Kate in her graduation gown, plainer than she was now and wearing glasses, gazed from the mantelpiece in a silver frame.

Even when he was a boy David had understood that the Flynns were unfashionable because they had their minds set on higher standards of good taste. Kate's father was already dead then, he had been some kind of musician; Kate was the only child. Her mother was Jewish. There must have been money at some point, to buy this big house; he couldn't remember that Mrs Flynn had ever worked, apart from giving a few piano lessons. Here and there around the room were incongruous contemporary things that Kate must have brought with her when she came home: a bright-coloured pot full of pens and pencils, a poster advertising a photography exhibition at the ICA, bright striped silk cushions, a pink-and-yellow blanket thrown over the back of the sofa, signs of the different life Kate must have in London.

She carried in the Glenmorangie and two glasses, also a pot of coffee ready to plunge. David never usually drank coffee in the evening, but he didn't care tonight if he was kept awake.

—So what did you think of *Jephtha*? she asked.

41

—I thought it was excellent.

—It was. But the staging irritated me.

He didn't want her to demur. He never cared, anyway, how the designer chose to dress things up, he took no notice of that. He hoped Kate wasn't going to fuss about it.

—All that Italian neo-realist bit, headscarves and Mussolini suits. They see that it's about authority and patriarchy, and then the ideas bulb pops on: oh, it's just like Fascist Italy. Wasn't that annoying?

—It didn't bother me, he said coolly, warning her off. —Music isn't 'about' things. Personally, I'd rather hear it sung as a concert.

She was a university lecturer; no doubt they got into the habit of holding forth, thinking they knew everything. Perhaps she would be tiresome after all. To his surprise she fished in her bag for cigarettes and a lighter; there was hardly anyone in his acquaintance these days who still smoked. She didn't ask him if he minded; slipping off her shoes and tucking her feet under her, she curled up in one of the big old armchairs, contemplating him sitting in the opposite chair through the cloud of her smoke. The black cat that had followed her into the room jumped into her lap. There was something familiar in the way Kate smiled at David, as if she knew things about him he didn't know about himself; it must come from when they were teenagers, and he was such an innocent, without a clue as to what you were supposed to do and say with girls.

He wanted to change the subject. —If you've moved

42

to live down here, does that mean you've given up your job in London? Are you working here?

—I've given up full stop. I'm not working.

—Not working at all?

—Isn't it amazing? Billie gets a care allowance, I'm renting out my London flat. We seem to manage. I live like an aristocrat. Lying in bed late, reading all day, going to concerts and the cinema, visiting friends. We watch all the detective programmes on television. I think I ought to take up cards. What do the leisured classes play in the old novels? Bezique? Piquet? *Vingt-et-un*? No doubt it all seems very dissipated, to a man with serious responsibilities.

—It's a big sacrifice to make, to look after your mother.

—I'm not the sacrificing kind. I really didn't do it out of goodness. I was curious. Is there anything left inside, after twenty years? Anyway, nobody cares any more: the students, the administration. I was bored with everything about academic life that had enchanted me at first. The obedient processing of the latest fad. I'm too old for it.

—Is that really all you think it is?

—Don't take me too seriously. I don't know what I think. Anyway, now I'm so happy, doing nothing. Of course it's early days. I may yet end up gibbering on the street, or murdering Billie in a moment of overweening rage. Or begging for my job back. I did leave that option open. I managed to arrange a year's unpaid leave.

—You're not secretly scribbling? We're not to expect

43

the publication of some great work of fiction one of these days?

She looked disappointed in him. —Oh no, she said. —Why does everyone think that? That's the last thing. Perhaps if you haven't had children they think you ought to give birth to novels instead.

Kate didn't know whether David Roberts could remember a little scene that had gone on between them in this house, years and years ago, when they were young and she'd made an awful fool of herself; she didn't care whether he could or not. He looked so imperturbable, sitting perched on the edge of his chair in his suit and tie, with his knees apart, twirling his drink and looking into his glass as if he never would unbend, frowning his disapproval of her thoughts on the oratorio. She would have quite liked to make him blush. The thing had happened at one of her teenage parties; she had had the best, the wildest parties (Billie had been so persuadable, usually she agreed to stay away for the night). David must have tagged along with Carol. The idea of those parties generally was that by the end of the evening the crowd of individuals was resolved to a number of inter-locked couples in a darkened room. They had had the folding doors pushed open to make this room and the library into one; Kate had been lying on the old chaise longue, she had patted a space for David to sit down beside her. Perhaps if the doors hadn't been closed now, the sight of the chaise longue would have reminded him.

For Kate and Carol in those days David had only been

an earnest little brother who could never be coaxed into trouble: he was still a child, with doubting eyes and a sober careful mouth. Experimentally, when he sat down she'd taken his hand – a boy's brown hand, with bitten nails, fingers stained with biro ink – and put it inside her blouse. She'd been wearing a wraparound crêpe top, a black print with gypsy flowers, and no bra underneath; she had expected David to be astonished and grateful, immediately in her thrall. David instead had snatched back his hand as if she had burned it, and jumped up from the sofa with an expression of absolute disgust, then gone to find Carol and let her know he was going home. Kate had told herself at the time that he must have been terrified – they used to say sagely that some boys were 'terrified' of sex – but she had known it wasn't that. And although a thousand worse things than this little humil-iation had happened to Kate since – infinitely worse things – she had held a grudge against David Roberts all the same, and thought him rather a bore, even in all the years afterwards when she met him sometimes at Carol's. She had only finally forgiven him tonight, when he called out her name in the Millennium Centre, and his pleasure at seeing her shone so transparently in his face.

He wasn't anything like Carol. They came from an old non conforming Cardiff family, which once had owned a steelworks; Carol had showed her the Unitarian chapel whose foundation stone was laid by a great-great-grandmother of theirs. Carol was dauntless and crusading; David seemed stolid and cautious beside her. He had trained as a doctor, and been a GP for a while; now Kate thought he did something in Public Health. His tight dark hair surprised her, growing crisp and close to his head; when he was a boy it had been silky and straight (everyone in those days had worn their hair long, even the science students). Its bristling tightness now seemed a manifestation of the effort with which he held himself back. He had lived, of course, through dreadful things. Kate had known Francesca, they had been at university together; Carol and Francesca had shared a flat at one point, before Francesca ever knew David.

—Do you know my wife? David asked her, and she startled, before she understood that of course he meant the present one, the one Kate had last seen weeping at the side of the motorway after that extraordinary thing with the swan; she had thought once or twice since, with curiosity, about the blonde farouche girl whose beauty had only gleamed out like an accident in the great luck of her escape. Kate had an instinct not to tell David how she and his wife were mysteriously linked; anyway, she wouldn't be able to explain why she hadn't made herself known at the roadside.

—I've met her, she said pleasantly, —at Carol's. But I've forgotten her name.

David gazed, burdened, into his Glenmorangie.

—Actually, Suzie was there with me tonight, at the oratorio. But she hated it, she left after the second interval. She doesn't really enjoy music.

While David and Kate were talking there came the sound of slow steps on the stairs, and then Mrs Flynn walked into the room. She was tiny like Kate, and had the same sculpted head with its drama of cheekbones, tautly curving nose and eloquent eyes; perhaps because she had no chin her expression was bland and sweet where Kate's was decisive. David was shocked at how Mrs Flynn's shoulders were bowed and her hair was pure white; she stepped with brittle stiffness as if she was afraid of falling. His own mother hadn't come anywhere near this phase of ageing; she was still brisk and busy with her voluntary work. Perhaps Mrs Flynn had always been older than the other mothers; perhaps she wasn't young when she had Kate. He had prepared, when he heard her coming downstairs, to see her in nightclothes or a dressing gown; but she was dressed up in a flowered skirt and pink cardigan, with white button earrings, as if she was going somewhere. Her white hair was neatly pinned up behind.

—I heard you had visitors, Kate. She held out her hand, smiling.

David stood up to explain himself; her hand in his was impossibly light, a scatter of bird-bones loose in their pouch of skin. —My sister Carol is an old friend of Kate's.

—How nice, dear, she said. —I do know Carol.

—Billie, said Kate. —What are you doing? You were all nicely tucked up in bed when I looked in. Whatever have you put your clothes on for? It's the middle of the night.

Mrs Flynn was unrepentant. —Is it really? she smiled. —I thought it was morning. I didn't want to waste the lovely day.

—It's late, Mummy. It's night.

—I don't often get the opportunity to listen in while you young ones talk.

—You see how mad she really is? said Kate. —She still thinks I'm one of the young ones.

Mrs Flynn made a comical face at David, sticking out her lower lip in a pout. —Why should I miss all the fun? And of course music. This is a great house for music. Music and books. Are you a reader? I've been lucky enough to be surrounded with art and beauty, all my life.

She lowered herself, clinging to the arm with her two hands, onto the end of the sofa, where she sat stiffly graceful, smiling from one to the other.

—David's a doctor, Billie.

—Well, that's fascinating, isn't it?

—I'm a Consultant in Public Health. Communicable diseases. Don't get me started on how fascinating: I love my work. But I should read more. Sometimes the only reading I find time to do is *Thomas the Tank Engine* to my son.

—I hate that 'should' of dreary obligation.

—We have so many books, Mrs Flynn sighed.

—Where are your books? David asked, looking around. —I remembered books, but they aren't in here.

—We have quite a library, next door. Would you like to see? Please borrow something. Please use it as your own.

—I expect, Kate said, —he thinks books are frivolous, in the face of the kind of work he does. Explosions, epidemics, disasters.

—Why don't you lend me something? David said. —
Poetry or a novel. If you lend me something interesting
I'll try. It would be good for me.

—Anyway, isn't your son too old for *Thomas the
Tank Engine*? He's surely in secondary school by now?

—You're thinking of Jamie, David said. —Jamie's
seventeen. I have a younger son who's only six.

—Seventeen? Oh, that's shocking. He can't be seventeen: it seems like yesterday. What is he like,
Francesca's son?

David for a moment didn't answer her: for some
reason he didn't want Kate to know that Jamie was more
like her than he was: clever and sceptical and difficult,
a voracious reader.

—He's a great cyclist, he said. —Out at all hours on
his bike.

After David Roberts had gone, Billie was supposed to
be putting the kettle on for cocoa (she would have difficulty getting back to sleep after the stimulation of a
visitor), but she had found her spectacles instead and
was sitting looking competent at the table in the kitchen,
going through an old pile of leaflets and pointless mail.

—What are you *doing*? Kate wailed. —That's all been
sorted! It's for recycling.

—I just thought there might be post that needed
dealing with.

—Fat chance, if there was, of your dealing with any
of it. Anyway, it's bedtime.

Obediently, Billie put down the free sample of fabric

softener. —Do you think that this stuff's any good?

—For Christ's sake. I can't forgive you for coming downstairs when I bring my friends in. What kind of social life am I supposed to have? What kind of sex life, for that matter?

—He's a very nice young man, isn't he? How do we know him?

Kate had always spoken to her mother sharply. When she was a child she'd hit her too, and bitten her: Billie had talked about her temper as if it was a force of nature, magnificent and inevitable, which had made Kate ashamed. When Kate was older, she and her mother had had grand shouting matches; they had also told each other everything. In truth, the quarrelling hadn't got any worse since Billie had been ill. But Kate knew other people would be shocked that she swore at her mother and raised her voice. She was occasionally shocked at it herself. Sometimes she pushed at her mother in exasperation, she smacked her legs when she was trying to help her get her shoes on.

Filling her mother's hot-water bottle, she reflected grimly that David Roberts tonight would have taken away a charming impression of both of them, the eccentric pair in the house of culture and music. He had insisted on borrowing a book, so in the end she snatched up something from one of the piles on a table and pushed it at him, to get rid of him: something in a green binding, God knows what, probably some collection of poems in Polish.

Three

In late March, when it was supposed to be spring, there was a fall of snow. Kate opened the back door last thing at night and Sim ran high-stepping into the kitchen, affronted, with spots of it on his fur; the next morning all the flowerpots in the garden, empty for years, wore white caps. It didn't last even twenty-four hours. The sun shone weakly and the air was busy all day with a persistent ticking of melt water; on the roof the softening snow slid about. Big drops plummeted past the windows while Kate rehearsed Schubert in the drawing room with the quartet she'd managed to get together. Even the birds' cheeping sounded liquified.

That afternoon Billie drove the dented Citroën down to the shops as usual, at a cautious fifteen miles per hour. They parked illegally outside the leisure centre at the bottom of the park, beside the library, in a spot they already thought of as their own, so that they were indignant if anyone had taken it; then picked their way through brown watery slush to the café, whose customers had tramped the slush inside. Their entrance was always conspicuous; everything had to wait, as if for royalty, for Billie with her stick and her gracious unseeing smile. The staff – girls and boys with piercings, pink- and blue-dyed hair, bared midriffs even in this weather – knew what they wanted before they asked: Kate always had black coffee, Billie hot chocolate and shortbread. Billie had developed a new greed for sweet things; effusively she thanked whoever brought them, calling them all Jenny and Polly whatever their gender. The newish existence of this particular café among the shops of the suburb had drawn out – from shabby Victorian and Edwardian residential streets, and a mix of white and Bengali families, and students, and solitaries either interesting or mad – the appearance of a little community. There were exhibitions of local artists on the café walls, along with posters advertising drum 'n' bass, yoga classes, online creative writing groups.

On the way back from fetching extra sugar for Billie, Kate was brought up short by a boy at the next table: she was certain that she knew him. One of her ex-students? She was used to the passage across her life of more or less golden boys and girls. The face – wide, with rich creamy skin and deep hooded eyelids, long coppery-brown hair pushed behind his ears – seemed too strongly significant. Guessing, smiling tentatively, she balanced her sugar packets by the corner on the edge of his table.

—Are you David Roberts' son?

She hadn't been interested in him, after what David

said: she'd pictured him in one of those unflattering biking helmets, absorbed in dreary self-punishing tests of physical prowess. He had to struggle to draw himself out of that raptness in which the young relate to one another; there were three others at the table, boys and a girl. She saw them register her middle age.

—I suppose I am.

—But you don't look very like him. You're like Francesca, aren't you?

He wasn't at all what she had carelessly imagined: at the mention of his mother his expression opened up, complex and conscious. He half stood up from his chair.

—Did you know her?

—She was my friend at college. And I'm a friend still of Carol's.

—OK, that's cool. I don't know many people who remember her. Apart from Auntie Carol. And my grandmother, of course.

—Is that Francesca's redoubtable mother? I haven't heard of her for years.

—She's pretty amazing. Yeah, she's doing really well. Do you live here?

—I've lived in London for years. But I've moved back. I grew up here.

—I wouldn't move back, one of the boys said: freckled and ginger, thickset.

Kate conceded. —You're eager to be gone. But that's how it is. Like being born: can't wait to get out, spend the rest of your life trying to get back in.

Kate could amuse these young ones; what else had

she got out of all those years of teaching? Teaching gave one a better idea of how to talk to them; mothers especially found themselves trapped inside that awful jollying, explaining voice. She smiled around the table and took in without a flicker that the girl was pretty, brown-skinned, possibly Iranian, with long eyes whose stiff black lashes were like kohl-lines. Probably she was Jamie's girlfriend, or if she wasn't, wanted to be. Weren't girls still made like that? Or perhaps all she daydreamed about was becoming an investment manager, or a dentist.

—And you're in the sixth form, Jamie? You are Jamie, aren't you? Are you bright? What's your subject?

—He's bright, said the girl, proudly envious.

Jamie grimaced as if it wasn't worth discussing. —I don't know if I have a subject yet. I don't know if it's English or Philosophy.

—Do English, Kate said, unhesitating. —Why waste your life learning clever ways to redescribe what everybody already knows? Art's much more complicated.

He smiled warily. —I'd like to talk to you about my mother sometime. If you didn't mind. I'd like to find out more about her.

—Is this Francesca your mother? the girl said, astonished: so, he hadn't allowed her far inside his privacy.

—I wouldn't be a reliable witness, Kate demurred. —We knew each other when we weren't much older than you are now. It's a long time ago. I'll only remember funny bits and pieces.

—I'd like the funny bits and pieces, I think.

She gave him her telephone number then, and told

him how to find the house, the name in black and gold letters painted on the fanlight over the door.

—You could cycle over. Your father said you were interested in bikes. He and I bumped into one another at the Millennium Centre.

Jamie laughed. —He has no idea. I go everywhere on my bike; but I'm not interested in it.

Kate wouldn't have minded him in one of her classes: a Tolstoy type, not a Dostoevsky type, who were two-a-penny. But Billie was waiting patiently for her sugar; and in all the ceremonial fuss of stirring her chocolate and tucking a paper napkin into the white Peter Pan collar of her dress, Kate wouldn't even have noticed the young people leave, if Jamie hadn't raised a hand in farewell to her through the window, straddled already half across his bicycle, hopping on one leg. She saw for herself then how shabby and ancient it was, not even a racing model (and that he didn't wear a helmet). She thought that probably he wouldn't ever turn up at Firenze. He'd be protective, on second thoughts, of his own idea of Francesca; which probably, considering some of the things Kate remembered about her, would be a good thing.

She had bought a postcard in the post office. Along with her fountain pen, she fished it out from her bag: a photograph of the triumphant figure of Justice from over the Crown Court in the city centre, with bandaged eyes and swinging scales. 'Dear Max,' she wrote, cramping her big black italic hand into one half of the space; she didn't want to have to put the card in an envelope, in case Sherie didn't get to read it too. 'Greetings.

55

I am well, amid more civilised *mœurs de provence*. My days are dedicated to art, and my nights to the cellist in our new quartet. And how are you? Kate.'

It wasn't strictly the truth. She didn't in fact find the cellist at all attractive, although she suspected he could be encouraged, if it amused her or she grew desperate, to harbour a moody thwarted passion for her. It would be in keeping with his sorrowful paisley shirts washed to pale thinness, his lion's mane of hair with its secret bald patch, and the divorce he clung to as part of the explanation for himself, as martyred saints in paintings carry round the wheels that they were broken on.

David came home from work one evening to find not only Giulia in his living room but also the new teacher, Menna, the fortune teller. David had been at a tabletop multi-agency exercise, rehearsing contingencies for a flood in the Bay area, in a big room hired out for functions at one of the leisure centres: behind his concentration all day there had floated the liquid echo and splashings from a swimming pool and the thudding chock of balls, perhaps in a basketball court. All the various authorities and agencies at these events competed to make their points, and public health came low in the order for commanding attention. 'We don't have time to wait for you to consult the books,' one of the policemen had said to him at some point.

The women were sitting with the curtains drawn and only the lamps switched on, drinking wine, huddled intimately on the floor among the cushions, their talk intent, their heads bent close together: Giulia's hair faded dark-blonde and Suzie's honey-coloured, the new girl's black and shiny as a china doll's, in a long plait. They looked up and paused when he stood in his heavy coat in the doorway with his briefcase, but only as if he were a stone fallen into their stream, interrupting its flow for a moment. The new girl's face was doll-like, too: with white perfect skin and too-small symmetrical features, eyes rather burningly coal-dark, outlined in black pencil. The children were in the snug, watching *EastEnders*, cuddled up one either side of Jamie. David and Suzie disagreed over whether the soap was suitable: the idea of its lugubrious quarrelling imprinted on their infant minds depressed him, but she said if he wanted them not to watch it then he had to be home in time to do something else with them. She said if they didn't watch it they would feel different to the other kids at school, and he kept to himself the thought that it was better, to be different. The house was burrowed deep into its comfortable evening; whatever they'd all had for supper was cleared away in the kitchen and the dishwasher churned. He poured himself a glass of wine – the girls were on their second bottle – and chose something from the freezer that looked roughly the right size and shape to microwave for his supper, not bothering to wipe away the ice crystals to find out what it was.

—I'm sorry, Suzie called into the kitchen. —I didn't keep anything for you. I didn't know what time you'd be finished.

When he'd eaten the gluey food and came with his

wine to sprawl on the sofa, their talk petered out conspiratorially. *EastEnders* was finished and Joel came running to snuggle in his lap, hooking an arm round his neck, the light little body just beginning to elongate out of baby roundness. Hannah showed off her series of ballet positions in the middle of the room, proficient but not graceful.

—Do you know, Daddy, that Menna can tell fortunes?

—Oh yes, David, Giulia urged him, an enthusiast for everybody's gifts. —Why don't you let Menna tell yours? Suzie, have you got playing cards?

—He never would, said Suzie, not looking at him.

—She's uncanny. She can tell you things about yourself you can't believe she knows.

—I can't say I find that an appealing prospect, David said firmly.

Instead Hannah dragged Jamie from the snug and made him sit cross-legged on the carpet to have his fortune told: he had always since she was tiny given himself up like this to her command. David couldn't tell what Jamie thought; he was smiling slightly, but that could have meant irony, or just dope. The women and the children watched intently, Hannah breathing noisily with her mouth open. The girl was probably closer to Jamie's age than to any of theirs.

—D'you want to do this? she asked him.

Jamie said he didn't mind. She shuffled and cut the cards with deft expertise, handed them to him to cut again, and then dealt them with crisp practised movements into rows. Her hands were small, fingers sore and puffy round the bitten nails; there was no elaborate mystification, but something was commanding in her matter-of-fact concentration. David couldn't help imagining she had been soaking up everything they gave away about themselves, to bring it out later as her triumph. With sudden significant slowness, Menna turned a card over, then another one; her glance flicked from them up to Jamie's face. —The watcher, she said, —from his vantage point: lots of sky.

Suzie nudged Giulia's arm in triumph. Jamie smiled steadily back at Menna.

—Books, she said, frowning, peering. —Lots of books. I can't read what's written in them, yet.

She lingeringly turned over another card, making it snap. A tiny jolt of surprise seemed to register in her shoulder blades. David thought it was an effective touch. —Oh, she laughed. —How interesting. She looked at the other women. —Trouble.

—What kind of trouble? Suzie said.

—The usual kind. What do you think, at his age?

—Oh, Jamie. Giulia touched him reassuringly on the shoulder. —You don't have to go on with this if you don't want to.

Jamie only shrugged and looked amused. —Perhaps I ought to know, he said.

David broke the spell, getting to his feet. —I think these children should go to bed. I'll take them up.

There were furious wails of protest; Menna paused with the next card ready to turn over.

Giulia pleaded. —Let them watch. It'll only take a few more minutes.

Menna turned the card over slowly, stared at it. Then she shook her head. —It's gone, she said: blankly, as if it didn't matter to her one way or another. —Something's blocking me. I can't see it.

She pushed the cards away, muddling the carefully dealt piles.

—Oh, David! Suzie complained, with real regret. —That was you. Your fault.

Hannah couldn't forgive David all the time he was putting them to bed; she sulked, and spat her toothpaste on Joel's feet, and stubbornly wouldn't even come to listen to the story. Joel was free to choose something safe; his favourites were all about railway cats or jolly postmen or good little trains, he endured Hannah's more frightening choices in a stoic stillness. David thought Joel liked the opportunity to have his father to himself; he recounted little muddled snatches of school life, wanting confirmation that what seemed only strange and arbitrary added mysteriously somehow up to sense. He put his hands on his father's face and held it looking into his, so he could be sure he had all his attention. While David was reassuring Joel, he heard Jamie pull down the ladder to his attic and then pull it up again behind him.

The women when he came downstairs were confiding together in low voices, so that he knew they didn't want him to join in. He could hear that Suzie was telling them about escapades from her teenage life, about going to rock festivals with her friend and bringing boys back to the tent. She had only been fourteen when they did this.

She had told David these stories – or some of them anyway – when they were first together, including the fact that she had caught herpes from one of these boys, and had had to attend an STD clinic afterwards. He hadn't been shocked; he was a doctor, he took a practical approach. But it did shock him – he couldn't help it – that she told the stories now, to this woman she hardly knew, and in a voice as if it was all funny or even glamorously wicked. He left them to it, and went into the study to check his e-mails.

By the time Suzie came to bed he could tell that she had drunk quite a lot more; she stumbled over her shoes on the floor, swearing under her breath, and instead of folding her clothes or putting them in the wash basket she let them fall where she took them off. She showered for a long time to sober up. When she climbed into bed he had already put out the light on his side, and he closed his eyes as if he was asleep; pressing up close against his back, she made him too hot.

—Tell me about Francesca, she pleaded into his pyjama top, her voice muffled so that at first he wasn't sure what he'd heard.

—Whatever for? I'm asleep.

—Tell me. It's important.

—You know all there is to know.

—No, I don't. We hardly ever talk about her.

—When someone's dead, after a while there's nothing new to say. That's natural.

—You treat it all so calmly. If I died, would you be this calm?

61

He turned over to face her in the dark.

—You used to not want to discuss all this.

—I know. But now I can't stop thinking about her.

—Don't think about her. It was a sad, awful story. Better to let it go.

—Which way did you go to sleep together, when you were lying in bed like this? Which side did she like to lie on? What did she wear to bed?

David dutifully thought about it. —I can't remember, he said. —I don't know what she wore.

—You must be able to remember.

—We kept such different hours. I'd be getting up to go to work sometimes as she was coming to bed.

He did remember then that when Francesca was very pregnant she could only sleep sitting up in an armchair. But that was also when she began to imagine it wasn't a baby growing inside her but a demon, which would split her open and kill her when it was born. He didn't want to tell Suzie about that.

The next day on the way back from work – he was early, a meeting had been cancelled – David decided on an impulse to turn right at a traffic light instead of going straight home, and to call in on Kate Flynn. It was weeks since he'd been to her house after the oratorio. Somewhere washing about among the tissue boxes and empty crisp packets on the back seat of the car was the impossible book she had lent him; he had felt so puzzled and slighted when he opened it at home and found he couldn't read it, that he had meant simply to drop it through Kate's letter box sometime, and not to go out of his way to see her again.

But she might have made a genuine mistake; and anyway he was disappointed now, standing in the dusk at Firenze's front door, when the bell chimed somewhere far off and in the long minutes he waited after it no one came to let him in. The pillars of the portico were crumbling and corroded; a black mould grew across the white steps. Through the windows to either side of the door he couldn't see anything but the porch with its checkerboard tiled floor and empty flowerpots and rotting deckchairs; the fringed cream blinds pulled halfway down were worn to threads. He hadn't known he was thirsty to talk with Kate Flynn until she wasn't there. He nursed her book under his coat, shielding it from a drizzling, sideways-blown fine rain that had started as he got out of the car; he didn't even try to post it through the letter box (which was anyway, simplifyingly, too small). He had never been any good at talking: Suzie complained of it, even his mother teased him for it. All the short time he was married to Francesca, he had kept a young man's silence like a seal across his lips. At work of course he talked, but there it had consequences, and was about substantial things. He didn't know where this urge to spill his private thoughts had sprung from, sharp and precise as other appetites.

Turning his collar up against the rain, he made his way back to where he'd parked the car; then lifting his head as he felt for the keys in his pocket he saw Kate and her mother crossing the road from the park, Kate holding up over them both a huge black umbrella. Mrs

63

Flynn looked more frail out in the open, wrapped up in a brown crocheted beret and scarf; she walked with a stick, head down, her mouth slack from her efforts. Kate in her black-and-white checked wool coat was not fussily solicitous but had adjusted her pace to her mother's slow advance, looking around with that high gaze of hers which although she was short seemed to glance across the tops of things, trees, roofs, passing cars. David was suddenly shy. He thought he could read the succession of expressions on Kate's face when she recognised him – blankness, surprise, faint irritation – and he was reminded of weekends when he was eleven or twelve and Carol and Kate, reluctant, had been detailed to 'keep an eye on him' when his parents went away; he had known with indignation at the time that he was more safe and sensible than they ever were.

—This is a bad moment, he explained himself. —I was only bringing your book back. I'll come another time.

—Oh, don't go, Kate said. —We need company. Perhaps you could get Mummy in. I'll put the kettle on.

Mrs Flynn gave no sign that she recognised David, but submitted to his care. They made their way together up the side path to the door; the asphalt was worn into treacherous pits or upreared over tree roots, and the old lady gripped David's arm with her free hand. The cold breath of the house, sour milk and damp towels, came to meet them from where the door stood open onto the entrance hall. He could hear Kate running water in the far-off kitchen. In the hall he asked Mrs Flynn if she would like to take her coat off, and obediently she began to unwind the scarf from her neck. Now that she was no longer in forward motion, a rusty old habit of deprecating charm started up in her.

—The park was glorious, she said. —They keep it up so well.

—Don't take anything off, called Kate. —That dreadful man still hasn't fixed the boiler.

—We love our park, Kate and I. It's such a joy. We've always been so lucky, having it on our doorstep.

—I think it's funereal, said Kate, still in her coat, carrying cups into the drawing room on a tray. —It's like a cemetery. All the new trees, and every bench you sit on, in memory of someone whose favourite place it was. I began to think I'd find one with my name. We had to go into the glasshouse to keep warm. Full of sparrows zinging about, drunk with relief, thinking it's summer.

—The borders were magnificent! murmured Mrs Flynn, although she obediently kept her coat on.

Kate frowned at her as if she had a headache. —Don't be silly, Mummy. It isn't even properly spring yet. Everything that had grown up had lain down again under that snow we had, we were dejected, our feet were cold, and then it began to rain. We clung to David when we saw him because without him we might sink into bottomless despondency.

She found matches to light the gas fire, and brought in the teapot in a dirty knitted cosy; outside it seemed to grow dark very early, partly because of the dead creeper that hung in a matted blanket from the veranda, sagging as the rain soaked into it. They sat in the gas-fire light; Kate on a cushion on the floor made no move to switch on the lamps, nursing her teacup for warmth, a mess of bangles clashing on her thin wrists. The cups were bone china, tiny, rosebud-patterned, and David had swallowed down his tea in half a minute.

—You gave me a book I couldn't read, he said, holding it out to her.

—Oh? Kate looked vague. —Which one was it?

—I don't mean it was too difficult. I mean it's in some language I can't read. Polish, I think? Did you realise you were doing that? What did you mean?

Kate opened it quickly and then snapped it shut with her loud laugh, that he flinched from sometimes.

—I remember now. You were very importunate. I couldn't think why it was you wanted me to choose your reading for you, so I just picked up the nearest thing. I did have a suspicion, afterwards. But I'm so sorry. It was awful of me, wasn't it? Can you forgive me? It is Polish. I'll find you something else. If you haven't gone off the whole idea.

—I don't know where to begin, that's all.

—It's rather touching, in your middle age, that you're ready to 'begin'. Like one of those adult baptisms: grocers and insurance clerks in white sheets, dunked in midwinter ponds.

David was disconcerted that she thought him middle-aged.

—Aren't we? Aren't you forty? Isn't that in the middle somewhere? I never really know how old I feel. Sometimes I think it's all hardly started; sometimes I feel jaded as some mummified immortal. You're much better balanced, aren't you? You seem to know who you are.

David turned his empty teacup upside down, frowning, interrogating himself. —I suppose that outwardly . . .

—Outwardly's good. Don't hesitate, don't tell me that you're not balanced, not yet. I'm liking to think of you as terribly steady. Billie, don't eat more biscuits, they're not good for you.

—I'm hungry, dear. What is for dinner?

—Hungry again already? Surely we've only just had lunch? Let me get you out of your coat now it's warmed up in here.

The old lady stood up and let herself be pulled about; unwound from her bulky outer layers, she seemed doll-sized. Underneath she was dressed in something lemon-yellow.

—Kate's looking after me so wonderfully. You know she's a brilliant girl? Her professor – I forget which one – said to me at her graduation: 'Do you know what we've got here, Mrs Flynn? She's something special.' We have to take great, great care of her, he said.

—Shut up, Mummy. Really, shut up. That professor's died since; and nothing came of all my youthful promise. It's too sad.

—It's her temperament, Mrs Flynn whispered confidentially to David. —She has it from her father. He was Irish. He was a brilliant man, too: a violinist.

—Billie's an absolute believer, when it comes to brilliance. She believes in other lovely things too, like civilisation and progress.

67

—As far as it goes, David said, —I'm a believer in progress. Is that so ridiculous?

—I suppose you'd have to be, in your line of work.

—Sewage and inoculations and sanitary housing: aren't these good things?

—I know what: you should read *Madame Bovary*, that can be your first assignment. For the purest contempt ever for the idea of progress. Only I'll think less of you if you're not at least half persuaded. One mustn't read like a prig, you know.

David wondered if Kate thought he was a prig.

—And you have to buy your own copy, I won't lend you one. You can get it for three-and-sixpence, anywhere. If you can't read French the translations are all equally bad.

He found himself somehow telling her, although he hadn't meant to go into so much detail, about John Snow and his researches into cholera at the Broad Street pump, and the beginnings of a scientific epidemiology; Mrs Flynn followed smilingly with every indication of deep interest. He wanted to communicate to Kate his passion for a certain tradition of pragmatic progressivism: gradual unromantic improvements in people's daily lives.

—I don't know how to live in this house, Kate said to him earnestly, suddenly. —Doesn't that sound strange? I lived here for all my childhood, I've come back almost every other weekend for years. But I don't know how to make my mark on it. It's as if all the years I've been away haven't happened.

David looked around the room, trying to be helpful.

—Why don't you move in more of your own stuff?

—I'm not complaining. In a way I'm quite enjoying the sensation. One gets so tired, of one's own mark; hearing oneself work through the same old performance. It's nice – for instance – to meet you again, for a change. You're very restful, after some of my friends.

She felt for a cigarette in a packet on the mantelpiece, scrutinising herself frankly, frowning, in the rectangular gilt mirror. —Where did I put the matches? People buy me those kind of sexy silver lighters that I love, but I lose them infallibly.

He stood up and found the matches; he didn't think to gallantly light her cigarette for her until it was too late.

—I ought to go, he said, addressing her in the mirror. Tarnish blotched it like a black lichen spreading from its corners. Her reflection, unsmiling, was more tentative than she was in the real air. —You find my enthusiasm boring.

She reassured him, shaking her earrings, tilting her head to blow her smoke away from him. —Not boring: it's romantic. We sceptics only long to be contradicted.

—Oh well. Perhaps we enthusiasts long for that too.

—I hadn't thought of that.

—Oh no. Oh no! Kate groaned aloud to herself as soon as she'd shut the front door behind David. —Oh no, not this.

She stood with her back to the door, gripping the cold metal doorknob in one clenched hand, pressing herself painfully against where the letter box was fixed inside with two protruding screws.

—Not this, I can't bear it.

—Kate? What's the matter? came her mother's voice from where she was sitting in the drawing room, obediently where Kate had left her.

—Nothing! Stay there!

She had watched David make his way down the path to the gate, hunching his shoulders under his coat against the rain. If she made an effort she could still just imagine seeing him impartially, casually: good-looking enough, absorbed in himself in a way that didn't promise well, limited, earnest. He didn't turn round to wave at the gate. Probably in a crisis, confronted with raw emotion, with anything improper, he would react with caution: he would show a superficial kindness and underneath it deep distaste. There were bolts of killing disapproval locked up under the thick pelt of his hair, and in the brown steady gaze that followed her conversation with only the slightest hint of lumbering. He was dangerous to her. She must use all her experience to guard herself against him, against the cold look of disassociation he was capable of turning on her at any time.

—Kate? What are you doing?

Sometimes this intimacy of shared life made it seem as if her mother lived and moved inside her skull. The creakings of Firenze were familiar as a childhood language; she heard Billie getting up from her chair.

—I'm doing nothing. I'm just standing here.

She hurried upstairs and locked the bathroom door

behind her, then sat down on the closed toilet lid, doubled over, holding her stomach. How had this happened? At what moment precisely had she allowed this longing inside to devour her? She saw David's face, wide and heart-shaped; his skin that in middle age had grown thick and resilient, with tough beard-growth kept cleanly shaved. She could still smell his soap, and the warmth that flowed from him, reassuring as toast; the idea of his serious conservatism melted her, made her weak. From behind his expression cloudy with self-preoccupation, his smile flashed unexpectedly crooked: he was more responsive than he knew, he was capable of intensities he hadn't tasted.

—I'm too old for this, she said aloud.— It will kill me this time.

—Kate? Her mother rattled the doorknob: she had pulled herself all the way up the stairs, guessing at a crisis even in her confusion. —What are you doing in there? What's going on?

—Go away. Leave me alone.

She ought to be back at work, she ought be keeping herself busy, keeping herself stupid and numb. This was what had always happened to women when they had too much time to think: they made themselves conduits to all the passions in the universe, they dreamed open all the possibilities that sane hard-working people kept shut away. She lay down on her back on the floor, on the ancient lino whose pattern of black lines and pink and white rhomboids was worn almost to whiteness in places. She knew she had done this sometime before, in the far-off past, in the thick of her teenage excesses. Her mother had been

71

outside the door then, too, rattling the handle, begging to come in, pleading to know what was happening.

Kate's head was between the pedestal of the sink and the side of the old huge bath, still the same bath as in her childhood, old-fashioned even then, with claw feet, hideously stained inside. It was so old-fashioned that people were having these baths put back in now, their popularity had come around again. If she was going to live in this house, really come back to live here, then she must have the bathroom done up; have a shower put in, have everything made new, and modernised, and bearable. From this angle she could see horrors underneath the bath where the lino ended and Buckets and Mops gave up: shadowy shapes of hair and dust and lost things, an old tub of some extinct brand of scouring powder rolled on its side and forgotten. She could smell urine down here, for all the cleaning it had had: decades of drops and spills of urine, soaked into the lino, into the boards beneath.

At this point, Kate knew, she could stand up from the bathroom floor, dust herself down, run her wrists under the cold tap, think of this momentary collapse with life-saving irony; walking out of the bathroom she could glance at her mother's anxiety with blank impatience. 'I have no idea what you're fussing about. Aren't I even allowed to use the toilet in peace?' Even when she was a teenager she'd always known that this thing, this falling in to a new obsession, was something you did to yourself. You chose to abandon yourself to it. Always, given that choice, Kate had gone in deeper and deeper still, as if the disorder was life itself.

Four

Through his closed eyelids David knew that his father was struggling into his bathing trunks under a towel tucked round his waist in the same routine he had held to for forty years; probably for fifty, sixty years, since whenever Bryn Roberts had grown out of being the lithe little boy who swam naked on this same Pembrokeshire beach with his gang of friends every summer holiday, when he came from Cardiff with his parents. These days the waist was expanded into a high assertive dome; they had a photo of him belly-to-belly with Suzie when she was pregnant with Joel. Bryn grunted with the difficulty of hopping on one leg while he changed, and although he still had broad muscled shoulders, the flesh had sunk on his breast, where the grey hair that used to sprout like wire grew soft and long: nonetheless, he insisted on swimming every day of their holiday if it wasn't actually raining, even at Easter, when the sea's cold was an iron blow. David didn't open his eyes for the triumphal roar when the towel was whipped away, or the strong old man's run into the sea, powering out and throwing himself dauntlessly upon the waves. The paddling children screamed at his splashing past; the women – his wife, his daughter, his daughter-in-law – applauded in mixed irony and admiration, the lifelong female accompaniment to his performance.

David's awareness was buried in the dark behind his glowing lids, deeply absorbed in the sea's rhythmic crash and drag: he was dozing and at the same time vividly awake to his situation. He dug his fingers into the secret cold of the sand with its grit of shell fragments, heard the tickling of tiny creatures moving at his ear, smelled the salty rot of weed on the rocks as the tide fell. The gulls' calls seemed closer than the women's talk, which was only another murmur like the shingle rolling against itself: Carol preoccupied with the barbecue improvised out of a baking tin and wire grill where she was cooking sausages for lunch, his mother watching the children over the top of her book, Suzie rubbing in suncream, rolling down the straps of her top, positioning herself to tan in the sudden unexpected spring sunshine. David sometimes felt he was coming awake for the first time, now he was forty: as if all the time that had been supposed to be his youth had passed in a muddled dream. He was surprised in those moments to find himself still connected to this collection of other people who filled the surface of his life and insisted that they knew him.

The children carried sloshing buckets of water up from the sea and Hannah marked out with her spade on the small horseshoe of sand that the falling tide exposed an overambitious square for a sandcastle. She began throwing up ramparts in a burst of energy; Joel, impressed, followed scooping and patting obediently in her wake. They squatted to repair the slipping walls, then lay on their bellies kicking their feet, reaching their skinny arms to make two tunnels that would meet underneath: David remembered the slightly sinister success, meeting eventually other fingers under the surface, alive as your own, grappling abrasively. After lunch he swam, surprising himself, tiring himself, far out, farther than Bryn had gone. He turned and bobbed in the rocking sea to look back at the small shingly beach, scooped out of black rocks crusty with barnacles and limpets, where he could only just make out his family; behind it was the square austere stone house on the Parrog, with its roof of thick old purple-blue slates, and its sloping front garden where tough seagrasses grew behind the walls built of some rough cement-like mix of shells and pebbles. It had been Betty's parents' home once, and now Bryn and Betty kept it on for holidays, for the family, for the grandchildren.

Only Jamie wasn't with them; he had stayed in Cardiff, saying he had work to do. David was relieved to be free of his adolescent son's presence, his long lope, his silences, the signs of his corrosive boredom. In the middle of a conversation or a family joke he would sometimes get up and walk away, leaving them to the spoiled end of it. It would be easier for them all when he went away to university next year.

*   *   *

75

Carol could imagine how insufferably solid the phalanx of their family might seem, concentrated in belonging in the old house. In Suzie's face that seemed at first sight so frankly open – its pale full mouth, the faint freckles that came right to the edges of her lips, the sandy-lashed blue eyes resting steadily on whoever was talking – there were if you watched for them signs of an unexpected wincing awareness. Bryn, who had been a general practitioner for forty years, had not lost in his retirement the habit of confident benevolence; Suzie blinked and smiled, caught in the bright stream of it, withholding her own thoughts as if she hung onto stones in her pockets. She was more carefully tactful, Carol decided, than Betty – who had been tactful all her life – ever quite noticed; Suzie deferred subtly to her mother-in-law when they cooked together in the inconvenient old kitchen, whose Rayburn stove had to be coaxed and propitiated by an expert. Sometimes when Suzie was in the room Betty spoke to Carol in Welsh; Carol would only answer her in English.

In the evenings, when the children were in bed, the family played solo whist around the rickety green baize card table (Betty's parents would never have allowed cards). Suzie didn't know how to play and wouldn't learn; she sat in their grandfather's big chair with her feet tucked under her, biting her hangnails and reading her book, some self-help thing. The old musty pungency of flagstones laid on an earth floor had survived the redecorating of the high plain rooms and the new furniture bought to make the place more comfortable, and still brought on Carol's asthma; the tall clock still ticked although it wouldn't keep the time. They had a log fire in the grate, because after the fine days the evenings were sharp. David wasn't concentrating and lost two good solo hands. When the card players took a break for Betty to make hot drinks, Carol and Suzie went outside together to look at the sea. They leaned on the wall of the little stone quay; a fat gibbous moon, dark pearly white, hung low above the horizon; the black water breathed coldly in and out.

Suzie pulled her cardigan tight around her shoulders. —Do you believe in life after death? she said out of nowhere.

—Golly. Even when I was a Christian, I was never able to persuade myself. I could only believe in the 'how to live' bits of it, not the magic. I'm so boringly rational.

—Were you a Christian? I suppose you were brought up as one.

—For ages. Until I was thirteen or so, and fell in with wicked friends.

—I've always been so solidly sure there wasn't anything, it never seemed a problem. Now there are presences: I feel them, I'm sure I feel them.

—Presences?

—As if everything's come alive. But not exactly in a benevolent way. Not evil either. Restless.

—Oh, said Carol kindly, sorry that she couldn't take this seriously: her own instincts were so exclusively earthly. —In the house here, it's obvious that my grand-parents are present in some sense, because we still have their things, it's their place, we're remembering them all the time while we're here. But that's all.

—Not that. More active than that. Like a pressure: with messages. As if the way we live is all wrong, sealed up in ourselves: but underneath the skin of things, there's a whole world of interconnections and meaning.

—OK, that makes some sort of sense.

—You think that the people who believe this stuff are all half daft and gullible, with crystals and tarot cards and things. But actually there are friends of mine, a new friend of mine from school, who really does seem to have some sort of gift, yet she doesn't make any fuss about it. Quietly and calmly, she reads your mind. She takes away my headaches, just touching me on the temple. She talks about spirits as if they were the most ordinary thing, around us everywhere.

—I don't know if I'd be comfortable with that.

—That's what I would have thought too.

Separated by their difference, vague to one another in the darkness, they stayed on, listening to the sea.

—Don't mention to David that we talked about this, Suzie said.

—Of course not, if you don't want me to.

—He freezes up if I even try to talk to him about anything that isn't just material and practical. I don't mind him not believing in it. But he seems disgusted that anyone could ever think differently.

—Oh dear, said Carol. —It's true, I suppose, he can be a bit inflexible.

David's son came to Firenze twice before Kate could find time to talk to him. She had made up her mind, if she thought about him at all, that he wouldn't turn up; and the first time when she opened the door to him – it was an awkward moment, she was on the phone to Max over some practicality to do with the appalling people renting her London flat (in her naivety she'd imagined that boring meant undemanding) – she half pretended she didn't recognise him. He must have seen her crumple up carelessly in her hand the piece of paper he gave her with his mobile number, meaning to lose it. That had been a grey windless joyless day, she had been full with her idiotic troubles; the sight of Jamie, who was like David whom she was hoping for, but was not David, had seemed an exotically cruel turn of the knife. David had called twice more since he brought back the Polish book. He talked, she had drawn him out. Scrupulously coolly, she had held back any signs of what she felt, then suffered for it afterwards. What if he didn't come again?

When Jamie called the second time she was rehearsing with the quartet, so that she arrived at the door where he stood with his bike – in sunshine this time – with her violin in her hand and a carelessly expectant sociability, thinking he was going to be the clarinettist who wanted to play with them. Behind her trailed impatient ends of music and laughing voices (dark note from the lugubrious cello). Jamie peered past her shoulder, longing visibly to be asked inside; Kate saw that he was calling now because he was curious about her, as well as interested in his mother. She said that she couldn't talk to him that afternoon, but that she would meet him the week following, in the café where she'd first seen him.

She almost forgot the appointment but didn't quite; and what's more, she arranged to pay the Buckets and Mops lady, whose name was Alison, to stay an extra hour and sit with Billie, because Billie in the café took up all her attention, and if she was to do her duty by the boy then she ought to concentrate – at least for this short half an hour, after all this time – on Francesca.

The park, on her way to meet him, displayed all the delicate first dazzle of spring: fresh yellow-green leaves the crumpled limp texture of kid shaken out of the hoary old branches; red slips of new growth sprouting on griz-zled standard roses. The first rowing boats of the new season were out on the lake. The great magnolia that shaded the herbaceous border was fat with waxy buds still tightly pink; later, they would open to cream. Kate remembered as she walked her old rage at Francesca, who had been so tall, so indifferent, so English; now the poor old dead had faded and gone out of fashion whether they liked it or not. She had chosen carefully clothes appropriate to the meeting with Francesca's son: a green dress, slightly Audrey Hepburn; her cream jacket with the big jet buttons; sunglasses. She was late, of course, and the boy had probably already decided she wasn't coming, although she admired him for sitting absorbed nonetheless in his thoughts and not giving away any signs of the shame of being forgotten: at his age Kate would have been agonised, and long gone. He had his mother's full loose lower lip, which Kate had forgotten until she saw him. It made their smiles slippery and equivocal.

—Remind me what you're going to do at university?

—I've had a new idea. Anthropology. I've contacted a couple of places.

—That's what I'd do if I got to choose over again.

—It's really good of you to come; you're probably very busy. What do you do? I mean: what's your job? Are you a musician?

—I gave up my job. Didn't your father tell you?

—He's never spoken to me about you.

Kate took that in without the coffee even quivering in the cup in her hand. She would have hated to think that David carelessly dropped scraps of information about her for his indifferent wife, in front of the children.

—Until this year I taught in the Slavic Studies department at Queen Mary. I worked on translations of Aksanov and Chekhov stories. Then I was bored with the academic life; anyway, my mother is ancient and dotty, and I was able to pretend I had to look after her. I took against the metropolis with all its uncomfortable excitements; I decided I would come home to Wales. I told myself that all the hidden poetry of life was in the in-between-sized cities where you can walk home from the theatre in the evening, and everywhere you go you meet the same crowd of people.

—And is it OK?

—It's almost too much: childhood, youth, the past. I was safer in London where my life ran shallowly. I may have made a terrible mistake.

—But you can always get away again. Apart from your mother of course.

—Oh, she'll live for ever! Then Kate put down her

cup in its saucer with an apologetic sigh. —That wasn't tactful, was it? Considering what we're here to talk about.

—I don't mind about my mother being dead. I can't really remember anything else.

—In future the therapists will drag it all out.

—Was she like you are?

—Don't tell me that's why you've wanted to see me? Because you think I'm like your mother? I can't tell you how much Francesca would have hated to be compared to me! She was to begin with – you must know this – tall and rather beautiful. A princess.

—I've seen photographs, of course.

—The photographs don't do her justice; she looks awkward, because she was self-conscious, whereas in real life she flowed. That was her grace, the flowing deliberate way she did things. In those days I was a radical feminist, or so I thought; Francesca was bored by the politics everyone else was going mad over, she wrote poetry. Do you have her poems? She had things apparently in the *TLS*: that was later. I don't know whether they were any good.

—I didn't know she wrote poems.

—You have her mouth, by the way.

—My grandmother says that.

—It's very subtle; it changes everything straightforward you have from your father.

—Did you like her?

—I admired her. She was Carol's friend really. They lived together in the second year, in an amazing flat in

Kensington, with marble fireplaces and bits of the ceiling fallen in, like a ruined palace. Francesca used to hold court in party dresses she bought from the junk shops. Carol and she were always falling out.

—Carol never told me that.

Kate was penitent. —I'm remembering, you know, an irresponsible time. We were none of us very kind: we were too clever, in competition to be the cleverest, struggling to block out some sort of shape of adult life for ourselves. Carol was always the kindest. We were all sad, as you are when you're young. We all went to bed for days at a time with misery, and mostly it came more or less all right afterwards. We didn't die, anyway. I don't know why Francesca did what she did later. I lost touch with her, I only saw her once, twice, in the years after she married your father, and had you.

—Why did she used to fall out with Carol?

—Carol's so reasonable. Francesca would make a fuss about ordering something special in a café, then leave most of it on her plate. She claimed to be allergic to all sorts of things: tea, cats, soap, God knows what. She had favouritisms and then she dropped people, and Carol had to lie to fend them off, pretend at the front door that she wasn't in when they could hear her laughing upstairs. But then all that was also just what Carol liked. You know, stout and watertight and sensible is drawn to fragile, flawed, pretty as hell.

—I suppose so.

—I've been too frank, haven't I?

—It's what I wanted to know. I'm interested.

—Was that your girlfriend: the pretty dark one? In here with you that day?

—Not really, Jamie said; not at all brutally, but as if it was an effort for a moment to remember who she was talking about.

—Poor thing. 'Not really.' If she could hear you: wouldn't it break her heart?

He was surprised. —I don't think it's like that between us, honestly.

Talking about the old days at UCL made Kate anything but nostalgic; actually, despite what everybody said about youth, most of her past made her shudder in sheer disgust, and relief that she didn't have to live it over again.

Kate and David left his car in Park Place and were chased by a sudden shower into the foyer of the Reardon Smith, behind the museum; she held her umbrella up over both of them, he stooped his head, and of necessity as they dashed she gripped his arm. It was exactly the kind of intimate manoeuvre she'd never been able to manage with Max, who was six foot four and had to have an umbrella of his own. Inside David bought tickets for the recital while she shook the rain off the umbrella, then he stood back to let her go first through the door into the gorgeous little 1920s lecture theatre, all subdued polished wood and white pillars and red plush, where the BBC Radio 3 man was already mumbling to himself and his listeners in his upstairs corner. They were hardly damp; Kate took off her jacket anyway, and put her hand on David's sleeve, to make sure. David held out the programme for them both to read. They were falling into a pattern of friendship that had been before Kate came back to live in Cardiff exactly her idea of the sort of thing that would evolve in a place like this, between grown-up cultured people. He picked her up at the house and they went to concerts together; he called in on her unannounced to talk about books, on his way home from work, or at weekends. (He had told her when he was halfway through *Madame Bovary* that he was interested in the medical stuff but that Emma irritated him; he thought she deserved, for her petty selfishness and credulity, all the disappointment and doom that he sensed was coming.)

They glanced at each other with eyebrows raised when some people clapped in the wrong place. After the slow movement in the Schubert E flat trio, which for God's sake she had heard a thousand thousand times and even played, Kate found she had tears spilling out of her eyes and running down her cheeks, and had to fumble surreptitiously in her bag for a tissue to wipe them away, hoping her nose wouldn't be red; as they filed out with the rest of the audience to have their free coffee in the museum, he held her lightly by the top of her arm, possibly simply holding her back to let somebody past, but also possibly out of comradely recognition of her emotion. All this was very poignant. But even Celia Johnson in *Brief Encounter*, Kate thought, wasn't satisfied with just this; and that was before 1968. I'll die, she thought, if more doesn't happen. They didn't wait with the crowd in the museum restaurant downstairs but went up to the nicer place you could get coffee in the pillared airy foyer under the dome.

David met people he knew; he introduced Kate – without, of course, any shadow of a hesitation – and stood talking with them, his mac over his arm, while she went to queue at the counter behind the little tables; to claim their free coffee she had to signal to him for their concert tickets in his pocket. She had never felt so domesticated; she was pleased with the chance to watch David as his public, responsible self: straight-backed, watchful, courteous. She had been in London for a few days, seeing people and arranging for some new translation work; from there this pleasantly genial, drearily dressed crowd might look like nobody worth knowing. But these were real people, getting on with substantial things, guarding their privacy as if it was worth something. At least everyone wasn't glancing around for something better happening somewhere else. David knew a man who taught music at the university (they had been at school together); Kate in her shallowness would not have given his meek beard and Marks & Spencer trousers, worn too short, a second glance. Talking with his friend – about music, of course, not gossip – David was animated and forgot where he was; she saw the hawk-flash of his authority from under the heavy lids he hid behind. He was tanned from his seaside holiday in west Wales.

They sat down at a table under a huge Frank Brangwyn oil painting of the trenches in the First World War: their awareness in the midst of chatting snagged occasionally on some bloody horror.

—So tell me, she said, hanging her jacket on the back

of her chair, giving him her smiling attention, —what have you been doing at work since you got back?

David smiled warily. —You wouldn't be interested.

—No: go on, I really am.

—I've been revising our immunisation guide for parents in line with new policy, and trying to get on with this report on the funding implications of the reorganisation.

—That all sounds so . . . solid. What are the funding implications?

He laughed. —Even I'm bored by the idea of going into that. Why don't you tell me how you got on? Are they keen on your idea for this new translation?

Kate put on a face of despair and gave an exaggerated account of the struggle she'd had to persuade them to be interested. —Who wants to read the Russians nowadays? she said gloomily. —In the Cold War it was all so glamorous, everyone loves a bit of suffering under totalitarian oppression. Now we're sick of it, the eternal moaning and groaning. What's the matter with them? Why can't they just get on with it like everybody else?

—I can see why you're drawn to Russia, he said. — There's so much depth to the culture.

She shuddered. —Depths to drown in. The place terrifies me. My family aren't from Russia, you know. From Lithuania; quite another thing. My grandparents spoke Polish and Yiddish.

Kate wondered if Jamie had told David that they had met and talked about Francesca; it seemed likely that the boy would keep it as his secret. She didn't know what David's reaction might be to her having discussed his dead wife with their son; anyway, she didn't want David's family, any of them, tangled in the talk between them, binding them fatally in a pattern of friendly above-board intercourse which would end in her being invited round to their place every year for Christmas drinks. She didn't know whether David told Suzie that they were going to these concerts together, or told her how often he was calling in at Firenze; he had definitely phoned Kate from work, not from home, to ask if she wanted to come with him to the Reardon Smith. Sometimes when she was with him, instead of feeling happy, she was filled with the sensation of having made a terrible mistake, not in falling for David, but in how she had lived her whole life before it happened, all her efforts not to be banal. The right way to live, the good way, had been invisible to her: now she was locked out of it, peering in through its windows. She set David tests, to find out what he thought their relationship was: today she thought perhaps something would show up when he drove her home after the concert, where Carol was sitting with Billie. (Carol was a brick, she had moved into Firenze while Kate was away.)

In the event, when David had stopped the car he looked at his watch and sighed: he didn't even have time to come inside. He asked Kate to give his apologies to Carol: he and Suzie were taking the children out to lunch with friends. He was always failing Kate's tests: on the other hand, he never failed them quite catastrophically enough, so that Kate could always excuse him (he sighed, after all, when he looked at his watch). She had told Max all about him when she was in London: how she didn't know whether he was shy and conventional, or simply unmoved. She had managed to prise Max away for at least one lunchtime from Sherie. For all his generous interest, Max had still seemed to feel some pain at the idea of her passion for someone else: Kate when she noticed it was sorry, and changed the subject. She had kissed him when they parted: he had had to stoop down for her to do it, from such a thin, blond height.

The Citroën was making alarming noises, and the cellist in his disappointed way offered to take Kate in his car to the big Tesco supermarket on Western Avenue, because he needed some shopping himself. She couldn't afford to turn down such an opportunity, although she wanted nothing less than to know the contents of his lonely supermarket basket. The bits of shopping they had to do were dwarfed by the booming gigantism of the place: it was for oversized families, trolleys heaped high with spoils, a couple of dresses or a pair of shoes or a plasma television topping off the bumper packs of oven chips and the seventeen varieties of French cheese. Defiantly, so that her basket wouldn't look anything like the cellist's, she filled it with flowers and fizzy wine and chocolates for Billie, who would be delighted. Actually it turned out that the cellist was a bit of a gourmet, buying duck-liver pâté and bottles of green peppercorns and walnut oil.

Then she met Suzie Roberts in the poultry aisle. Kate saw Suzie first, but too late to pretend she hadn't and hurry away. Suzie was bending over the organic chickens, the little yellow free-range corn-fed ones that had had happy lives. She was wearing cut-off pink jeans and a short white cotton vest that showed her freckled tanned belly; Kate imagined they were both shivering and goose-fleshed in the emanations from the chill cabinet. Suzie wasn't wearing any make-up. The children were beautiful: the girl with David's deep eyelids and conker-brown hair chopped off at her shoulders, swinging like corn-silk; the little boy with his mother's fairness and white lashes. The girl daydreamed, pivoting on one foot, and the boy attended conscientiously to his mother's choosing: this chicken or that one? Suzie let the boy decide; solemnly he pointed out his favourite with a finger, and then checked quickly against his mother's expression, to see if he'd done well. Suzie squeezed his shoulders and pressed her cheek against his, sun-flushed flawed adult skin against his perfect childish creaminess. From where she crouched down slightly to her little son, she looked up and saw Kate watching beside the turkey portions.

Of course there wasn't anything between Suzie and Kate: nothing had happened, except in Kate's thoughts, that might not have been shown to the world in broad daylight. But it was possible that Suzie knew that David her husband phoned Kate from work sometimes (although nothing could have been more innocent than those short businesslike calls); and she surely knew they had been to concerts together. David's daughter lifted her dreaming lids and inspected Kate frankly. It was too late not to say anything.

—Kate Flynn, isn't it? Do you remember we met at Carol's? I'm David's wife.

Kate had forgotten Suzie's voice: husky and steady, with traces of an accent, not Welsh, more Essex. Suzie didn't put out her hand to shake, but tightened it on the boy, and even touched the girl's shoulder lightly with her other hand, as if she presented them as a collective.

—Of course I remember, Kate said. —I'm surprised we haven't bumped into one another before. I've moved back here to look after my mother.

—Yes, I heard. How is she?

—Doing very well, thank you.

—David said you're both music-lovers.

—My mother and I?

—You and him.

—Oh well, we both come from musical families. Doesn't Bryn Roberts sing? He looks as if he ought to sing. I believe my mother taught David piano once – I mean long long ago, in the Stone Age. Or was that Carol?

—It's nice, that he has someone to go to the concerts with. I expect he told you that I'm no good at his kind of music.

—I suppose with children it's hard to get babysitters.

—We've got Jamie, Suzie said. —My stepson.

—Of course, said Kate. —I'd forgotten about him.

They managed to move past one another, smiling and pretending they were in a hurry. Hardly noticing whether she put anything useful in her basket, Kate hurried to find the cellist and make him take her home; but he was only halfway through his list, and fussily determined to get every ingredient for some fancy dish he was cooking up to eat all by himself. In every aisle Kate walked down while she waited for him, she seemed to meet Suzie and her children walking up, so that they had to acknowledge one another.

At home Kate unpacked the shopping carefully. She made Billie a sandwich and coffee, gave her the chocolates, put the television on, put the flowers in the sink, and then said she needed to lie down for half an hour. Billie turned on her a bland, chewing, acquiescent face, then went back to the advertisements. Half an hour or three hours, she wouldn't notice; all the clocks in the house had been left to run down long before Kate came home, the ones that wanted winding and the ones that wanted batteries; only Kate's watch now ever showed the real time. She retreated to her bedroom and lit a cigarette, pulling the curtains shut across the day that was anyway muffled with grey cloud against any sign of the sun. She kicked off her shoes and lay on her bed, smoking and giving herself up to hollowness, staring at the Pied Piper in the nursery frieze who loomed with his jaunty uplifted beckoning trumpet through the purple paint, in such promise of adventure and pleasure. How could she have imagined for one moment that she mattered except as an occasional Sunday-morning friend to this David whose other life was so actual, so unalterably good-looking, so substantially made flesh? She must have thought he was a man with a paper life to screw up and throw away, like some of the people she knew in London. She had screwed up her own professional life as if it didn't matter, and stepped outside it into where she was no one.

Five

David arrived home from work one evening to find a two-man mountain tent, orange, in the back garden. Suzie got up from where she was kneeling to hammer in tent pegs, wiping her hands on her jeans, smiling in a way that was somehow strained and challenging.

—I borrowed it from Giulia's girls, she said. —What do you think?

—It's all right. Holes in the lawn. What's it for?

—I thought I might take the kids camping: if the weather's fine. With Neil and Menna; they go away nearly every weekend. I had to make sure I knew how to put it up. It's years since I had a tent.

—You seem to have managed OK.

—Actually Jamie had to come down and rescue me.

David didn't in the least want to go camping: the idea of its play-inconveniences had never appealed to him, he wasn't the type renewed by close contact with the earth. He was taken aback nonetheless by Suzie's presumption that he wouldn't come.

—I know you've got work to do, she said, conciliatory. —I thought we could leave you to get on with it in peace.

The children were in ecstasy over the tent. They wanted to sleep in it that night, in the garden; Suzie said that they could if Jamie would stay out with them. Hannah zipped up the front and sat inside in the hot orange light with her phone, telling her friends about it; Joel brought down his Beanie Babies. But Jamie had disappeared with his bike, and he didn't come back. Avoiding David's eye apologetically, Suzie fetched her pyjamas from under the pillow in their bedroom; they all three undressed and got into their sleeping bags while it was still light enough for them to see. David worked in his study and then watched *Newsnight*; every so often he was surprised by the looming outside the window of the tent's alien faint fluorescence, and remembered his breathing, dreaming family afloat in it. He heard Jamie come home late; they met once in the kitchen, where David was getting a glass of water and Jamie was shovelling in his usual overflowing night-time bowl of cereal head down, hair falling in his face, book propped inches in front of him on the table to keep conversation out. David supposed that his son was revising for his exams, which began in a couple of weeks, although there was not much evidence of it. Whenever he had tried to play the part of the concerned parent as he felt he ought to do (hadn't Bryn when David was doing his A levels all those years ago even checked topics off against his revision list?), Jamie's teachers had met him with an amused reassurance that made him feel foolish. Jamie would sail through, they said. He couldn't fail to do well. Arts subjects anyway, David told himself, were so different to the sciences.

Before he went to bed, David stood outside the back door to check the deep chill in the garden now that the sun was long gone: he worried about them in the tent. He carried out a spare duvet and fiddled with the tent flaps, peering through; in the light from the kitchen he could just make out their huddled shapes, Suzie lifting her head to stare at him. Inside the tent the air was sweetly frowsty as a mouse nest.

—I brought another duvet, he said. —I worried you wouldn't be warm enough.

Suzie didn't answer for a few more moments, as though she couldn't find her way out of her sleep. —We're fine, she said eventually, still blurry. —We don't need it. But thank you.

On Friday evening Menna and her boyfriend drove up to collect the campers in a shabby old Bedford Dormobile van, painted with giant flowers in some unsuitable paint that was flaking off. David wanted to ask, is it safe, is it MOTed, have you checked the tyres?; but he bit down the words, kept his hands in his pockets, knowing his disapproval made him prim, fussing while his wife was carried off by gypsies. He saw perfectly through Menna's contemptuous black-button eyes, ringed round with black kohl pencil, what she made of where they lived: the shallow-rooted, expensive little brick-built estate with its pointless cottage porches, its raw gardens newly scratched on the red earth. The boyfriend was amiable and competent, he had a ponytail and hard brown hands (apparently he worked for the Parks Department, on a project conserving the old Cardiff cemeteries). He stowed Suzie's tent and luggage neatly in the back of the van and hoisted the children inside. Their noisy exit – the children at least turned and waved – hollowed out the evening; David could still hear the drone of the motorway when he went inside, as if the walls of his house had lost their solidity. He stood at the kitchen window, looking over their garden with its new-planted trees, past the green folds of the golf course and the clotted evening shadows of the old estate behind its wall, where the rhodo-dendrons would be in flower now, to where the first line of hills swelled in the north: intently he listened to the crunching of cars on the gravel drives, doors banging, mealtime pots and pans, an insect slamming into the window, cats padding along the tops of fences.

On the way back from Sainsbury's the next morning (Suzie had left him a list), David called in at Giulia's. He had been afraid that Giulia's face would close regretfully when she saw him, but he was enveloped immediately in her capacious interest and clouds of the flowery perfume she wore. She was in her dressing-gown, with cream patted on her cheeks.

—I'm so glad it's you: I meant to invite you round, I know you're on your own. What kind of weather have the campers got? It's not brilliant, but at least not raining. How's Jamie? Come on in, you're my excuse for coffee. It's a dreadful mess in here as usual: nobody's cleared the breakfast things. Larry's escaped into the studio. You wouldn't think it but honestly we've been up for hours: why doesn't the morning ever get started?

Giulia and Larry lived in the big dilapidated house Larry had inherited from his aunt along with the dance studio; while they were talking the thump of feet and snatches of disco music drifted from where Larry was taking classes next door. There were always visitors at Giulia's, drinking coffee or something stronger, eating pasta when Larry cooked it: family, staff from Ladysmith, the girls' teenage friends, a brain-damaged neighbour in a wheelchair, refugees from every kind of crisis. David wondered if he counted as one of those. Sometimes when he and Suzie were invited for drinks a very thin old lady, another of Larry's aunts perhaps, would be perched on a tall stool in the corner, taking in everything, prompting in brittle bursts of Italian when the guests needed their glasses refilled. Giulia put the coffee on and went upstairs to change; the girls, with tight golden skin and tight clothes and hair the same dark blonde as hers, erupted with loud bird-chatter into the dining room where David sat at the table with the crumbs and eggshells, not minding that he couldn't answer their questions. When were they going to go and feed the horse? Was Larry going to take them into town when he'd finished? Did anyone think this navel piercing was festering? Giulia, hurrying down, tying back her hair, apologised that the coffee was poisonous: only Larry could make it decently and he was never there.

—I'm so angry, she said. —One of my asylum-seeker families was deported yesterday: Sudanese. Do you know how they do it? They pick up the children and threaten to take them into care unless the parents proceed to the airport. Do you think that's civilised?

David really didn't, and in fact he'd done some public health work recently for the Refugee Council; they conferred for a while. The girls melted away, uninterested. Giulia wanted to work out some strategy with the Council so that she and her school governors could prevent this happening at Ladysmith again; David didn't think it would be possible.

—And what do you make of this Menna? he asked, regretting it as soon as he had spoken. —She and Suzie seem to be great friends all of a sudden.

—Do you mind it? Giulia's open attention was expertly kind.

—It's not personal. Just all the fakery: the fortune telling, the old hippie bus, the ankle bracelet. Suzie used to be more impatient with that New-Agey stuff than I was.

—It doesn't do any harm, does it? They've only gone camping. And I quite liked the ankle bracelet. I was thinking of getting one. Am I too old? I daren't ask the girls, I know what they'll say.

—Of course it doesn't do any harm. Only Suzie surprises me, that she can't see through it.

—There's more to some of that old nonsense than

you and I would like to think. My grandmother – a horrible old woman – had second sight, I swear it. She used to have a certain dream – always of water – the night before any accident happened in the family.

David could only look blankly then, embarrassed for Giulia: what was one supposed to say, confronted with the cherished superstitions of one's friends? His own rationalism was so complete, penetrating all his instincts, that he felt any unreason almost as a mistake of taste as well as judgement, shaming and silly.

Jamie had taken to calling in at Firenze. The first time he came, after their meeting at the café, Kate was painting Billie's toenails in the middle of the afternoon. He persisted at the front door, which she answered holding the pot of cherry-red varnish, her own fingers splayed because she was drying them.

—I told you everything about Francesca, she said. — There's nothing else.

—I was going to offer to help. I wondered if you needed anything. I could sit with your mother. I could cut your grass.

She sighed and let him follow her into the drawing room, where Billie was waiting with her bare feet up on the sofa. Kate took them on her lap and began painting again, bending low over the gnarled old toes in concentration. Billie was still vain enough to enjoy asking for a size three in the shoe shops, but her feet were swollen and purplish, and she suffered with bunions so that Kate had sometimes to cut her shoes away.

—Forgive our dreadful manners, Billie smiled graciously at Jamie. —How very rude of us.

He sat on the edge of a chair, blushing, staring round everywhere but at the nail-painting. —It's kind of you to let me in.

—Who is he? Billie asked loudly, but Kate pretended not to hear.

—I love this house, he said. —What an amazing place.

—See the grass. Kate signed to him to look out of the French windows. —Not so lovely. You'd need a scythe.

—There is a scythe, offered Billie unexpectedly. —In one of the outhouses.

—It will be blunt. If it's there at all. She's probably remembering something from half a century ago.

—I'll sharpen it, Jamie said. —If it exists.

Reluctantly, when she had finished Billie's nails, Kate found keys and opened the outhouses where she hadn't looked for years. Cobwebs were thick as filthy rags on all the accumulated rubbish: ladders, paint pots, her old stereo player from the seventies, a pedal sewing machine, a birdcage, bicycles, a workbench with jamjars full of nails rusted into one mass. Jamie wondered and exclaimed – look at this, it's an antique! – but Kate refused to be interested. Then, when they'd found the scythe, and he had decided it wasn't too rusty, sharpening it on a whetstone he'd also found, the afternoon was altered by the rhythmic swish of Jamie at work on the lawn: Kate opened the French windows and the room was filled with the perfume of the cut grass. The weather was close and grey. After some experimentation he found the right measured swing to make the grass fall cleanly; he took his shirt off and his face ran with sweat. Kate was exasperated by the careless young power in his brown back and shoulders and couldn't concentrate on her book. It was Billie's suggestion when he'd been working for an hour or so that they should make him tea; Kate brought out a table and chairs onto the veranda, carefully because the wood was rotten in places. Sim, displaced from the lap he was allowed on while she was reading, wound cabbalistic patterns round her feet.

—It's a good scythe, Jamie said to Billie, the rosebud teacup improbable in his fingers swollen hot and red from the work. He had already swallowed a pint of water at the kitchen sink.

—My father bought it. Although he was a businessman, he knew about the importance of working with good tools, he would only ever buy the best. Once, our property here stretched all the way up the hill, you know. When Kate was a child she used to play in our own little wood. All the trees are gone now except for our apple trees and that great beech behind the flats.

—Billie thinks sometimes she's a White Russian exile. A princess probably; there were so many princesses. I'm sure she blames the Bolsheviks for our reduced circumstances.

—I don't think anything of the sort, Kate.

—I taught with a few White Russians when I first started – the last of them, they must have been in their nineties at least – and they were much, much, madder than Billie. But we do have to remind ourselves sometimes that our money came from haberdashery. Stockings for the miners' wives.

—What's haberdashery? Jamie asked. —What's a White Russian?

—Oh, said Kate. —Don't you know anything? I thought you were supposed to be a clever boy. Anyway, I'm regretting letting you cut the lawn now. I think it looked better with the grass long. That grass was beautiful, it blew in the wind, it was blond like hair, the sound it made was like the sea. Now what does it look like? Stubbled and ugly, a poor cropped head.

Jamie was crestfallen until Kate laughed at him and gave him a cigarette.

—Don't take any notice of my daughter, dear, said Billie. —She's such a tease.

She asked Kate again later, —Who is he? How do we know him?

Kate would only tell her his name was Jamie: she didn't want to risk some connection sparking suddenly, and Billie spilling out to David, if he ever came, with admiration for his handsome son. Jamie squatted with his back to the veranda, squinting at his labours, and smoked at least with proper grown-up insouciance. It was the first thing you ever learned to do like a grown-up: Kate could remember practising in her bedroom, in front of the mirror.

The next time Jamie turned up he took them for a row on the lake. Kate was busy, she didn't want to come out, she had a paper to write for a conference she'd been invited to; Jamie insisted that Billie had told him she longed to go. It was a nightmare getting Billie into the boat, anyway: she hesitated in brittle indecision on the brink, prodding with her stick and grappling Kate's arm, until the boat-hire man and Jamie lifted and swung her in between them. There was only one other boat out: it was a Tuesday afternoon. The sunlight was hazy yellow and the water white-pale; the dipping oars puckered a milky skin then dripped with light; bread bobbed in the thick unrolling of their wake near the shore, where people overfed the ducks. Jamie rounded the clock tower and then they moved to the sound of the small splash of the oars down the lake to where the islands at the other end were cut off by orange floats on a nylon rope.

—Shouldn't you be at school? Kate said.

—It's exam time. We don't have normal lessons.

—Then you should be revising.

He smiled at her, heaving backwards.

—Isn't this heavenly? said Billie, sitting very upright, gripping the side of the boat, looking round with that expression of hers as though she was witnessing wonders. —You used to be able to row around these islands. And we got off and picnicked. We made a fire once and picnicked at night. Someone brought a guitar and we sang.

—Do you want to go around them now? Lift up the rope and I'll slip under.

—Do you think we might? What fun!

—Don't be silly, Jamie, said Kate. —There'd be a scene

103

with the hire-man shouting at us: and outside our own front door. You forget we're elderly and respectable.

—You're not.

—Don't you think we're respectable?

—Not elderly.

But obediently he pulled with one oar to turn the boat, then rowed back to the other end again, gliding so lightly that his passengers felt themselves suspended in the silver light reflected from the water.

—How do you get on with your stepmother? Kate asked.

—All right, now. We used to have a hard time.

—That's traditional, with stepmothers. Leaving you in the woods to starve, throwing you down wells. It's all in the literature. You were the cunning child, dropping little stones so that you could always find your way back home.

—She really wasn't wicked. I was awful, I think. I woke up ten times a night asking for drinks, and I only ate crackers and tinned tomato soup. We quite like each other now.

—Where does she come from? How did she and David meet?

—She has an insane family. Her parents do a magic show for children, they're working in Spain at the moment, for the expats: hopeless with money, Suzie's always having to bail them out. There's a brother who's done time for credit-card fraud and a sister who chooses the wrong sort of men and turns up at our house with bruises and black eyes. God knows how they met. We don't talk about real things at home.

Jamie with panache made the boat skim through the narrow channel between the clock tower with its tiny locked red door and the steep stone bank under the promenade, where passers-by leaned over to be made serene by the vista of lake and blue-distant wooded hills; their passage set rocking the surface mess of duck feathers and bread and ice-lolly wrappers. Kate asked Jamie as they disembarked – Billie locked rigid from sitting – if he knew anything about computers. He said he only knew the usual stuff, but Kate thought that was bound to be more than she did: when they got back to the house and while Billie was unbending in the heat of the gas fire burning pale in the bright daylight, she took him upstairs to show him where the iMac Max had bought with her still sat in its chaos of wires on the table in her bedroom.

—Could you make this work?

—You mean, just put it together and plug it in?

—Exactly.

He laughed because it was so easy.

—Is this your bedroom? he asked, when she came up ten minutes later to see how he was getting on, and found the screen humming. —It isn't like an ordinary bedroom.

—It's an idiotic room. It's a child's bedroom, made for the charming kind of child I never was. I haven't made up my mind yet how to live here as myself. What is an ordinary bedroom like, anyway?

—Oh, you know, fitted wardrobes and carpet and all that.

—Fitted wardrobes. They sound awful. Do you have those?

—I kept them out. Suzie tried to force them on me but I wouldn't let her.

—You know I was born in this house, Kate said. — Not in this room. I'll show you where. It's probably the opposite kind of room to fitted wardrobes.

She sat Sim on her shoulders: he was jealous of Jamie, and wouldn't leave her alone with him. Mostly the door to the master bedroom was kept shut; occasionally she sent Buckets and Mops in with a duster. It was shaded as it always had been with the old blinds pulled down: they were so moth-eaten that this afternoon the gloom was peppered with tiny beams and pricks of sunlight. Mirrors glinted like dark pools, over the dressing table which stood with its back to a side window, and in the door of the frowning massive carved-mahogany wardrobe, all naiads and fruit and sheaves to match the bed with its spilled cornucopia. Maids had once cleaned the mahogany, or so Billie reminisced, with rags wrung out in vinegar and boiling water. Kate couldn't remember anyone ever sleeping in here: her grandparents had been dead for years before she was born. Always the same smells – moth-balls and wool carpets, and something sweet like old-fashioned face powder – had hung unchanging in the close air, only fading and mingling over decades, and yielding now to a sour damp; the rain must be coming in somewhere here, too. The room ran almost the whole length of the house; one end was arranged as a sort of boudoir, with a sofa covered in red silk faded to pink, and a writing desk.

Jamie took a few shy steps inside.

—What an amazing room.

—What was my grandfather Sam thinking of? How many tribes of children did he dream of engendering in that bed? What had he seen in Vilnius that made him want this: don't you think, it's a poor little Jewish boy putting down his barrow on a winter's night and peering through lit windows? He really did have a barrow, I believe, although it sounds like poetic licence.

—Are you Jewish? he said.

—Not really. Not really Jewish, not really Welsh, not really Irish (that's my father). Not at all English.

Kate crossed to the windows and pulled at the blinds; the mechanisms jerked and choked and gave out puffs of dust as they rolled up. Outside the three floor-length windows was a long enclosed wrought-iron balcony overlooking the lake, whose silver had healed itself seamlessly behind their intrusion: there were no more boats out, the swans were in possession. This was the best room in Firenze. When Kate imagined doing the whole house up, modernising it, making it a place where she could have a real life, she always planned to turn this room into her own bedroom and sitting room. The day after she made her plans, though, the labour and banality of actually carrying them out would fill her with ennui. And perhaps there wasn't the money for it anyway.

—Poor grandfather Sam. Actually there wasn't much engendering. For all the dynastic fantasy of that bed head, it's been a thin little, weak little female line, trickling to a halt with me, running away into the ground for ever. They only had Billie. My grandmother had miscarriages; Billie was a late miracle, after they'd given up hope. Doesn't she look slightly unearthly, against nature? She was born in this room, we both were. She only ever had me: I was late as well. I suppose we were conceived in this bed, both of us. And my grandparents both died in here, not knowing that there would be any grandchildren. My father also died in here: the interloper. Better they never knew about him. So we've shut it up: too much momentousness, too cumbersome for daily use.

They stood squinting slightly at one another in the low late-afternoon light, filtered and made pearly through windows that hadn't been cleaned for years; with the blinds thrown up, the room behind them leaped into bleaker distinctness, made more strange by the invasive present: the wallpaper torn, the carpet stained, great hulks of furniture marooned.

—I love it that you've left it, said Jamie. —No one else would do that. Granny Bell has an old house but she's always changing it, it's always up to date.

—I haven't lived in this house for twenty-five years. When I was a teenager it made me sick: I used to nag Billie to change everything, to buy everything new. Now I haven't got the energy, though it still makes me sick sometimes.

—Why do you have that white lock in your hair?

—Sorrow, of course. For my wasted life.

—Really?

He put out a hand to touch: Sim batted at him with a paw, claws unretracted.

—No, silly, it's heredity. There's another one at the back, growing on the nape. I have them from my father apparently, though they don't show in any of his photographs. I suppose mine are going to be lost, now, as the rest turns to white as well.

Kate pulled her head away from clumsy boy fingers, although later when Billie asked Jamie to play the piano she saw that the fingers weren't so bad, despite what the scything and the rowing might have seemed to mean: the hands were long and fluent, with good movement, and he had the broad-stubbed finger-ends that promise intelligence of execution rather than elegance. He played appallingly, though: his style was execrable and he stumbled, blushing, through the easy pieces he professed to know. He hadn't ever got very far, he said, he had given up years ago. He had only very reluctantly – shoulders hunched in expectation of humiliation – agreed to play for them, because Billie persisted beyond what was quite sane in pleading with him, and Kate, wanting to get on with her book, couldn't be bothered to intervene. He could have left, couldn't he, if he hadn't wanted to make a fool of himself? Jamie confessed that he hadn't ever had a real piano to practise on, only one of those electric keyboards. Kate watched pity and purpose light up in her mother like lamps; patiently Billie propped herself behind Jamie, crooked as she was, working his shoulders until they dropped and his arms fell into the right line.

—Put your hands over the keys. Not like that: imagine you are holding oranges: curved, curved. Now play: just this simplest little exercise, listen. 'Climbing a Stair'. Keep those fingers curved. Weight down, drop your wrists, on the first note; lift off, lift the wrists – only lift, not staccato – on the third. Curved. All the way up. There: now do you hear? That's better, isn't it? Try this one: 'Opening the Door'.

After this, whenever Jamie called, Billie made him work with her at the piano for at least an hour, teaching him through little games as if he was seven or eight years old. Billie's old competence roused from murky depths when she was teaching him, she was incisive and exacting; even if she thought he was a child, she insisted he play his easy pieces and exercises to the highest standard, as she had done in the old days when she gave lessons and ran her Suzuki classes. Kate listened to Jamie stumbling, stalling, trying in vain for the same simple thing over and over. She thought it was good for him to struggle and fail: he had the sleepy indolence of clever boys for whom everything has been too easy. He read a lot – he'd read already much more than his father – but unsystematically, with huge gaps in his knowledge which he imagined he could supply with guessing and intuition.

Jamie's presence in the house began to bother Kate obscurely. Sometimes she turned him away when he called; but then Billie asked where he was, the lessons made her so happy.

—Why aren't you with your friends? Kate frowned.
—Don't you have friends?

110

—I do have friends, Jamie reassured her, —but I'd rather be here.

—Why?

—Everything here is different. You're not like anybody else.

—How would you know? You don't know anybody.

He went cycling out to the countryside at Cefn Onn, behind the new estate where he lived with his family, and brought back for Kate a great bouquet of wild flowers stuffed under his sweatshirt; when he pushed them at her they were half wilted, and she scratched herself on something, drawing blood.

—Isn't it May blossom? she said. —Don't you know not to bring that in the house? It means bad luck. Take it away. I don't want it in here.

The first weekend Suzie went camping with Menna, the weather wasn't very good. A fortnight later, the forecast was better, and she told David they were going again, to the same place, a site in a meadow beside a river beyond the Hay Bluff. David was surprised to find himself indifferent this time. He was busy; he hardly looked up from his computer when he heard the old Bedford van arrive on Saturday morning (its puttering filthy exhaust more polluting, surely, than anything they could make up for with their puritanical veganism). Suzie stood in the door of his study to say goodbye, hesitant as if he might want an explanation for her defection again, so soon; but he didn't, he had work to do, he kissed her quickly.

111

He had spent most of his week out of Cardiff, coming home very late; he was monitoring an outbreak of meningitis in one of the valleys towns where a fifteen-year-old girl had died and a couple of others were ill. It was difficult to trace all the friends the dead girl had had close contact with: the night before she was taken into hospital, she had been driven around, up and down the mountains in the dark from one house to another, in the crowded back of someone's beat-up car; they had been drinking and taking amphetamines, she had complained of feeling ill. David tried to imagine this teenage life, this careless jumbled contact, like fox cubs nuzzling and tussling together in a den; when he was their age he had kept himself scrupulously apart. He didn't know what Jamie did when he went out at night. He telephoned Kate Flynn and asked if she wanted to come with him to see a film at Chapter Arts Centre. There was a Bergman season on; he wasn't sure it was his kind of thing, but he thought it might be hers.

Virgin Spring rocked him with its violence. He disguised his shock from Kate as they made their way out with the seven or eight other members of the audience from the small studio cinema; nothing could surprise her, she had seen everything before. He avoided someone he knew from the hospital, not wanting to have to talk shop. They stopped in Chapter bar to have a beer, and David drank something heavy and cold and sweet that Kate recommended.

—My wife's taken our children and gone off with the hippies, he told her, —in a van painted with psychedelic flowers. Probably they're drawing up their astral charts at this very moment, somewhere in the Black Mountains.

Kate leaned her chin on her hand bristling with rings to listen. —Just like that: without warning?

—The signs have been there for a while. The dream catcher over the bed, candles everywhere, marijuana in an old tobacco tin, a copy of Kahlil Gibran in the toilet.

—That's bad, sighed Kate. —Kahlil Gibran in the toilet. Sometimes it's the *Rubaiyat of Omar Khayyam*. It can lead to the Desiderata beside the front door.

The beer went straight to his head. He told her about his meningitis outbreak.

—You have the power of life and death, she said, as if she was reading it in his face.

—I'm afraid not.

—No, no, you do. Isn't that an extraordinary thing? Because of what you decide, individuals live or die.

—It's a system; I apply it. Nothing in the least heroic, although the system's very admirable.

—It makes what I've done seem a kind of dream, a mistake. A life lost in books. What an abyss of difference, between your usefulness and mine. How did I choose it: this play-life? I should have been a nurse. We carelessly make one choice after another and our lives pile up.

He laughed at her. —I don't think you'd have made a good nurse, I'm afraid to say.

—You mean I'd have been useless. Too selfish, indolent, disobedient.

—Not for those reasons. But why are you denigrating

your real expertise? You don't really think that books and music are only play.

—Oh, if I was really any good at the violin, or if I was a real scholar . . . Are you happy?

—Happy? I don't know.

—You see yourself as instrumental, Kate said. —Your outer life is given form by structures larger than yourself, the inner life is left alone. There's a kind of bittersweet glamour in that. It makes men very attractive at this point of life you've reached, with youth behind them.

—Surely it could apply to women just as well, these days?

She made a quick disclaiming face. —But not to me.

Kate suggested he come back to Firenze for coffee. He drove knowing he ought to feel irresponsible because he was slightly, uncharacteristically drunk; actually he felt exalted and confident, and when they climbed out of the car he breathed in deeply the cold night exhalation of vegetation from the park. The woman Kate had asked to come in and sit with Billie was watching television in the library; David hadn't ever noticed before that the Flynns had television. Kate thanked her effusively, called her 'my lifesaver', got out her purse to pay, hurrying her off in a performance of patrician condescension that Suzie would have bristled at.

—Put the kettle on, she called to David. —I'm going up to make sure Billie is all right.

He wandered through several rooms whose light bulbs when he found the switch were either blown or grimly dim, and found himself eventually where he remembered a glassed-in conservatory area led down to the kitchen at a right angle to the main house, beside the garden. The cavernous space with its pantomime-sized table and gigantic plate racks on the walls was comically disproportionate to Kate's and Billie's needs; when he searched for coffee most of the cupboards were empty. An electric cooker had been installed long ago beside the disused gas range. Water thundered into the kettle from a high tap over the square enamel sink; the kettle at least was electric, although its flex looked dangerously frayed. Kate's black cat mewed throatily to be let out of the back door. David couldn't find instant coffee, and then guessed that Kate might only make real, and found that in the huge old cream-coloured fridge whose loud motor with its changes of mood was insistent as a personality in the room.

A small plastic-framed mirror hung askew from a hook over the sink and while he waited for the kettle David looked at his reflection, skin greenish in the bleak central light. He saw himself as Kate had suggested, authoritative and complete-seeming, mysterious just because he didn't have any time to spare for introspection; then looked quickly away, ashamed of the falsity of consciously seeing this. It occurred to him for the first time that Kate might be expecting him to make a pass at her. He didn't think of himself as the sort of man women wanted to do this: but Kate's type – London types – might take it for granted that if two people liked each other enough, finding themselves conveniently alone, they would end up in bed together. Why not, after all? His wife had abandoned him and gone off with strangers. Why not make it simply an extension of friendship?

But he knew he would only be appalled and embarrassed if anything like that started up. Hadn't Kate tried to kiss him on some occasion, when they were teenagers, and he'd made a humiliating mess of it? Francesca had once called him 'unimaginatively monogamous'. He made the coffee hastily, the glow from the alcohol all subsided. Kate came and leaned in the kitchen doorway, watching him doing it, telling him funny stories about Billie, directing him to where the coffee cups were kept, and the sugar. They were proper old porcelain cups, green and gold, with saucers; if you held them up to the light you could see it shining through a woman's face set in the base. He avoided looking directly at Kate. He didn't think he was attracted to her physically, anyway. There was something off-putting in her extreme thinness under all those layers; the idea of peeling them away was more forensic than sensual. Also, she smoked, she was smoking now, blowing smoke at the ceiling, knocking her ash into the sink, waving the cigarette carelessly in a dangling hand. He said that actually he was tired, his exhaustion after the busy week had just hit him, he must hurry off to his bed as soon as he'd drunk his coffee. Even the word 'bed' seemed too intimate; he winced as he used it. He imagined that Kate could see through him; that her eyes, if he'd been able to meet them, would have been full of mockery at his predicament.

Halfway home, he was furious with himself for his gaucherie and for his ridiculous idea. How rude he must have seemed, falling over himself to get away. And he regretted now the stupidly squandered opportunity; so bitterly that he almost turned around and drove back. But how could he have explained? He had wanted to sit with Kate in the library with its pink-shaded lamps and walls of books, unravelling himself: the ache of longing for companionship, now he was cheated of it, was overwhelming. At home he sat for a long time outside in the car before he could face going into the house that seemed by contrast so transparently empty.

For half an hour on Sunday evening David thought that the film he and Kate had seen lived on in him: in his voice quaking with rage and his trembling hands he was horrified to feel that same righteous male violence. Suzie came back late, hours later than she had told him to expect them; he had been frantic with worry. And when she came in, she was stoned, really stoned, so that looking for her in her eyes he couldn't find her, she was veiled and blurred and lost to him. The van with its farting exhaust had dumped them and made its derisive exit: when he came out from his study, his family crowded in the hallway seemed transformed by their short time away, tanned and dishevelled and staring with exhaustion. They even smelled alien: of some mix of smoke and earth, pee and petrol. He was outraged at the idea of Suzie's irresponsibility, getting into that state while she was in charge of the children.

—It was good, Hannah and Joel insisted, but unsmiling.

He bathed them tenderly and put them in clean pyjamas; they didn't even ask for stories, they melted into their sleep almost as he lifted the duvets over them. While he did all this he heard Suzie throwing up noisily in the en suite bathroom.

—What is this about? he said. —What are you doing?

She was propped against the sink with her T-shirt off, in only her bra and trousers, her hair dripping wet as if she'd been pouring water over her head to try and sober up.

—Having fun, that's all, she said idiotically, with the water running down her face and neck. —But you wouldn't know about that.

—It's a peculiar kind of fun. Look at you. The children are wiped out. They have to go to school tomorrow. So do you: but that's your business.

—What are you accusing me of?

—You can go where you want, he said. —But you're not taking the children away with that crew again.

—They had a fantastic time. Just because they're tired now.

—Who was driving? David said. —What had he been smoking?

—Oh, I'm going to go and sleep in Joel's room, Suzie said, pushing out of the bathroom past him, picking up her pillow from the bed, rummaging unsuccessfully in a drawer for pyjamas, slamming it shut with the clothes still hanging half out of it.

—I'll go and sleep in there, sighed David, performing weary patience. —You stay here. You might need to be near the bathroom.

He moved to close the drawer.

—I don't want you to touch me! she exclaimed, backing off, hugging the pillow to her chest. —Don't even touch me.

He hadn't thought of touching her, but when she shrieked at him he felt vividly a tingling in his hand, as if he'd slapped her face with all his strength, knocking her head sideways with the blow; he stood away from her quickly, letting her go. Slumped down onto the side of the bed, he felt the blood pulsing thickly into his ears and his throat. He heard her vomiting again, in the other toilet.

In the morning Suzie was chastened, she reassured him that Neil had been perfectly safe to drive, Menna had been fine, only she had been poorly, she must have reacted badly to something, she was sorry. And the children, although they drooped and whined all week from the late nights, dropped fragments of delighted narrative of their adventures for him in voices that didn't expect him to be able to understand: the nights so dark, the torch that failed, the barbecue built from stones, the thieving goats. Jamie remarked conversationally that the skunk Suzie's friends had been smoking was probably hydroponically grown and much stronger than anything she had been used to; that would be why it had made her ill. David heard him out in silence and then shrugged, as if it was a matter of indifference to him. Suzie didn't

119

talk about going away for any more camping weekends; in fact, he knew she gave the tent back to Giulia. She didn't mention Menna, although he presumed that when she said she was going out for a drink with friends it was with them. She went on sleeping in the top bunk in Joel's room.

Six

Billie was baking: over her dress she had tied an old-fashioned apron, frilled, with heart-shaped gingham pockets outlined in red piping. She looked absolutely competent, turning a hand whisk, beating egg whites into a froth. Kate was frowning into a book, sitting upright at the big table with its white enamel top. The kitchen smelled strongly of something like marmalade.

Carol had called in on her way home from work.

—Billie, you look so pretty, she said. —You remind me of a waitress in a Danish pastry shop.

—Do you know, said Kate, —there are carrier bags full of her clothes in every room upstairs? Lots of them not worn yet, with the price tags still on, which I try not to read.

—We had such lovely times in the old days, Billie reminisced, —shopping for outfits together. Didn't we, Kate?

—Long after she stopped paying the gas bills or calling

121

the plumber in, she must have gone on visiting Howells and David Morgan, trying things on, having all the assistants running round after the sweet old lady.

—She is sweet.

—Everything suits her, everything fits: but the trouble is it's all white and pink and pale yellow. She just forgot to buy the other stuff, the black and the brown, the sensible part. She looks every day as if she's dressed for a wedding. Talking of plumbers, that heating engineer's in the house somewhere. He's bullied me into buying a new boiler. We were having to heat our water in saucepans. Go and spy on him, tell me if you think he's any good, or if you think I should make a scene and demand my money back.

—I knew you'd have to see sense and get a new one sooner or later. What is Billie cooking?

Even in her vagueness Billie didn't forget to be winning, tilting her face to one side, pursing her mouth, looking at the whites in her bowl as if she was surprised to find them there. —What am I cooking, Kate?

—Cake, said Kate shortly.

—Oh yes, cake. Her face cleared. —My mother's cake: orange and almond, very moist. You'll love it.

—But look at the size of me! What are you thinking of, tempting me with cake?

—Darling, it's good for you.

Billie's pretty clothes were stained and spotted with dropped food ('And they're all dry-clean only,' Kate moaned), but her hair was immaculate in its perfect pleat, sensuous as snow.

—How I wish I could do my hair like this, Carol said, kissing it, sniffing the dry-leaf faint odour of Billie's scalp.

—I'll teach you, sweetheart. Easy-peasy.

—With my old straw? You're joking. Anyway, what would I look like with my hair pulled back? She showed them, baring her teeth and growling. —Pretty scary, huh?

—Billie's making cake because she thinks I don't feed her properly.

Billie was distressed. —Is that what I said?

—I'm with Billie, you're an awful cook. It's because you don't like eating.

—Oh it's true, when she was a baby she was so fussy. She wouldn't have the breast milk, she wouldn't have the Ostermilk. When she was a little girl, she lived on bread and butter: cut so thin, only I could do it right. Swallowed down like medicine, in tiny pieces.

—I have to sit here for anything involving machinery or heat. Or for when she forgets what she's making.

Carol took the lid off a pan. —Are these oranges really supposed to be boiled?

—So it says in the recipe. Put the kettle on, make tea, stop stalking up and down. You're making me nervous.

Carol emptied the teapot in the garden, tea and leaves an amber arc against rain-soaked grass and foliage brilliant in sunshine. Kate shivered, hunching her shoulders under her jumper.

—It's a lovely day out there.

—Don't want to know.

—I came to ask you how the conference went.

Kate didn't smile or look away from her book. —It went fine.

—They liked your paper?

—They adored it.

—Meet many people you knew?

Kate scowled and put the book down. —Your solicitude is showing, she said. —You know, like a bra strap or a droopy petticoat.

Penitently, Carol measured out spoons of tea into the pot.

—You're bored, she said to Kate later, upstairs, when the cake – exotic, made from beating the boiled oranges to a mush and mixing them with ground almonds and eggs – was in the oven, and Billie was resting in front of the television, and the boiler-man was paid off. —You're not happy. I told you how it would be. We have to think about respite care for Billie, at the very least. Why don't you try and find some work down here?

—Look, said Kate. —D'you see what I mean? Bagfuls of clothes, not even unpacked. Cupboards full.

In a back bedroom, dust motes swam indolently in a thick bronze light; they explored in the bags, pulling out dainty tops and skirts and dresses, throwing them on the bed (untidy as if Billie might have slept in it recently), agitating the dust to frenzy so that Carol began to wheeze, finding a little dusky-rose-coloured cashmere pullover to like, a sleeveless broderie anglaise top. Kate stripped off her jumper and unbuttoned her shirt; she didn't wear a bra. Her skinny nakedness was always

124

frank as a curt statement; meagre palm-scoops of breast, big chocolate-brown nipples, a narrow ribcage the same silky brown as the skin of her face and hands. Carol imagined how her friend's body would age by diminution, shrinking and concentrating, while her own would blow up and dilute; their bodies didn't show much ageing, yet, only their faces and hands gave signs of it, like first flares of yellow in green summer trees. Kate tried a silky dress with a Peter Pan collar and a pattern of tea roses.

—I hate to think of you stuck here all day every day, doing nothing with that brilliant brain of yours.

—It never was brilliant. Anyway, who keeps these books, to see who's used themselves wisely and who's wasted?

Carol felt smothered inside her T-shirt and gasped her way out of it, turning her back to Kate because she didn't want to see their different flesh too cruelly juxtaposed.

—As a matter of fact, I'm fine. I'm going to give a musical party: isn't that a good sign? Max has said he'll come down, and a few other friends from London. I may invite your brother. Try this one on, it's summery.

—My brother? David? Oh, Suzie did say that you'd met him at a concert.

—She's a bore. I suppose I'll have to invite her too.

—Suzie's not a bore.

—And she sleeps around.

—Kate, be ashamed of yourself. Wherever did you get that idea?

—David told me.

—I just don't believe you.

—Or I intuit it in the gaps between the bits he tells me. And you can smell it on her anyway: one of those feral women, short on words, itching to leap into bed.

—That's not funny, said Carol. —You've got a horrible imagination. What are you up to; what's all this about my brother? You're not developing some sort of thing about him?

—I know I'm getting very provincial, but I'm not quite that bad yet. I think I can do a bit better than your brother. Don't get me wrong, he's a really decent salt-of-the-earth type. He's the type you'd be grateful for in an emergency, when the more interesting and attractive ones were falling apart or saving themselves.

Carol was mollified. —I didn't think he was your sort. She grimaced at herself in the mirror, in a chintzy cotton dress too short and too tight. —And Wales isn't a province by the way, it's another country.

Kate preened beside her. —I could never wear anything this optimistic.

—I look like an armchair whose loose covers have shrunk in the wash.

—Why did Francesca choose him, do you think? Of all the ones who were queuing up to get inside her silk knickers?

Carol stared quickly at the real Kate not reflected. —What made you think of her, all of a sudden?

—Perhaps because we're looking like the ugly sisters. That's how she used to make me feel. That rope of pale hair of hers, and the long nose and close-together eyes:

126

I suppose it had all taken centuries of breeding. Do you remember how she talked?

—I can't. Carol was pained to realise she'd forgotten.

—Nasal, fastidious. As if she was picking a slow path among the mistakes that other people might have made. Not that she was clever: clever was another mistake.

—David wasn't queuing up, I suppose; perhaps that was what interested her. He didn't really notice her until she set to work, attracting his attention.

—She thought he was a fortress, she thought he was deep and still, and that she would be healed if she could lose herself in him. Do you remember how she used to parade him round with her, after they were first together? Petting him, talking about him as if he wasn't there?

—He was just starting as Senior House Officer.

—Her talk must have been a torment to him, don't you think? Wasn't he one of those young men ashamed of letting anything out from inside?

Carol was thinking about Francesca. —How sad it was, she said, sitting down abruptly on the bed, on top of all the clothes. The smell of baking cake was spreading through the house. —It's the saddest thing that's happened in my life, really.

She lay down and closed her eyes, as if to dream about it, and fell immediately asleep.

Kate Flynn sent the Robertses an invitation to a musical evening: Suzie pinned it on the noticeboard in the kitchen among all the other notes from school and swimming club, the photo of Hannah winning the sack race, Joel's drawings of bird-people with hawk-faces and wings in place of arms. On its stiff plain cream card, Kate's spiky black italics written in fountain pen seemed a sign of stern difficulty, and neither David nor Suzie mentioned the card's arrival or discussed whether they would go. Eventually David's mother brought up the subject, sitting at the kitchen table when David came in one evening, late from work. Suzie was cooking at the stove amid steam and a clattering of pans: David's awareness these days went obliquely at once to his wife when he came into the house, so that he could know how their quarrel stood. The fish pie and carrots and frozen peas were a performance for his mother, not to deceive her but to appease her. Jamie was laying the table carefully, even putting out bread and paper napkins; he was better at charming and courting Betty than David had ever been. Betty's quiet domestic ideal was substantial in any room she was in, so that none of them while she was there could move without edging past it; even though she often came these days to escape from Bryn, to complain how he didn't have enough to do, how he followed her round the house, pestering her over the tiny details of shopping and tidying.

—I didn't know you were in touch with Kate Flynn, Betty said, seeing the invitation. —Poor thing. You know she's come home to look after her mother?

—David is in touch, said Suzie. —I don't really know her. We've bumped into one another once or twice.

—Carol worries about her. She thinks she's taken on too much. I must say that of all people I wouldn't have

128

expected it of Kate: she didn't used to treat her mother very well. Of course you remember, David, Mrs Flynn used to teach Carol the piano.

—I know them, Jamie said unexpectedly, pausing with his hands full of knives and forks as if he might have added something more.

—You're bound to have come across them at Carol's, Betty said. —Carol and Kate have been friends, not for ever, but from when they were in the third year, in the same class at Howells. Have you been to their house, Suzie? You ought to go to the musical thing, just to see it. It's an extraordinary old place, a bit of Cardiff history. The grandfather must have had a lot of money, but I should think they've spent most of it by now. Carol says they haven't changed anything in there, they could open it up as a museum.

—I've been there, Jamie said. —I'd like to live like that.

Suzie was amiable, draining vegetables. —What, in an old ruin? That would suit you.

—Like what? said David. —How've you been there?

—They live as if they'd just been dropped onto earth from outer space. As if all the boring stuff didn't matter.

Suzie only laughed at him now but she and Jamie had fought once, literally, pulling hair and scratching faces, over his refusal to tidy his room. Their truce wrong-footed David, after all the years he had dedicated himself to looking out for his impossible son (Jamie wouldn't eat off coloured plates, he wouldn't go to bed in his own room, he wouldn't socialise with other children). No

129

one would think, looking at the grown boy, coolly self-sufficient, that the child had taken such an effort of love.

—I expect they had servants once, said Betty. —To do all the boring stuff.

—Will we go? Suzie asked, from where her face was hidden behind the oven door. —To this musical evening?

—Do you want to? David hadn't been to the Flynns' for a while; he'd held off as if he imagined Kate was disappointed in him somehow. He didn't want Suzie looking round at the dilapidated old rooms, making a story out of them for her girlfriends; he felt protectively that Firenze belonged to him, he couldn't bear it spoiled. And yet if she said she wanted to come, how could he not take it as an encouragement, when things were poised so uneasily between them?

—All right, she said carefully. —I'm curious, I suppose. Probably I'll regret it, I'll get stuck talking to someone with a beard and a collection of early instruments.

David didn't know why Suzie was sleeping downstairs (she'd moved out of Joel's room onto the spare bed in the study); she wouldn't speak about it. She had once even put her hand over his mouth when he tried to ask her, shaking her head to warn him off, pushing him away from her with her fist against his chest: not unkindly but urgently, as if someone was watching them and she was under a vow of non-communication, although they were all alone.

Kate looked brilliant in a dress of some sort of flimsy transparent black stuff that came halfway down her calves, embroidered with green and gold beads; she wore tall green shoes and dramatic glass jewellery like pantomime emeralds. For some reason when David had pictured the evening in advance he had imagined it – tenderly – as rather subdued and old-fashioned: a few of Billie's old friends from the other houses around the lake, Kate's string quartet, perhaps a couple of Carol's colleagues. He knew as soon as he and Suzie got out of the car, from the hubbub of voices and the lights blazing, that he'd been stupidly mistaken. How could he have forgotten Kate's teenage parties that had had to be crazier than everybody else's, and where the police had invariably been called? They climbed the zigzag path and saw through the lit uncurtained dining-room windows the long table spread with fashionable food (Kate must have had a caterer); Billie's old friends, propped chatting animatedly on their sticks and frames, were having the time of their lives in a press of animated interested strangers, dressed up and wound up, making party talk. There were children, too – surprising in this house – weaving their unnoticed paths among the adults. David's mood withered: he remembered that he hated parties.

The front door stood open, the porch was full of lights and flowers: a dark-haired woman he recognised as Billie's babysitter offered to take their coats upstairs. Borne into the hall on a tide of hostess-importance – she almost seemed to have an entourage – Kate kissed them and welcomed them enthusiastically; the next moment there was someone arriving outside on the street, dropped by a taxi, and she was carried past them down the steps to greet a tall thin fair young American. They were shyly helpless in her wake, David wondering how he had ever thought himself Kate's intimate.

—Sherie couldn't make it, the American was apologising to Kate: they came inside clinging together, Kate even in her high shoes having to tilt her head to see up to his height, he bending over her, youthful and easy, taking off his gold-rimmed glasses to wipe them. —You look great, Katie. At least I think you do: can't see a thing.

—Sherie's always so busy, Kate sympathised. —We'll have to make do with you all by yourself.

—She's got a deadline, writing something for *Guardian Weekend*.

—David, Suzie, this is Max. We're privileged that he's prised himself away: Max is very domesticated these days.

—Do you have children then? smiled Suzie, hopeful of some earthy common ground.

—They'd like children, Kate said.

—We don't have children, Max said firmly, frowning at Kate.

Suzie shrank, Kate waved them towards the drinks and then carried Max off to meet someone; for ten minutes after they'd taken glasses of something with bubbles from a girl with a tray David and Suzie were stranded foolishly together in a corner of the drawing room, searching for anything to say. Suzie asked whether it was champagne and David said he didn't know, he couldn't honestly tell the difference between that and fizzy wine. The French windows were pushed open onto the garden and couples were moving about out there in the close grey evening; the chopped-off grass lying on the lawn smelled heavily sweet, and coloured lanterns, still pale in the late daylight, hung in the trees. Children were taking turns to roll down a sharp slope at the far end of the garden, into the fence. David had an instinct that if he and Suzie once went outside they'd be lost, they'd never be able to join in the party; after strolling round pretending to smell the roses they'd have simply to make a humiliated escape through some back gate or over a wall. They looked around them instead with exaggerated interest and talked about the house: filled up with life like this it didn't look so much eccentric as privileged. The screen-partition between the drawing room and the library had been pushed back to make one vast space running the whole length of the back of the building; David had never properly noticed the chandeliers before, because when he visited Kate had only switched on the lamps. Suzie took in the grandeur: white dints came in her cheeks where her jaw tensed in resistance to it.

Max the American seemed to know plenty of people, which suggested that lots of the guests were Kate's friends from London. They were striking in ways which David thought of as belonging to the metropolis: a girl with a feathered cap, bird-face and bright vermilion lipstick; a small middle-aged man, light on his feet, with face expressively lined and a heavy Central European accent; a beautiful fat woman in a sari exposing satiny folds of

133

bare midriff. They might have been simply the kind of Cardiff people David never met. Kate was continually tearing herself away from one group to bestow herself upon another: she waved plaintively at David and Suzie once, as if she yearned to arrive with them but couldn't yet. David would have gone out of kindness to talk with Billie, except that where she sat like diminutive royalty in a tall velvet chair she was surrounded by admirers, so that his own claim on her memory seemed recent and shallow. Then Carol was suddenly in the room – late, loud, fearless – dressed in navy blue cut low on her freckled bosom.

—We waited for you! Kate complained. —We couldn't start anything without you.

—But I had to get my glad rags on! You wouldn't have wanted me all sweaty and dirt-streaked, honestly.

—Sweaty and dirt-streaked? I thought you were supposed to be running the Housing Association, not building the houses yourself.

David and Suzie were weakly grateful that Carol crossed the room to them through all the other claims on her sociability; Suzie hung on to her in relief.

—This is an awful party, Carol. I don't know anybody here.

Carol's arm was round her straight away. —Darling, you know me! Won't I do? Come on, let me introduce you to everyone. David can look after himself.

David obediently circulated. And after all he did know a few people: the viola player from Kate's quartet (friend of a friend in the music department at the university), a consultant on the Public Health Committee who lived somewhere along the lake, a woman who knew Betty from the Cardiff Amnesty group (the musical evening was to raise money for Amnesty). He had a fragment of an interesting argument with Carol at one point, over problems with Assembly health policy (she was always ebulliently positive about the whole devolution thing, he wasn't); by then it was time, anyway, for the music. They sat for the performance in chairs arranged around the baby grand at one end of the long room. David looked anxiously for Suzie and couldn't find her at first; then when it was too late to offer to change places he saw she was standing propped alone in the doorway, tall in her white trouser suit, with a remote artificial smile, and a shy flush across her cheeks that made her eyes glint as if they were watering. When David looked round for her again in the applause at the end of the first piece she was gone.

The playing wasn't, of course, brilliant – there were some mistakes, the intonation was occasionally off, there was one false start to a movement in the Haydn (the cellist bungled it) – but the music touched him nonetheless with calm: he never knew how knotted his tension was until music undid it. Kate led the quartet in what attack it had. Her technique wasn't perfect but she was brave and made a warm strong sound; he took pleasure in her confidence, her lifted authoritative head, her swaying back, the ferocity with which she dipped to turn the pages; he forgot to wonder why she hadn't showed herself his friend this evening. Sometimes it

135

seemed to him that her gaze rested on him while she played; not seeing him, only absorbed in private concentration. Returned to themselves at the end of each piece – after Haydn, Schubert – the quartet turned laughing eyes on one another, admiring their safe arrival, triumphant and diminished because it was over. As an encore Billie joined them on the piano for one movement from the 'Trout'; the notes unfolded obediently from her blind hands with an eerie shallow deadpan like a musical box wound up, not unaffecting.

David afterwards joined the crowd bringing Billie their compliments. She shone with dignified modesty, apologising for her old fingers, making perfect sense until urgently she put her hand on someone's arm.

—Is Michael here anywhere? Where's Michael? I wonder what he thought.

None of them intimates, they looked around blankly but hopefully for Michael, they asked for him: Carol was quickly there, squeezing Billie's hand, cuddling her shoulders.

—Michael would have thought you were wonderful. He really would. What a shame he couldn't be here to hear you two play together.

—Oh, isn't he here? Billie was disappointed but not overthrown. —Such a gifted musician. I trust his judgement implicitly. Does he know Kate? Of course, he must know Kate, mustn't he? She smiled puzzling into Carol's face as if there were some conundrum there to tease out, an irritating blockage in possibility which must come clear if she persisted stubbornly enough.

—She was asking for Kate's father, Carol explained to David later with tears in her eyes, stricken by the music, or the old lady's mistake; her tears always burdened her brother, he had longed for her sake, when he was a boy, for her to learn to conceal them.

—Oh: is her father Michael?

—Just as if he were in the crowd here somewhere. She's never done that before, I don't think; she's been muddled, but not actually lost forty years. The father died a few months after Kate was born, you know: in the bed upstairs.

—I've never asked.

—Some sort of tuberculosis: of the spine? He was a violinist, he'd come over from Ireland to play for an orchestra here in Cardiff, that's how they met. Isn't it romantic; isn't it poignant? You can imagine, Billie went out to all the concerts in those days: her mother and father were dead, she was a rich woman, she lived here all alone, she was nearly forty. Kate says she thinks he only married her for her money, and that he drank and slept around. But then you know what Kate's like.

—She's not romantic.

—Or it's just another kind of romance, isn't it?

David looking for Suzie – thinking they could leave with their honour intact now the music was over – met Max in the dining room, eagerly friendly, glasses glinting, making bobbing dives into the various dishes – heaped up couscous salad, pink rolls of cold beef – from his great height, like a heron fishing.

—What a fantastic evening! Like being inside a

Chekhov story. The lake, this amazing old house, people gathered to make music, all the generations socialising together. I want to come down here and live like this. So civilised!

David thought that Max's account of the party wasn't like any Chekhov he'd read. Kate had recently lent him her translations of some of the stories; the characters mostly seemed to grind unhappily against one another, locked in misunderstanding. Kate told him they were funny but he didn't see it.

—Are you a colleague of Kate's at Queen Mary's?

—Just an old friend. Not smart enough to be an academic. I work for English Heritage.

When David said he was looking for Suzie, Max put down his plate in concerned helpfulness, as if he would start a search. —She's been around, she was in here earlier.

Recrossing the hall, David bumped into her coming out from the downstairs lavatory, the one he knew from his other visits to the house: at the end of a tiled passage, with a long wooden seat like a hinged shelf.

—It has a cistern on the wall and a chain hanging down, exclaimed Suzie in wonder. —I've never used one like that before. You can buy them in reproduction now, I know: but they're terribly expensive.

Their coats regained, their farewells left cowardly unmade (when they'd peeped round a door, Kate had been too deep for interruption in some group joke), absolved of public performance, they were suddenly uneasily thrown together in the car; aware of the near-audible ticking of thought. The engine starting up was a relief. Always on such occasions, without ever having discussed it, they used the car in the archaic configuration: David in the driving seat and Suzie the passenger. Used to the convention, apart from the first glass of fizzy wine, he had only helped himself to water; she could have had several more glasses of wine if she had wanted to bolster herself, but she struck him as bleakly cold sober.

—It wasn't too bad? he hoped, not really believing it.

Instead of talking to him she exhaled as if she was getting rid of something, and threw her head back, staring up through the dark at the felt lining of the tin roof.

—Will you let me out? she said then, as they drove alongside the lake, which sent its pale signal flashing like a code between the passing trees.

—Let you out?

—Not here. I'll give you directions.

He pulled up in the middle of the empty road. — What?

—Just drop me off somewhere. I'll get a taxi back later. I'm not ready to come home yet.

Baffled, he held his hands spread in the air above the steering wheel. —It wasn't that bad.

—You don't know.

He had to drive off again: it wasn't late enough for there to be no traffic.

—Well, perhaps it was that bad: I hate parties anyway. You're supposed to be the sociable one.

—Between the time the music stopped and when we left, said Suzie, —what's that? Three-quarters of an hour?

forty minutes? In all that time nobody spoke a word to me. I didn't speak a word to anybody. I just moved around from room to room as if I was always on my way somewhere else. Then I went into the toilet and stayed there for as long as I dared, only I was afraid there'd be a queue and someone would come rattling at the door.

—But you have to make an effort. You can't expect people who don't know you to talk to you when you're hurrying past them. You have to go up and talk to them. They weren't being unfriendly as such.

—You're right, of course, I know that. Only I got in a state where I couldn't.

—And now you want to be by yourself for a bit.

She looked at him; her directness was only equivocal because he couldn't return it, he had to watch the road. —Not by myself. With my friends.

Her face was impossible to read, anyway; when he did glance over its point was overridden by the shifting street lights, car lights, the muddying orange city illumination.

—Turn left here, go back down the park. They live in Splott: it isn't too far.

Dumbly, he drove where she told him to go, down past where the park became a wide-open recreation ground, through Roath and onto Newport Road, then over the Beresford Road railway bridge. He knew most of the streets they drove through even if he didn't know their names; but they pulled up eventually in front of an improbable little row of cottages he'd never noticed before. He couldn't make them out very well in the dark: they might have been built for railway workers, and were probably older than most of the surrounding late-Victorian development. Behind the huddle of their overgrown front gardens they seemed to promise a cosier secrecy than the austere long terraces with their doors opening more or less straight onto the street.

—This is it, said Suzie. —I'll see you later: but don't wait up.

His reluctance wasn't exactly passionate jealousy. Perhaps it ought to be: but he couldn't really believe, however opaque Suzie's behaviour had been in these last weeks and months, that she could have instructed him so calmly to drop her off at this house if she was planning to meet some lover inside it. Anyway, he presumed the house was Menna's, where she lived with her boyfriend, so the lover wasn't a practical idea. But whatever did Suzie imagine justified her stubborn refusal to explain herself to him, to give him a word, even, or a clue? Why couldn't she learn, as other people did, the grace to carry off a party like this one they'd been to? No one required her to enjoy it. Well, so he was free, again: she pressed his freedom on him.

—Can't I come in with you?

—No, she said, and put a hand on his arm, as if postponing something, promising something else for some other time.

He watched her pick her way up a path whose faint paleness was blurred by overgrowing shrubs and then lost in the thick overhang of shadows from the house;

141

he knew she turned to look at him once because he made out the weak blob of her face. Then another car, lights glaring, came up behind him and he had to move. He drove round the block to come past the house again, and paused with the engine running, peering into the garden. There was no sign of habitation to be made out beyond the shrubs, apart from the dim gleam in a glass fanlight above the front door. But Suzie in her white trouser suit was vanished, swallowed presumably inside.

The party did not do Kate any good. Some of her friends stayed on afterwards, filling up for the weekend the empty bedrooms, feasting on party leftovers round the dining-room table, taking their wine over to the park in afternoon sunshine to sprawl like a Watteau *fête champêtre* on the grass, in the flickering shade under the trees, while the children some of these friends had brought played ball or pestered for ice cream. As long as her friends were with her she could pretend to herself that it had worked, that she had been restored – by the jokes, the confessions, the touching and kissing, her own rather showy performance of ironising contentment – to what Carol called her 'old self'.

But when they went it made things even worse. Her old self anyway had been a precarious entity: now it was seized for a few days, not by a depression as she might have expected, but by a mania that burned her up. She was possessed all the time by the idea of David. Passion, she thought, must have seized wealthy women like this – like cramps or fits – in the old days, when an abyss

142

yawned in the hours between breakfast and dressing for dinner, with nothing to fill them but reading novels and gazing in the mirror, imagining things, gasping and moaning all alone. Work ought to be the cure: Kate tried to get on with her translation, but either she stared at it stupidly or her thoughts raced as if she was speeding. Whatever semblance of order she had begun to establish in her life in the house with Billie disintegrated; they sometimes didn't get up until the afternoon, and she never knew what time it was when they went to bed because she had lost her watch somewhere over the party weekend. Jamie had connected her DVD player to the television; she rented old black-and-white Hollywood films which she and Billie watched in drugged absorption, sometimes two or three times over, Billie forgetting each time what was going to happen. Only the arrival of Buckets and Mops on their appointed days gave any kind of shape to time passing.

Kate picked up the telephone, dialled David's number, put it down again. She had wanted at the party to see past this fixation that she had surely, after all, erected for herself: she had wanted to expose, by positioning him alongside her cleverer lively friends, how dull, how ponderous and inconsequent he was. Obligingly when she had asked Max what he thought, he had said that David seemed like the kind of fellow who'd set your bone straight if you broke your arm.

—He isn't that kind of doctor, Kate said dully. —Or is that supposed to be some weird kind of sexual clue?

—I just mean he seemed like a nice man who'd be

good at his job, but that I don't quite see what it is you're so hung up on.

—It's precisely the aspect of it you can't see, that makes it fatal. What do you think he thinks about me?

She dreaded herself, asking.

Max was cautious. —Possibly, he seemed a little uxorious.

—Uxorious? Oh, crap, Max, thanks for that.

She had seen for herself how David looked round everywhere for his wife when he was sitting waiting for the music, and again while he was applauding at the end of the first piece. She had thought he and Suzie couldn't wait to get away from the party together, they had hated it, they would have escaped sooner if they'd known how to, only they were too innocently, decently polite. She was haunted by David's kind slight bewilderment at her treatment of him, her betrayal of their friendship. She groaned aloud, remembering how once when she played a false note his shoulders had contracted wincingly as if she drew the bow across his nerves; she imagined the scene sometimes, although she knew this was exaggerating, as if he had been the only one genuinely hearing the music, among all the other blank, bored, pretending faces.

For several nights while Kate paced the house – her reading glasses propped abandoned on her open book in a pool of lamplight, Billie put to bed upstairs – police helicopters came hovering over the streets outside. You never knew what they were looking for, or whether they actually caught anybody; the agitating loud turmoil of their rotors came and went sometimes for what felt like

144

hours. They seemed a visitation from a different world: Kate thought how, up here in the peace beside the lake, she was getting used to being privileged and set apart, like being forgotten. In London this wasn't seriously possible anywhere: her nice first-floor flat, for instance, in a Georgian square with an enclosed residents' garden, was two minutes' necessary walk, on her way to the tube, from the bleak roaring Walworth Road with its metal-shuttered shops and minimarts plastered with fluorescent posters, selling stolen goods. Carol said the daily reminder of trouble was at least an inoculation against fear; that was why she preferred to live quixotically among her tenants in Adamsdown, even if it meant noise and scenes often, and difficulties with the dominatrix with samurai swords who lived upstairs. She said, goodness knows what hallucinations of danger and siege people are subject to, if they live anywhere too beautiful and too sequestered.

One night, late, the Firenze doorbell jerked in the passage to the kitchen with its usual weakly expiring clatter. Absent-mindedly, even though it was an impossible time for anyone to call who didn't have urgent or terrible news, Kate made her way in the dark through the little entrance vestibule with its empty shelves that still smelled sometimes of the bitter-peppery ghosts of past geraniums. When she pulled the door open a blast of warm night forced its way inside: importunate, humming with summer.

—Oh, Jamie, no, she said. —It's too late, I'm on my way to bed.

This wasn't true, but there was every reason for him to believe it; the house was in darkness behind her, she was reading, she had been pouring herself whisky in the kitchen. She couldn't see his face: he was an outline, shamblingly youthful, hunched over his bike, smelling of booze and dope, his voice arriving out of the dense centre of shadows. For the first time she noticed that he spoke with a Cardiff accent; or perhaps he forgot, because he couldn't see her, to make the adjustment between voices middle-class children learn to make according to the company they're keeping. That accent, with its oblique flattened teasing, had moved and seduced her when she was a little posh girl at Howells.

—I need to talk to you, he said. —I've finished my exams.

—Seriously, you came to tell me that?

—I've been out with my friends. But everything I had to say, I wanted to say to you. So I cycled round for a long time and then I came here.

—Come back tomorrow.

Jamie persisted, not moving, as if tomorrow was unthinkably another era; she made out in bulky silhouette against the fainter dark some top tied by its sleeves around his shoulders: he loomed especially large because she'd kicked off her heels earlier and was barefoot in the warmed grit of the floor. Resistance was insubstantial against his invisibly exerted pressure; reluctantly Kate permitted him to thud his bike across the threshold and prop it against the shelves of empty flowerpots. He

146

followed her into the kitchen, breathing heavily: he must have been cycling fast and long. A forty-watt light bulb under the old plain white shade dispensed its gloom into the room's farthest corners; it turned Jamie's usually cream-coloured skin – as he paced round the room's perimeter not seeing anything – crumpled and grey, gave him blue hollows under his eyes, showed up that his hair wasn't clean and hung lank across his forehead. She knew how horribly, if he looked like this, the light must expose her: she took grim satisfaction in it. She poured him whisky – she had no idea what he drank but surely he drank lots, he was a young person, she had read about their drinking in the newspapers – and sat down at the kitchen table whose white enamel looked at that moment better suited to vivisection than to sociability. He drank the whisky down in thirsty swallows.

—So how did they go? she obliged him without much interest.

—How did what go?

—The exams, stupid, that you came to tell me about.

—Oh: that wasn't that I came for. They went OK. I'm thinking maybe I should do Economics, to really understand how everything works. Only I should take a year off before I go to university anyway.

—You're lacking in vocation, it occurs to me.

The fridge quivered to an end of one of its gulping, rattling ecstasies: Jamie, still standing, was suddenly frowningly aware of where he was. —Do we have to be in here?

Kate shrugged. —I'm on my way to bed, remember?

—But I need to talk to you: it would be better some-where – less bright.

His youthful self-absorption (he had hardly looked at her) was overbearing; he was full of portent, her scepti-cism was weightless and dry by comparison. What could it matter anyway where they sat? Passing through the hall again, carrying her glass and the bottle in one hand, she felt with the other for the old Bakelite switches, which sprang noisily but made no miracle of light: they were left picking their way through floating patches of jewel-colour where the street light in the curve of the road outside shone through the stained glass on the stairs.

—I must get up a ladder tomorrow and replace these bulbs, she said irritably, knocking into Jamie who seemed to have stopped short. —I've been meaning to for weeks.

—It's better, he said, turning on her, his voice thick. —It's what I wanted, so that I could talk to you. In that bright light I couldn't. I've been here to the house already three times tonight, and gone away again and then come back.

She decided he really was quite stoned, or drunk – not only from the whisky but from the beer he smelled of, that he must have had earlier with his friends – and she said so disgustedly, pushing him away; only he seized her free arm, clasped it tightly so that she felt the damp of his hot fingers through the loose knitting of her cardigan.

—No: he seemed to consider impartially. —I've cycled it off.

—Oh, listen, Jamie, let go of me. This is stupid.

148

—It's not stupid, he insisted. —You know what it is. You know it isn't stupid.

—I don't want to know. Stop it. I'm old enough to be your mother, remember? I am precisely as old as your mother.

She tried to pull free, he grabbed clumsily for her other arm, and seemed to be searching out her face with his: the bottle smashed down onto the floor tiles with a crash as loud as an explosion. Kate managed to hang onto her glass by the rim: she felt the bottle's whisky pool around her toes. —Oh, don't move! she cried out fiercely. —Broken glass absolutely everywhere!

Her hands pinioning Jamie to the spot – as if he was a child, so that he wouldn't step on the shards – weren't tender.

—And now you've woken Billie, she moaned. —You absolute idiot.

Breathing into one another's faces blindly at close quarters, inhaling the rising whisky fumes, they seemed to be able to hear the old lady's bed creak upstairs as she sat up; then wakeful tentative silence.

—It's all right, Mummy, Kate called. —I've only dropped a glass.

—Is it you, Kate?

—Go back to sleep, darling. Nobody's hurt.

—Are you all right, Kate?

—I'm fine. Go back to sleep.

They listened until the bed creaked again as she lay down.

—What I was trying to tell you . . . Jamie continued:

149

he hardly seemed to feel responsible for what he'd caused, or even notice it, though he did lower his voice.

—No! Kate hissed. —Don't! Do you realise that I don't have shoes on? She pictured herself marooned in a pool of viscous spirits and jagged glass pieces.

—It's all right. Jamie surrounded and encompassed her. —I have thick soles, I'm not afraid to walk in it. I'll lift you.

—But I don't want to be lifted!

Clumsily he landed kisses – on her hairline, and, stooping, on her collarbone.

—Stop it! she protested.

He lifted her across the mess and carried her into the library.

His heat and urgency were a force; what was there in her to resist it? There was enough light at least for him to see to put her down on the old creaking protesting chaise longue.

—This is a terrible mistake, she insisted, pushing him off. —You've just got a crush.

—I'm completely serious. You don't know how much I feel. I think about you all the time.

—But you've got no idea about me.

—How do you know what ideas I've got?

He stroked back her hair from her face with the hot palms that she imagined calloused from his cycling, lowered himself beside her, kissed her so that she tasted through the drink and the cigarettes the young, strong cleanness of his mouth. He was awkward, inexperienced, anxious, but his youth was absolute; his weight pinned her down painfully, there wasn't room for both of them side by side. She could have pushed him away again, she could have told him to stop. She told herself she would, in a moment. If anything, she yielded to him out of disappointment in herself: and out of boredom. She had nothing else to do.

—At least take your boots off.

Obediently, without letting go of her, he pushed them off one after the other with his feet; with shaking fingers he failed to unbutton her blouse, then thrust it up out of his way instead.

—I knew you didn't wear a bra, he said.

In her shame she only lay passively, not allowing herself to move or to respond.

Needless to say after all the clumsy manoeuvring it was too quickly over; almost as soon as he was inside her, Jamie cried out in sharp regret and collapsed on her heavily, breathing wetly against her ear.

—I was no good, he lamented, muffled.

—It doesn't matter.

Coldly she looked past him, between her raised bare knees, a tangle of tights and knickers draggled from one ankle, at the dim room changed by what had happened in it. Well, it had been changed before, nothing would show, it wouldn't make any difference.

He lifted his head to search her face. —Was it any good for you? He was chaotic with the audacity of what had been accomplished.

—For me it was the deepest possible disaster.

—Next time, he tried to promise tenderly.

151

—Next time? Kate rebuffed him. —Go home. Leave me alone. Don't put the light on. I don't even want to see what we have done.

—But I can come back again?

—Never again, she said. —Never.

She lay turned away from him, staring into the back of the chaise longue, refusing to look while Jamie stumbled about, pulling up his trousers, finding his T-shirt, trying to lace his boots. She knew that he stood for a while mutely still, desperate for her to turn round and be kinder; then she heard him pick his way through the mess in the hall, sending some piece of glass skidding. She imagined, without herself stirring, that she heard the soft pressure of his bike tyres on the path, on the road. Half an hour later, in bed upstairs alone – she'd swept the whisky bottle, in the light from the library that she put on at last, into a sticky heap, in case Billie wandered downstairs in the dark – she was overwhelmed suddenly with a crowding detailed awareness of his body. The smooth hairless brown skin taut across his ribs, impregnated with flavours of marijuana and sweat; the hot nape of his neck, his hair pushed behind his ears; the jawline tensed and intent, the swallowings in his throat; the undainty big man's feet still in their socks: these pressed in on her so that she had to bury her face in the pillow, trying to shut them away.

Riches, heart-twisting riches: but not for her.

Seven

Suzie's sister (a few years older) arrived to stay with them, it wasn't clear for how long. The first they knew about it was when the doorbell rang, on an evening when the sun had so blazed all day, raising a miasma of shimmering pollution above the city, that their house had seemed too flimsily paper-slight to offer any respite. They had looked longingly over at the dense trees of the old estate, but it was too hot to walk there and no one could bear to get inside a car again if they didn't have to, once they were back from school and work. No sooner had the bell rung than Evie was inside the house, humping her large suitcase – pale blue, battered, decorated with pink hearts – over the threshold, the tail end of a taxi turning the corner of the cul-de-sac; Jamie arriving home at the same moment had opened the door for her. Evie immediately, urgently, stripped off the cardigan and mac she'd worn for ease of carrying; the extra layers must have been a torture. Her face – like Suzie's, foxily cinnamon-coloured, freckled – was splotched with pink, and the dark roots of her short spiky blonde hair were wet.

—So what's Jamie up to? she asked, effortfully cheerful. —Are you off to college?

—Perhaps, Jamie said. —I might take a year out. I'm thinking about it.

—You know the fees go up next year, said David, insisting on a point he'd already made several times over, as he came out from the living room where he had been helping Hannah with her homework. —Make sure you've secured your place before you defer, don't leave it too late.

His son gave him a look whose mask-like tragic contempt was surely disproportionate to the offence.

—And you ought to wear your cycling helmet.

—Hiya, David, said Evie.

Jamie took the stairs two at a time, they heard the crash of the attic ladder pulled down, then pulled up after him. Later he'd come foraging in the kitchen, after they'd cleared up supper.

David kissed Evie absent-mindedly. —Did Suzie know you were coming? She didn't say anything.

—Isn't she here?

—Out.

—She's always out, said Hannah. —She's gone mad, about her new friends.

—Actually I didn't tell her, Evie said. —It was on an impulse.

Suzie and Evie had that disconcerting sibling resemblance, alike enough – in height and shape and the rough idea of the face – to be mistaken for one another in anyone's peripheral vision: so that David would walk into a room and think Suzie was standing there until Evie moved (or spoke: her voice was throatier). There was always an instant of shock before adjustment: everything about Evie seemed more exposed, the eyes bigger and more startled, the lines deeper-incised, the mouth fuller (Suzie said Botoxed). They dressed in the same casual clothes: only Evie's things were skimpier, tighter, lower cut (also, she had a ring in her navel). One night David walked into the bathroom and didn't see for a long minute, while he searched for Calpol for Joel in the medicine cupboard, that it was Evie soaking, with only her head – fortunately for their embarrassment – visible above the mass of foam.

—There isn't any lock, she apologised.

—It's so the children can't lock themselves in.

—No worries.

—I can't believe I didn't look: sorry.

—Don't be silly. Find whatever it was you wanted.

That surprise seemed to bring about a new intimacy between the two of them: easy-familial and not sexual. No one asked how long Evie was staying. Whenever she came she had an air of escaping just ahead of some damage or danger on her tail, men or money. She and her daughter Cara, the same age as Jamie, had stayed for weeks at a time during various catastrophes; Suzie was seen by her family as the one who had lifted herself out of their patterns of bad luck. This time Evie told David evasive stories about a job she had left, an insurance office and

155

a boss she'd been involved with; and about Cara, who had gone to live with her father recently after some row whose outlines were unclear.

Evie must have seen Suzie's bed made up in the study, she was bound to notice that Suzie was out almost every evening ('doing yoga', she explained perfunctorily, or 'with her singing group'). Menna and Neil had got the use of some chalet in the Gower Peninsula for the summer, and Suzie was there almost every weekend, on her own or with the children. The children loved the chalet and the beach and the sea: they were uneasy that David didn't come with them. They nagged him, they tried to bribe him with odorous carriers full of seaweed and crab-bits and stones which had been special when they were wet; he told them he had too much work to do.

—Why don't you go? Evie asked, scrupulously casually, not to be seen to be prying.

—I really have been busy.

—And they're not your kind of crowd?

—Perhaps not.

Evie went out with Suzie's new friends a couple of times, but she confided to David that they made her feel a hundred years old, and she couldn't join in the singing: she said she hadn't known that Suzie had such a lovely voice. He didn't ask for more details. At home Evie slipped into a domestic role, shopping for the family and cooking (she was a better cook than Suzie). She even cleaned the house, not badly, although she didn't have Suzie's perfectionism; the rooms were heaped with piles of ironing, the vacuum cleaner was left wherever she'd last used it. Suzie couldn't complain, she'd stopped doing anything in the house herself. Suzie always kept Evie at a sceptical, brittle distance when she visited. Sometimes when Evie and David found themselves watching the news companionably, he suffered from an eerie hallucination that Suzie had left a surrogate to keep him quiet while she went wandering, like shape-changing trickery in a fairy story. He didn't know whether Evie had asked Suzie what was going on in her marriage, or whether if she had Suzie would have confessed to her, or put her off.

One weekend when Suzie was away he took Hannah and Joel to call on Kate Flynn. Marshalling the children up the zigzag path, he thought that bringing them would make a difference in his relationship with Kate, and was shyly proud of their unflawed transparent skin, of the plaits he'd made – not very well – in Hannah's hair, of their awed demeanour in the shadow of the big house, with its turret like something from a children's picture book. He thought that Kate was bound to like them; meeting them, she would know him more completely. When no one answered the bell even after David rang three or four times (they put their ears to the flaking paint and heard it sound improbably far off), Joel was visibly relieved not to have to believe his father had friends who lived in such a place.

Hannah spotted the play park with swings and slides and an ice-cream van, madly crowded in the summer heat. For an hour he pushed Joel on the swings and watched while they slid. They kicked around a football on the grass, then flopped in the shade under one of the great trees; David, on his back with his eyes closed, felt the earth turn and his life passing. It struck him that he was always vulnerable, lying down: he needed to meet life on his feet, upright. They tried Firenze again before they got into the car to drive home, but this time he didn't really expect an answer. The children anyway by now were overheated, and sulking because he wouldn't buy them soft drinks from the van (they'd had ice cream).

—Mummy lets us have Coke, Hannah complained, easily indignant. —She says, what harm can it do, in the long run?

Kate wasn't sleeping. She had to go to the doctor for more pills, performing competent and un-addicted in order to be rewarded with a prescription. The ones she got in Billie's name, from a different doctor – not for Billie, who didn't need them, who slept like a baby – were much easier. The doctor said she must try to establish regular times for going to bed and getting up: she thought he was right. She found light bulbs in an understairs cupboard, got out the stepladders, and replaced all the ones that weren't working, even in the rooms they didn't use: if the lights exposed stained wallpaper and furniture jumbled meaninglessly together, she turned them off quickly and went on finding her way in the dimness, with the blinds drawn down. She washed the hall floor with a mop and hot soapy water; the whisky smell, however, persisted, she couldn't get rid of it, it

158

made her sick for days. She tried for a while getting up at seven and cooking porridge for Billie (she couldn't eat anything herself at that hour). Billie slept on her back, her eyes were never screwed up or squinting in sleep; her huge lids swung wide open when Kate shook her, and showed the flash of her dreams escaping. She clung onto the bedclothes, and had to be coaxed into putting on her dressing-gown with promises of syrup on her porridge.

—You know, dear, Billie said thoughtfully after a few days, —it's very hot for porridge.

Kate had hardly noticed the blazing weather. Carol said how lucky Kate was at least in Billie's good nature, that senility usually brought changes of personality, resentment and aggression. Sometimes Kate could hardly remember what her mother had been when she was adult and in command: she had to focus on particular moments, Billie waiting with her neat little shopping basket at the school gates, Billie giving herself into the hands of the hairdressers while Kate stood looking on, having her hair coloured, brown honey, for all those years before she gave in to white. She had been compliant always; but with an inward resistance like a stubborn sweetness, a secret of superiority, that made her gently deplore other people's lives not led in the same light of beauty and taste as hers. This princess-air used to drive Kate to distraction. Now the reality of that resistance was dissolved away, leaving only its shape behind; Billie watched all kinds of awful programmes on the television, and particularly loved the advertisements.

159

Kate bought batteries for the clocks; she sorted her bookshelves, she tried to work on her translation. She hammered nails into her walls to hang pictures; she spent all day in her pyjamas without getting dressed and didn't wash her hair. The balance of her attention always swung like this between her self and her surroundings: when she was at her physical best, dressing well, she could live in a mess; when she despaired of herself and her clothes, she lavished care on her room and her possessions, paid bills and took broken objects in for repair. At least the sleeping pills made a fog in her head so that she didn't have to feel anything very sharply. She didn't answer the front-door bell. She told herself that if she and Jamie never saw one another again, then what had happened wouldn't exist, she could prevent it from having existed, it needn't ruin everything. Sometimes Billie answered the door; twice she let Jamie in. Kate heard his voice while she was upstairs in her room puzzling in leaden doubt between different ways of expressing the nuances of mastery and subservience in Tsarist Russia. Awareness of him in the rooms below was only physical, like a cramp; she refused to think differently about him because of one moment's stupid error of judgement. Billie, labouring, climbed up the stairs.

—That boy is here, she said. —What is his name?

—Ask him what he wants, said Kate. —Tell him I won't come down, I'm busy with this.

—Oh, we mustn't interrupt your work, darling. Has he come for his lesson?

—Mummy: how can I concentrate?

Billie stood hesitating, then tiptoed down again. After a while Kate heard Jamie at the piano, playing his scales, trying and failing, stumbling, going back to the beginning and starting all over again. While she was listening to this she couldn't do a thing, she couldn't think, she sat with her stomach muscles painfully squeezed (she hadn't eaten anything much for days, apart from crackers and apples and tea), pressing her hands over her face until her rings left marks. It was a kind of torture, waiting for him to play a wrong note and then hearing it: but it wouldn't drag her downstairs, she would endure. After all, she was the grown-up, she was the one on guard against blunders happening. At last Billie let him go, or he wandered of his own accord into the hall: she guessed that he stood longing to come and find her but also dreading it. She kept still, afraid that if he heard her make any ordinary movement he'd be somehow encouraged, and come up. Apart from anything else, her hair was scraped back in an elastic band, she was wearing her glasses and old ghastly stretch pyjamas, her face looked bruised and sallow as it always did when she was in one of her states, when she wasn't eating. She owed it to Jamie at least that he shouldn't see he'd embraced a death's head, an old woman. Eventually she heard him give up and go.

The second time he came, Kate locked her bedroom door. He knocked at it, and called her name twice; she stayed motionless on her bed, not answering, hugging her knees tightly. Then she knew that if she stayed living

161

like this something would break; so she took Billie to London. They went to the Bloomsbury hotel where they used to stay in the old days, before Kate left home, when they had tickets for London concerts or theatre; she was surprised when she telephoned to find it still existed. On the train she wore dark glasses, with a scarf wrapped round her hair and her summer mac buttoned up: luckily the hot weather had broken.

—Wouldn't Mother have loved this? said Billie, looking eagerly out from the train window at the countryside cut across by swathes of rain, watery gleams.

—I wouldn't know, said Kate. —I didn't know Mother.

—She spoke five languages. Her French was exquisite. They meant her for a high school teacher.

—We could always go back, if you liked: I mean Lithuania. We could look for our roots: people do these days.

—Oh dear, I don't think so. She touched Kate's hand consolingly as if Kate might not know what had happened there. —I don't think there'd be anything left for us. I never liked the children's books my aunts and uncles sent, the pictures were too frightening, I thought of it as a primitive place. But Mother loved the books, she pined for it. After they came here, she never had her health.

—That's because old Sam was strong as an ox, wouldn't leave her alone.

When Kate talked like that, Billie pretended not to hear.

They had to make a fuss at the hotel, to change their room to one on the first floor, so that Billie didn't have to climb too many stairs. Kate told herself she'd done the right thing, getting away from the old house, leaving behind her disasters. She began to calculate how long their money would last if they led a hotel life here as people did in old novels, blessedly irresponsible, not having to worry about leaks in the roof or throwing out sour milk; they weren't very solid calculations, she wasn't really sure how much money was left, she had never quite got round to searching through Billie's papers and making the necessary calls to find out exactly. Their room was plain and high, painted white, with an austere handsome marble fireplace, a window overlooking the street where taxis splashed past in the wet, and a framed photograph of lions in the Serengeti; partitioned from next door, the elaborate plaster coving sliced through abruptly. The television was small and black-and-white, with a twisted coat-hanger stuck in for an aerial. It rained all that first day, so that they couldn't go anywhere until the evening, when they found an Italian restaurant round the corner; Kate ate a third of a plate of pasta and then smoked, Billie polished off three courses, finishing with a glass of something sticky and yellow. Back at their room Kate telephoned Max, while Billie, with every appearance of deep interest, watched through a fog of interference a police drama already halfway through.

—Max, I've run away, I'm here in London.

—Katie? Whereabouts: 'here'?

—Something dreadful has happened.

163

—I thought everything was going so well.

—Because you've no idea.

—Where are you? What's happened? D'you want to come round?

—I can't tell you now: I'm not alone.

—Oh, Katie: I hope you haven't made a terrible mistake.

—We're too tired to come tonight. We're in our pyjamas already. We'll come tomorrow evening.

—I'm not at all convinced it's the best thing, us meeting him.

—Not him, silly: it's Billie I'm here with.

—Ah. That's OK, I think: I'll just check with Sherie.

—Anyway, I have made a terrible mistake, she confessed. —Only not that one. I'll tell you tomorrow.

She and Billie visited the Wallace Collection the next day; they drank tea and Billie ate cake (Bakewell tart with lavender sauce) in the glassed-in central courtyard. In all the rooms Kate met herself reflected in the rococo slender-framed Louis Quinze mirrors, a dark spirit haunting among the blissful nymphs of the paintings: tarnished, concentrated, bitter. She bought a postcard, a girl in a pink satin dress, roses at her waist and in the round bosom pushed high by her corsets, watched by her lapdog, carving her lover's initials on a tree: it filled Kate with desolation. Billie talked to all the attendants, a charming old lady made happy by art. They took taxis everywhere, Kate was rich with cash, she paid out notes off a fat wad in her purse. To go out to Max's that evening she dressed severely all in black, pinned back her hair tight to her head, only painted her mouth red, left her face bleak, wore her dark glasses again; if Sherie had to see her in this state, then she owed it to herself at least to make a drama out of it. When they arrived in Max's Highbury flat, the tall windows were open to the refreshed summer night, Jill Scott was on the Bang & Olufsen, and there were the usual heaps of new novels and journals on the coffee table whose top was glass an inch thick, semi-clear like Glacier Mints, the base a precious twisted piece of an old elm. In the States before he moved to England Max had worked on two lucrative contracts on Madison Avenue.

Sherie, coming out from the kitchen in a pretty apron, flinched visibly at how ferocious Kate looked. Kate was sorry, and tried to be nice to her, exclaiming at the delicious food even if she couldn't eat much of it, asking how her writing was going, making an effort not to gossip with Max about friends Sherie didn't know.

—You must be working out, Kate said to her. —You look so fit! I'm so unfit. I don't do any exercise. What will become of me? It'll be such a tragic waste, I'll die young. Or is it already too late for me to die young?

Sherie sat stiffly and was not seduced, her round face pale with unbelief. Unfortunately Billie, enjoying herself, chose to be garrulous on the subject of Kate's unusual giftedness: if Max and Kate had been on their own with her, this would have seemed simply funny. Nervously Kate got out her cigarettes; the others hadn't finished their crème brûlée.

—Actually, would you mind smoking on the balcony? Sherie said.

165

—All by myself? Kate made a mouth of mock sorrow.

Max was gallant, wan, propitiatory. —I'll come out with you. Shall I?

—You go, said Sherie, stacking up the plates briskly without scraping them. —I'll stay and look after Billie.

Outside Kate and Max leaned on the wrought iron side by side, looking through the moonless dark at stately trees flirting their leaves in yellow patches of illumination from the street lamps; the rain had raised rank smells from the pavement. The warm thick night was full of movement, her cigarette smoke blowing heavily around them.

—I wish you'd be nicer, he said. —I wish you and Sherie could get on.

—As a matter of interest, I really was trying my best this evening. Obviously not good enough. You've forgotten that I'm really not very nice.

He sighed. —Well, I'm enough of an idiot, then, to like you.

She remembered what it had been like to yield to Max and have him look after her, she smelled his two-showers-a-day cleanness, his Acqua di Parma aftershave, his lawn shirt: invitations to peace, to pleasantness, to play.

—Oh Max: I've made such an awful mistake.

—It must be awful, for you to think it is. Is it to do with the good doctor?

—Yes. No. Yes.

—Tell me about it.

She opened her mouth obediently to tell him: and then shut it again.

166

—But maybe not. I can't.

He turned his blurred face to her – they stood outside the broad panes of light that fell from the windows – whistling low and admiringly. —Uh-oh. Katie's actually done something she's too ashamed to tell. Are we talking wrong side of the law here? Penal sentence?

—Don't make fun of me, Max. I'm feeling bad enough.

—Katie? He was apologetic: offered himself, patient and neutral, bending down his tall height to extinguish the difference between them. —You can tell me anything, you know that. If you need to talk. You don't look well. You look awful.

—I know I can. She touched her hand, the last end of cigarette a stump between her fingers, lightly on the back of his. —But, maybe this one ought to be my secret: I'm not sure I can find the words. Anyway, perhaps I quite like the idea of having a secret from you. From everybody.

—I'm sure you've got so many.

—No: no. She weighed judiciously. —Actually this is the first one for a long time. Not all that much happens to me these days, you know.

—I'm devoured by curiosity, about the secret.

—Don't be. I think it has no consequences, it doesn't count: don't think about it.

—Like the white bear.

—Hmm?

—You know: if someone says, don't think about the white bear. Then every time you try not to, you do. Isn't that Tolstoy?

167

—This isn't even a full-grown bear, she said. —It's just a cub.

The next day Kate left Billie with Max at his office ('she won't be any trouble') and went shopping in all her old favourite places. Max had said – she reminded him – that she looked awful; he must support her then, in recovering herself. She promised she would eat lunch, and did. She pleaded with her hairdresser, begged him to fit in an appointment to cut her hair: she paid him extra on top of how expensive he already was. She didn't think about the white bear. She watched herself emerge out of bleakly bedraggled beginnings in the salon mirror, gossiping with Antony: she hadn't been beautiful ever, but perhaps she was not too bad yet. The dramatic hollows and sharp points, crowded in the narrow face, could still be intriguing and seductive, hadn't yet absolutely failed. She bought new shoes, although she'd told herself they were the one thing she really didn't need. When she had thought she was finished and was looking out for a taxi, laden already with bags, they claimed her incontrovertibly from a shop window: dark pink soft leather trimmed in black, decorated with a black suede rose, impossibly totteringly high.

David awoke sweating from nightmares. They weren't about avian flu or terrorist attacks or any of the things he was supposed to worry about at work. He was in a group of people conversing intently, whose words were somehow not audible to him except as blunt needles jabbing under his skin; or he was submerged in complex and frantic plots, carrying messages between people he'd never heard of.

—Are you leaving me? he had asked Suzie one evening, confronting her in the study where she was undressing for bed. —Is this marriage breaking up? Are you having a relationship with someone else?

—Please don't come near me, she said, pulling her nightdress over her head with hasty hands, hiding herself: it didn't seem to mean anything between them now that he'd seen her naked in her extremity, giving birth to their children.

—You have to talk to me, for Christ's sake. Tell me what's happening.

She wouldn't look at him, she shrank away. —Please, she said. —Wait. I don't know. I can't talk about it yet. Don't shout: the others will hear.

—Do you think they don't know?

David hated it particularly that Jamie was a witness to the collapse in his marriage: he couldn't meet the boy's eyes, he winced at his physical presence in a room, as if Jamie had absorbed and was contemptuous of every twist in his father's humiliation. When David lay awake in the small hours, Jamie's quiet movements around the house agitated him as if they were his own fears, preventing him from sleeping; when he heard Jamie leave on one of his night bike rides to God knows where, he had to get out of bed and come downstairs to check he hadn't left the house perilously wide open behind him. In fact the doors were always safely closed, Jamie was perfectly sensible about these things, even if he did leave his dirty dishes heaped in the sink. Evie asked David if he didn't think there was something wrong with Jamie. He spent such long hours shut up alone in his room, not even playing his music. Surely, whatever he said, he couldn't be reading books for all that time?

—He's smoking, said David. —I think he smokes himself into a stupor sometimes. Don't think there's anything you can do about it: short of chucking him out altogether. There's nothing we haven't tried. He goes his own way, he doesn't listen to us.

—I wasn't criticising him, said Evie, startled. —He's lovely. Isn't he lovely with the kids? I just thought he might be unhappy.

It was true that Jamie was good with the children; they adored him. He had picked up a board game for a pound in a charity shop: Hero's Quest, with tiny metallic warriors and orcs and wizards. He invented missions and wrote them on pieces of paper for Hannah and Joel to follow – *The Masters of Morion have to recover the Red Stone of Zelton from the Chest of Azeriac* – then sat with them cross-legged for hours on the floor of Hannah's bedroom, seeming as wrapped up in the stories as they were, earnestly explaining why they couldn't cross the threshold of Morion without the right counters. It was surely better than the children watching endless soaps on the television.

One evening when David came home the house was full of people. At first sight he might have thought they were Jamie's friends, if they had ever visited: sprawling over the furniture in their bright-coloured play-clothes, communicating in noisy call-and-response like a bird-flock, they seemed younger than he could remember ever being. They jiggled to music as if they might break out into dancing; something folky was playing on the CD player in the study (Suzie had taken over his study, he had moved his computer into the living room). He looked around at first in vain for anyone he knew, fool-ishly displaced, still hanging on to his briefcase, as if he'd put his key in the door to the wrong house: then he saw Giulia and Larry in the kitchen cutting up pizza, and Menna with her stark china-doll's face and upright dancer's posture on the sofa. Anywhere she sat, she made a little court and was queen: staring unsmiling, she stiff-ened under his proprietorial survey. Two girls on the floor at her feet chattered, comparing their bare dirty soles, not seeing him.

The French windows were open; on the patio, among Suzie's bright-blooming pots and hanging baskets, male heads he didn't recognise at first – then he identified Neil, Menna's boyfriend – were bent in consultation over the barbecue. It hadn't been used this year: the charcoal surely would be damp, after its winter in the garage? Hannah and Joel held their breath as they did for him when he lit it; Evie, animated, hunkered flex-ibly down on her heels with her back to the patio wall, was gesticulating with her roll-up at someone he didn't know. Her sociability, he was reminded, was rash and overexposing: the marijuana smell (would the neigh-bours notice?) mingled foully with the smell of the fuel they were using to start the barbecue. David didn't like to see the children being around so many people smoking, he turned back into the hall. Suzie, running downstairs, stopped as abruptly at the sight of him as if he'd put out a hand.

—It's my birthday, she explained on the spot, out of breath, a few feet higher than he stood on the ground.

At a blow dignified wronged restraint was knocked away. —Oh: love, I'm sorry. Of course it is. How could I have forgotten?

—No, it's all right. I really don't care.

—I can't believe I didn't think. I've been writing the date over and over all day.

—Don't worry.

If her eyes glittered it wasn't from hurt tears: she was exalted, brimming with some glee closed to him; he was sure that until she saw him she had forgotten even to expect his coming home. Giulia brought him wine from the kitchen. —Come and eat pizza: from the Dolce Vita, where Larry's cousin's the chef.

Humbled (and anyway hungry), he went with her. — Did Suzie tell you I forgot?

—Oh don't worry! Larry never remembers my birthday.

—She didn't say anything about a party.

—It was impromptu, Giulia said. —We decided today at school, when she told us she wasn't doing anything. We phoned around.

—Let them get on with it, Dave, Larry said. —Take it from me: when the girls get it into their heads to enjoy themselves, there's nothing for it but to light the blue touchpaper and retire.

Larry's big handsome Italian head was marked with inherited strong lines that looked like sorrow, but he was jovial, tied into Suzie's apron, serving pizza; afterwards he lapsed into the *Telegraph* with a glass of David's whisky. David poured himself some too. He made his way round the party after he'd eaten, fuelling himself with the whisky, and found out that Suzie's friends were care-workers, actors, shop assistants; one worked on a council play scheme, one made furniture. Perhaps she preferred them because they were funnier; the more he drank, the more he was aware of his earnestness weighing him down like a clumsy coat. Neil had triumphed with the barbecue. His tanned skin was taut against his small fine-shaped skull, puckered in crinkles beside hazy eyes; there was a dope smoker's considering delay between his thought and his speech. David knew he ought to be more resentful of the man than of the girl, but it was Menna somehow whose self-possession goaded and exasperated him.

—Someone likes their music, Neil said, admiring David's CDs, shelf upon shelf, carefully ordered by composer and chronology.

—David only listens to classical, said Suzie. —Way over my head. When I went with him to a concert, all I could think about was that I was afraid I was going to cough, because I hadn't brought any cough sweets. I didn't even have a cold or anything; but I began to feel this little tickle, rising in my throat; I could picture how all those disapproving faces would look round at me, if I spoiled everything. So I kept saving up little bits of saliva and swallowing them down, to stop my throat being dry. It was all I could think about, I didn't hear a note.

A girl asked if David was a musician.

—He doesn't play anything, Suzie answered. —He's in public health. He works out which ones of us will get into the bunker. Or who to vaccinate if the flu epidemic comes.

David had an idea that he stood swaying his head like a dumb ox between them as they talked. —Is that really what you imagine I do?

She shrugged. —What do you do then? You work with death and disaster all day, don't you? Sometimes I imagine you bring it home with you on your hands.

—But David's working to prevent all these awful things, said Evie. —Somebody has to.

—It's a kind of power, Suzie said. —Don't try to tell me he doesn't enjoy it.

David was confusedly nauseated, he closed his eyes, leaned back against the wall, and felt the room dip drunkenly under him. Later Suzie pushed the furniture recklessly back for dancing and the children came squealing and jumping into the new space. They wanted to make peace between their parents, they tugged at David where he sat slumped with his back to the wall on the floor in the study (Suzie had tidied her bed away out of sight of the guests); but he wouldn't, couldn't, move.

* * *

Kate and Billie arrived home on a Saturday evening. As the train rolled into the station, past the end of St Mary's Street, they saw that the centre of town was given over to milling seething crowds of young people, the girls almost undressed in the hot summer weather, the males in the white shirtsleeves that were the minimum required by club dress codes. The swaying pale mass, moving sluggishly perhaps between venues or simply possessing the outdoors, seemed mysterious as restless spirits in a vision. Their taxi took them the back way, and still had to nudge at first through flesh that wouldn't yield to traffic: faces leered in at the windows, one boy dropped a pie on the road in front of the taxi and, lordly, waved them to a halt while he recovered and bit into it. Billie laughed, captivated; as they got away to the suburb and the lakeside, the restored empty quiet was both a balm and a diminishment. Sim (Carol had been feeding him) greeted them inside the house in angry ecstasy, butting his hard head affrontedly at their stroking hands. Kate took Billie up to bed.

She fell asleep herself, eventually, in her clothes, on the chaise longue: and woke to find Jamie standing a few feet away in the lamplight.

—The front door was open, he said.

—Was it?

—So I came in, although I hadn't meant to. Are you still angry?

She didn't lift her head to adjust her new apprehension of him, which had fear in it for the first time: he wasn't exactly as she had been imagining him, or refusing

175

to imagine. Even in the interval since she'd last seen him – was that two weeks ago? three weeks? – his presence had gathered density: he loomed, to her sideways perspective, her head still snuggled on the cushion, differently deliberate, taller, his hair pushed behind his ears as if for concentration, hands in his pockets, his roundish boyish face newly sharpened and marked, the creases under his eyes more deeply squeezed. She hardly knew him: he wasn't what she remembered, he was more important. Of course if he was worth anything, he would be changed by what had happened.

—No, not angry. Careless of me, leaving the door open.

—I wanted to ask if we could go back to how we were before: me calling round, not too often; us just talking. Would that be possible?

—Is that what we did? She sat up, stretching with her arms above her head; she was wearing one of her new dresses, maroon, slippery, tight across her breasts. —Is that what you want?

He brought his hands out of his pockets and opened them. —Anyone could have come in, you know.

—You mean: and forced themselves upon me? That's already happened once, hasn't it?

He stared at the floor.

—It's all right. She put out her hand towards his. —Forgiven. You didn't exactly force.

—I thought you'd be angry: you said never to come again.

He wouldn't touch even her hand.

176

—Did I say never? Well, I didn't mean 'never'; not actually 'not ever'.

—Oh. Humbly he nodded. —I didn't know.

—You did: you see, you're here. Anyway, perhaps I did mean never, when I said it.

—It's been terrible, he confessed. —Thinking you meant it, and that I'd completely fucked up.

—So, is that what you want then, to be just friends?

—I don't want to lose that.

—We weren't very good friends, really. Not my idea of good friends. You're too young to be my friend, exactly.

He exhaled noisily. Kate stood up – shoelessly short again, like last time – and fitted herself closely against his boy's warm shape, inside his arms that closed around her raggedly, timidly; she pretended to herself that the difference in their mass – his overwhelming hers, making her tiny – blotted out other asymmetries. She pushed away his hair from his forehead with both her hands to smile up at him, framing his face; his eyes under their curved hooding bluish lids stared back, unreadable. Out of her adult experience, she was in command; she mustn't let him know how powerful his reserves of youth were. She took him upstairs into the master bedroom; Billie wouldn't come looking for them, she superstitiously never went in there. Kate had thought of that bed before-hand, but hadn't made it up with sheets in case she tempted bad luck, so they made love tangled in damp dusty scratchy blankets and a silk counterpane, naked on the old sour-smelling striped flock mattress. Under reaching fingers at some point Kate found unexpectedly the polished hard convexities of the carved headboard, its cornucopia of spilled fruit. She had pulled up the blinds, and their shoulders and his long back were silvered sometimes by moonlight: the moon was huge, full, operatic, reflected in the lake. Jamie was somewhat better at it all this time, with her help, although so shy, and making touching efforts of concentration; she gratified him with little noises of pleasure. Her own naked, sexual self surprised her, exposed again; it had been buried recently under such rubble of complications.

—This has to be our secret, she made clear. —This isn't a relationship, in the daytime. I have to trust you that no one will ever, ever know that this has happened, even after I'm dead.

—You won't be dead, he said reassuringly, as if he could promise that.

Eight

Evie's going hadn't been discussed; and then was suddenly precipitated in a flurry of calls on her mobile, which she took hurrying out of the room, then murmuring subduedly, jackknifed on her heels on the patio or in the hall, crouched over nursing her words as if they were dragged out of her in painful cramps. Then, after all, she wasn't going back to whoever it was she spoke to for those long sessions (Suzie said, 'another one of her all-too-married men'), but was flying out instead to spend a week with their parents in Spain.

—You must be mad, said Suzie shortly. —I'd rather spend a week in a police cell. In fact that's probably where you'll end up. Don't get involved in any of their scams, don't bring anything back for them in your suitcase. Don't lend them any money.

—It'll be Spain, said Evie. —I can just toast mindlessly on the beach, can't I?

—It'll be too hot to go out of doors.

—I want to make a new start.

179

—I suppose those have always been their speciality.

—They're getting older, you know, Evie said apologetically.

Suzie drove down with the children to the Gower chalet: it was the first week of the school holidays, and she and David had talked about the possibility of his going with them, catching the train back in time for work on Monday, as politely as if they were seriously considering it. Hours after the others had left, he looked up from his e-mails in the study and saw that Evie, finished packing, had gone to smoke at the bottom of the garden; she observed the house rules exaggeratedly scrupulously, though David didn't care about smoking as he used to. A clematis that Suzie had planted and then neglected drooped against the rawly new larch fencing; Evie on the bench with her head tilted back among its leaves waved up at the house; Jamie must have hailed her from his skylight. It was a muffled grey evening, with a warm wind stirring up in fits and starts; the garden roses glowed garishly and the brown soil, brought in for the beds when the houses were built, was parched around their roots. David wandered out to sit with Evie, stopped her grinding out her half-smoked cigarette.

—I ought to turn the hose on this lot, he reflected without much interest.

She looked at him kindly with her blue used crinkled eyes, and he thought she might say something about his marriage, but she didn't. Perhaps she was afraid of her younger sister: Suzie's bright contemptuous glance flashed sometimes these days with a glint that made David think of a sword or a gun. She made her entrances and exits as if, all the time she was home, she had to be braced heroically, enduring something difficult. He had to try hard to remember all those ordinary years when they had seemed to be coexisting affectionately enough. Evie's attention was drawn up again to Jamie's skylight, open wide, and his head framed in it, leaning on his arms: he must be standing on a chair. David wondered what you could see from up there.

—Such a nice kid, Evie said. —Jamie. Remember when he had that awful duck he took everywhere, he wouldn't let it go into the wash.

—Called Groggy. David had forgotten. —Smelled groggy too.

—Poor little thing: I mean, what he was like then.

—Yes.

—You were very patient with him. Now, he's gorgeous. You don't often mention his mother. How could she do what she did? Jamie wasn't actually there, in that flat, at the time?

—No. She'd left him at her mother's. She was supposed to be feeling better: going to a friend's party. Who knows when she changed her mind? Actually, the flat was full of her clothes all over the place. She was always untidy, especially when she was depressed. But it looked as if she might have been trying things on, thinking of going out.

—Oh, that's awful. I've done that same thing, tearing clothes off and on in front of the mirror, and nothing's

181

right. I mean, not the same thing, of course. But it is a kind of despair, I do understand it.

—And after all she was wearing her dressing-gown.

She made her voice small. —You mean when she died?

—Fell from a sort of tiny balcony, where people dried their washing. On the ninth floor.

—It couldn't have been an accident?

—Oh no. The wall was up to here. He showed with his hand. —Quite safe for the child. For anyone. Pierced through, so that you could see out.

When he came home after dropping Evie off at the coach station, David went in search of his son: unusually the attic stairs were down. The chair was still where Jamie must have been standing on it to look out (perhaps he often did that), but he was at his desk, working on the old Mac Classic he'd had from Granny Bell years ago, when she'd replaced it. David had offered to buy him a new computer and arrange for Internet access up here, but Jamie didn't want it. The little postcard-size black-and-white screen glowed in the gathering dusk, humming with importance, making grey the austere mess of the room, where the boy's possessions were thrown around carelessly as if to show they didn't have enough weight, yet, to tie him to the spot. Nothing was pinned on the sloping walls. David sat down on Jamie's bed. He didn't ask what he was working on, now that all his exams and school work were over – too many of his conversations with this son recently had seemed to be interrogations. Jamie stopped tapping keys and closed a document.

—I was wondering about that cycling trip, David said.

In the winter – David making an effort he had failed to live up to since – they had desultorily discussed going off together for a few days in the Beacons; David had a bike, newer and smarter than Jamie's, shamefully less used.

—What, now? Jamie was puzzled rather than hostile.

—I could take a few days off work next week. I could do with a break.

The boy's face was obscure in the shadows. David could still be taken aback by the bulk and broad shoulders of this child whose once-smallness, limbs tiny and perfect and quick, he could still imagine under his hands.

—I don't know, said Jamie warily. —It's not a good time for me.

—No?

David might have protested that Jamie – extraordinarily, surely – wasn't doing anything whatsoever, not preparing for the college place he hadn't applied for, not working to earn money.

—I'm kind of tied up here just at the moment, Jamie said.

David was relieved anyway: he was unfit, he wasn't on form, probably he'd never have been able to keep up with his son on a bike. —Never mind then. It wasn't important, just a thought.

—Though I suppose a bike trip might be OK: if it was just for a couple of days.

—Only if you were keen.

—I'll think about it, shall I?

183

—Do you still have that duck?

—Duck?

—Groggy. Evie reminded me about it.

Jamie, obviously remembering it for the first time in years, looked around for a moment vaguely, as if his old toy might really be in one of his heaps of things. —I should think Suzie burned it, he said, but without rancour. —Wasn't it a health hazard?

—You know, you should invite your friends round, David said.

Jamie was blank.

—We'd like it if you brought them here. Or girlfriend, if there is one.

—There isn't one.

David guessed that Jamie reddened, though the light was so bad that he couldn't be sure of it, and he felt remorse for embarrassing him all the way down the folding stairs: descent was noisy and comical, heads gliding out of sight through the trapdoor in stages. Jamie managed his exits in style, throwing himself in a twisting movement, one hand on the stair, from the third step, landing bent kneed with a single more or less muffled thump (the children were strictly forbidden to imitate this). Safe on the landing David paused, until he heard the typing resume. Jamie's childhood diaries – the last a beloved five-year one with a gold padlock, only kept up for three – had once been given to his father to read; David had searched them in vain for signs of whatever inward misalignment had driven the little boy's troubled outward life, his

184

tantrums and obsessions. The diaries had been all hope and light: 'We went to the park, it was good. We fed the ducks, it was a nice day. We came to Grany's and I had chips.' Now – David's honour was impeccable in such matters, he was incapable of reading anyone else's letters even left lying on a table, or looking in their opened e-mails – he would never know what his son had to write about.

He was surprised that he had told Evie about the clothes thrown all over Francesca's flat: the picture was mostly one he warded off successfully (he didn't think he'd ever told Suzie about it, and certainly not Jamie). That flat had been a bleakly ugly place, and while Francesca was still alive, for the months she lived there, he had blamed her in his thoughts (at that point they had hardly talked, they met to hand Jamie over) because she hadn't made any effort to superimpose her own taste over the previous tenants' dreadful brown and orange paint; it had seemed part of her wilfulness, her dramatised performance of suffering. When she was dead he thought he should have guessed what she would do, that the brown and orange paint had been a sign of it; which hadn't made him any less angry. He and her mother together had had to empty the place out, sorting Francesca's things from Jamie's clothes and toys: he would have done it by himself, but Jane Bell insisted. She had chosen certain things of her daughter's to keep, the rest they put into sacks for the charity shops. She had not broken down once all that day, that was the sort of woman she was; although she told him afterwards that it had taken seven years before she was ever surprised by happiness again, after Francesca's death. 'The funny thing was,' she had said, 'that although I knew she had meant to do it, I became terrified of accidents happening, to the other people I loved. I couldn't not mind, that they weren't safe. I mean, as nobody's safe, that's all.'

Without Jane Bell, in the time before Suzie moved in with him, David couldn't ever have managed Jamie's childcare while carrying on working for his Part One exams, and then as Senior Registrar. She was someone he admired uncomplicatedly; he didn't see her more because he was afraid he bored her. He went out and watered the garden with the hosepipe in the dark. If he had been asked a few months ago, he would have said he was in essence a family man, bound up in those other lives overlapped with his; now he didn't love his children any less, but felt his connection to them less permanent. His attention was newly drawn to those parts of himself that had been shrouded in abeyance, in the strong ordinary daylight of family fuss.

Kate found that after she had made love with Jamie she could fall asleep, without pills; not into her usual shallow nerve-racked half-doze, but an abandoned deep repose, voluptuous, full of dreams. One of the dreams – or an imagining that she had of herself curled up against him which drifted into a dream – was that his body lying on its side was a sheltering continent, the curve of it a great bay in which she was moored, hardly rocking on

186

the sea-swell, safe. Once she was fastened there she could let herself fall down and away inside the strong ring of his arms, his breathing against her hair. Even that first night she'd slept, under the scratchy blankets. It was quite absurd, she thought, that out of all possible couplings this one – which also harrowed her with guilt, and seemed the most awful mistake – made her the gift of this peace. Max after all was so nice, everyone had approved of Max, she had approved of him herself; but distinctly she remembered that she had always had to jump up from his bed at a certain point as if it was intolerable, gritty or itching, or the sheets too rumpled; she had had to put on her dressing-gown, and find her cigarettes, and talk, or read her book. Often she fell asleep long after Max did, in one of his expensive Swedish posture chairs, with her feet tucked up under her.

Sometimes Jamie must have slept too; but mostly when Kate did come awake, like swimming up from deep water, she found he was watching over her. Then in her sleepy state she would slide languidly into making love again, yielding to it as an extension of dreaming. Probably Jamie made up for his wakefulness, sleeping all day at home: he had nothing else to do. What had happened was a revelation for him – moored against him, she was his new continent. She could remember first discovering at his age, hidden inside ordinary life, the bliss of sex, running counter to everything else experience was teaching, the bustling commonsensical entropic drive. Jamie really wasn't doing anything else in his life apart from his relation with her: she was impressed, although she took care not to show it. No wonder his father worried about him. He had friends he liked, but she guessed that he didn't tell them much about himself: he said they didn't share his tastes in books and films, that mostly what they did together was drugs; they listened to music, they went dancing at certain (superior) clubs in town. 'We joke about things,' he said. 'Already, we're reminiscing together over our schooldays.' He made music on a computer (what he called music, not her kind) with one of them, the ginger-haired boy she'd met.

She asked who he'd had sex with before her, and made him tell her in detail about the two girls his own age, both at parties, neither time very successful or satisfying. What were their names? she wanted to know. What did they look like? How do you get on with them now? What about the one I met in the café? Did you ever have any homosexual experiences? He had a pent-up articulacy, unpractised, bookish; obediently he told her everything. She was pleased with his irony, forgiving himself his inexperience without angst, but keen to leave it behind.

—I'll bet lots of the girls like you, she said. —You're just the type. With your private life only showing in little clues and signs, just enough for someone to make a cult of. Cruelly indifferent, just because you're not trying to be. Your lovely wide child's face: thick curdy skin, like a hero in a fairy tale, gleaming in expectancy, waiting to be marked. When you're a man it will be a moody face, d'you know that? People close to you will watch it nervously.

—Curdy? he wondered, smiling into her face close to his, stroking her skin with his finger.

—Curds and whey. Creamy. It's a thing nobody eats any more, we only know about it from nursery rhymes. I would have liked you desperately, if you'd been in my sixth-form class. I would have done everything, awfully, misguidedly, to catch your attention and impress you, and you'd have been disgusted at my showing off, embarrassed for me.

—It's rubbish, he said. —I would have liked you. I would have known. But I'm glad you're not a girl.

—They're awful, aren't they?

He frowned, perplexed how to answer; but only pleasurably. He didn't wish she talked less in bed: some men had. —Not awful. But perhaps: chaotic.

—You see? How cruel you would have been? Chaotic: that was it, exactly.

—How many lovers have you had? he asked her once, shyly.

—After a certain point one stops counting. It wouldn't be dignified.

Another time he asked, in a pause in their lovemaking: —What do you think of me?

—Think of you? I don't think I'm thinking exactly, at this moment.

—No, but. When you do think, what do you think?

—Well: try to imagine how ignorant you seem to me.

—Oh. He was disconcerted.

—It's not reproach; just a way of describing the deserts of distance between us. I don't only mean things in books, although I do mean those.

—And I suppose by the time I catch up with you, you'll know more: you'll always be ahead.

Kate laughed. —It doesn't work like that. By the time you catch up with me I'll be an old woman.

She always made him go before it was light because it was tolerable somehow – even touching – to watch him dressing in the almost-dark, belting his jeans and tying up his trainers with unconscious grace; in the daylight she couldn't have borne it.

—When can I come back? he asked before he left: flatly, humbly, so she knew that in between times he only waited. —Tonight?

—Not tonight, she said. —I'm busy. Not tomorrow. Thursday, maybe. Come in the evening and play the piano: Billie misses you. Then we'll see.

—Thursday. OK.

Left alone that first morning, seeing the welter of blankets knotted with the counterpane, she had been afraid that Buckets and Mops would guess more than she wanted them to know about what had happened, when they came to clean; in the dawn light, wrapped in her kimono, she stripped old Sam's bed down to the striped lumpy mattress and made it up again properly, the cat winding obstructively around her feet or jumping into the sheets as she spread them. In the airing cupboard there were tall piles of clean white linen sheets, smoothly ironed from the laundry, the laundry mark written with

190

indelible ink in every corner; shaking them out she saw that they were full of holes, or worn thin as tissue in places. They smelled of bitter damp; the smell of semen, that she was aware of when she spread out the blankets, seemed clean and youthful by contrast. When she was a teenager, that new male smell had been associated proudly for her with triumphs of initiation; in her adult relationships she seemed to have forgotten to notice it. In those promiscuous teenage years Kate had set herself an appalling kind of game, to try to have sex in every room in Firenze. She'd run out of interest in the game, or never achieved it anyway, before she went off to university and different quests. Certainly she couldn't remember ever making love in Sam's master bedroom before; perhaps she'd held it off for last, because the room seemed daunting, haunted.

Somehow, on the bicycle trip that was meant to be an occasion for David's healing his estrangement from his son, Bryn invited himself along. David was incandescently angry with his father for about an hour on the evening before they set out, but Bryn didn't even realise that he minded; he brought round maps and sat planning with them at the kitchen table in transparent boyish enjoyment. In his cycling helmet Bryn looked – Jamie said – like an ancient Celt, long white hair sticking out all round; under his ungainly too-short shorts, zipped tight round the out-thrust belly, the huge knees and ropey calves made his light racing bike comically insubstantial in contrast. They had reduced the distances they planned to cover for Bryn's sake, and as it turned out David was grateful; Jamie seemed to idle effortlessly while the two of them laboured and sweated. Freewheeling downhill, Bryn bellowed out Welsh hymns or extracts from the Bach oratorio he was rehearsing with his choir, and Jamie joined in with loud hootings; on the long uphills Bryn and David got off and walked, while Jamie, standing up on his pedals, legs pumping in a low gear, strove all the way to the top.

A tiny window of perfect weather had opened for them, between too hot and too wet; the freshest and best of the summer was past but David liked the lush, fagged, despoiled late season. The hedgerows, machine-cut, showed a coarse stubble of broken stalks; the cruder flowers thrived, escapes of rapeseed blazed from the hillside, frothy rank slews of rosebay willowherb or Himalayan balsam flourished on waste ground or in mud. A small red deer scrambled, ungainly in its fear, up a steep bank; a fox glanced back in contempt over a gingery-fierce shoulder; they swerved, hitting the stink before they saw it, round a rotting badger corpse. With sagging wings and drooping undercarriage a hawk uplifted from a post so that its updraught seemed to cut David's cheek; plunging from dry heights into the hollow beside a river, submersion in its cool ripe dung smell was ecstatic.

David prudently, luckily, whatever the others had advised, had booked them in advance into pubs where they could eat and sleep; these turned out to be packed full and turning away holidaymakers, who cast regretful desiring looks around the calculatedly enticing oaky nooks, flagged floors, red-shaded lamps, wall-displays of old farming implements; the cooking aromas were more likely to be boeuf bourgignon or Thai chicken than lobscouse. After their physical exertions they succumbed in the evenings to an exhaustion that felt to David sensually velvety, unlike the parched one that came from long days in the office; they ate and drank greedily. David didn't know what, if they'd been alone, he and Jamie would have found to talk about for all those hours. Bryn – replete, expansive, delighted to be out of the house, triumphant at his proved cycling potency – ranged round a roomy, archaic masculinity, in his accent resonant as a bell: they talked rugby, politics, medicine until they were felled by sleep. Bryn was moderate Old Labour with Plaid sympathies; David was cautiously Liberal Democrat. Jamie said he didn't know what his politics were: smiling evasively, with his hair hanging into his face, he drew signs on the table in the beer that he had slopped. Bryn courted his wayward grandson more assiduously than he had ever made up to the steady son who picked his way in Bryn's oversize footsteps.

—At your age shouldn't you be wanting to change the world?

—I'd be useless at it.

—We never stopped to ask if we'd be any good at it, we just wanted to defeat capitalism.

—I don't like capitalism all that much.

—But it looks as if it's here to stay, said David.

193

Theatrically Bryn put his head in his hands. —We'll have to start the revolution, then, without you two.

Suzie (who had been all in favour of the holiday) had told David not to go on about what Jamie was going to do next; Bryn enquired so tenderly that Jamie didn't mind it, in that best flirtatious manner he had reserved for the lady patients who adored him, looking coyly over the top of his glasses brought out for reading the menu.

—I can't make up my mind whether to go to university.

—Whether to go? said David, dismayed. —I thought you just weren't sure which subject to take.

—He doesn't care for our kind of hard empirical knowledge. He's going to be a poet, don't you think? 'The unacknowledged legislators of the world'?

—Who says 'the unacknowledged legislators of the world'?

—Don't they teach you anything at school these days? It's Shelley. He's probably gone out of fashion, like revolution.

—Anyway, I've never written any poetry.

—I used to write poetry, said Bryn.

—What kind of poetry, Grandpa?

—Lugubrious, probably.

—Jamie, are you seriously thinking that you might not go?

—It's different in arts subjects. I could take out a year or two – you know, just messing about – and still get back in if I wanted to.

—Messing about?

—He means, supplied Bryn, —messing about the world. That's what they all do.

—Or here. I could get a job.

David was taken aback. —I thought you were so eager to get away from here. What kind of job? You'd soon be bored.

—I might not be.

—Results come out next week, said Bryn, who couldn't resist being interested in the competition. —He'll do well, I suppose?

—I don't know, said Jamie. —I can hardly remember what I wrote. It seems like I did them in another life.

The window draped in net curtains was cut into the two-foot thickness of wall (the place must be very old); beyond it the light descended through a scale of brilliant blues. A restless force radiated off the boy that was not merely the stored heat of the day; every so often he jumped up to go outside without explanation. No doubt he was smoking (his clothes smelled of it when he came back in), or he might have been trying to get a signal on his mobile, to make a call out from the obliterating folds of the valley. They understood that he was consumed by the exulting moment of his youth, driving him up the hills in those exertions where he couldn't tell himself apart from his labouring body. How could he care, what happened next?

On their last evening they all drank too much; Bryn waxed confessional about his marriage, tempestuously monogamous for forty-five years, still – David wasn't sure he wanted to know this – sexual. David clammed up about his two, both failures he felt sure now, disasters: although even as he gave them mentally up he thought how much he liked women, how he preferred their company, yearned for it, missed it. He remembered also how when he'd first brought Francesca home to meet his parents she'd come climbing (still in her besotted phase) into his bed in the middle of the night, and he'd been made quite impotent by the idea of his father on the other side of the wall. Bryn was buying them all whiskies as well as beer. Jamie wouldn't be drawn by his grandfather's teasing, he wouldn't say if he had a girlfriend; then somehow those two ended up at the pool table, Jamie winning easily, loser buying the next round. After the whisky David had to be sick (for the second time in a few weeks: he'd been sick on Suzie's birthday too, he who never drank too much); he sat on his bed in the strange room with his head in his hands. Jamie brought him a pint glass of water.

—Drink this, Dad. You'll feel better for it in the morning.

He touched him on the shoulder. David felt the strong warmth of his son's hand through his shirt and his skin's clammy reaction to the alcohol; it was so comforting that he was embarrassed to feel tears pricking into his eyes, although Jamie couldn't see them. They shared a room; Jamie still slept as he always had done, on his belly with his arms flung out, his head pushed half under his pillow.

* * *

196

Jamie and Kate took Billie walking in the park, in all the crowds. The flower beds had been planted up with blocks of astonishing shocking-pink, lemon-yellow, vermilion; the lake was jammed with boats; there were wilting queues in the play area for the slides and the swings; rapacious garden enthusiasts carried nail scissors surreptitiously in their pockets, for cuttings.

—Fair-weather park lovers, Kate said. —They should be here when we are, when it's miserable and wet leaves are blowing about, and everything growing has died or gone underground.

Billie in her pretty cornflower dress looked around her surprised, but ready to be enchanted. —We do live here, darling, don't we? she said doubtfully. —This is our park?

—Mummy: you've never lived anywhere else.

Kate wouldn't buy Billie ice creams from the van, she said they were made of whale-oil. A gaggle of Muslim girls photographing each other in a triangle of shade between three trees – some in headscarves, some without, one in a baseball cap – gave off almost a hum, like bees, of steady energetic pleasant chatter; one, hurrying away, checked her face hastily (perfect) in a tiny mirror. Billie wanted to sit down to rest: as they entered the rose garden to find a bench, a girl coming out had a creamy-orange rose against her hair, above her ear.

—Of course you looked at her, Kate said, as soon as they were as alone as was possible, keeping Billie in sight, inspecting the beds where the bare soil was grim between the grizzled old leggy rose-bushes, for all their blooming.

Jamie was amiably blank. —At who?

—Whom. The girl with the rose.

—Oh: I suppose she'd picked it here. She shouldn't have, do you mean?

—People will think you're my son, Kate said. —Or my nephew. I might be your mother's sister, keeping an eye on you, childless myself, slightly forbidding. Do you mind?

—I have got an aunt on my mother's side, he said. —But she's nothing like you. Why do you care what people think?

—You're such a nice boy. Temporarily, I suppose you're my fate. But you've no idea of the trouble you've made for me.

—Temporarily?

—Of course. Do you picture yourself pushing my bath chair?

—What's a bath chair? He was looking among ruby-dark tea roses with an air of choosing.

—Don't pick one for me now, after we've seen her: it's too late. Anyway, I don't like roses.

—Being young isn't like what people think it is, Jamie said to Kate that night. She had plugged in beside the bed her steel lamp from London with two creamy glass globes, like little moons, so they could see one another. —Before I knew you, it was like looking at real life – people actually feeling things and being things – through a closed window.

—The people on the other side of the window, of course, were looking back enviously at you.

—I was afraid of never getting to be actually real. Having Dad and Suzie's life: driving round picking the kids up from things, or dropping them off, booking two weeks' holiday a year, machines at home to do everything, that nobody uses. It's like a picture of a life. Only in here is real, because it doesn't pretend to be. That's a paradox.

—You're so clever, aren't you?

Propped on her elbow, she traced the effort of thought on his face with her finger.

—You know how to do things, he said. —Everything you touch, you know how to do it. As if there's a hidden pattern.

—If only you knew. Everything I touch, I spoil: apart from Billie. What would decent people think, of what we do? You ought to be afraid of me.

—I don't care about decent people.

Carol called at Firenze to invite Kate to supper.

—Get a Billie-sitter, she said. —Ask Alison. It would be good for you.

—Do I look as if I need good doing me? Kate, measuring out tea from the caddy in the kitchen, turned herself full-frontally for her friend's appraisal. Kate had recently had her hair cut; her badger-stripe was swept strikingly back from her face and her head seemed lighter, freed from the thick bob.

—I had a bit of colour put in, she confessed, approving

herself in the little skewed mirror over the sink. —On the hairline where there was some grey.

—As a matter of fact, you do look well. Carol ducked to peer in as well. —My whole wretched mane is grey, she complained, flattening it brusquely. —Not true grey; just as if the blonde had gradually leached out. Actually it's not you I'm worried about: I'm worried about the other person I want to ask. But, seriously, how are things?

—I have my music, Kate said, imitating her mother. —All my life, I've been consoled by art. Oh, and also in the evenings we've started backgammon: a different Billie steps out from behind the confused one, ruthlessly competitive, sharp as nails. We keep a book: I'm losing. And I hate the idea of work, I'm ashamed that I didn't liberate myself long ago. Everybody should try it.

—Not everybody of course could afford to, murmured Carol conscientiously.

—I'm sleeping like a baby. Aren't you amazed by that? Who is this other worrying person you want to ask to supper?

—My brother. You do like him, don't you? I know you used to think him a bit of a prig. Only I've got a feeling something's going wrong with him and his wife: she's away, again, with the children, he's all on his own, working too hard. I thought we could try and cheer him up.

Kate poured boiling water into the teapot from an impressive height. —I don't know, she said. —I'm awfully busy.

—You could talk to him about music. In the evenings on his own I think that's all he does: plays CDs from his collection.

—Surely no one uses that word these days: prig? It's out of an Edwardian children's book.

Kate came late to the supper party, so that they had started eating without her. Carol had invited a couple of other friends: someone who worked for the Refugee Council and a publisher from one of the subsided Welsh presses. The first-floor flat, bright and jolly, opened off a bleak common stairwell with timed light switches; as soon as the door swung open Kate knew she was in the wrong mood. She was hot and she had chosen to wear a tight-fitting black dress; Carol and the other woman, Angharad, were in T-shirts and trousers. Kate explained that the taxi driver had been late bringing her sitter.

—Have you left children? Angharad the publisher asked sympathetically.

—No: senile old person.

Kate stalked on loud heels into the kitchen to find gin. David half got up out of his chair to greet her, but when she sat down she made sure she didn't sit by him; she knew her discomfort settled on the conversation like a cloud, despite the wide-open windows and cheerful dishes of salads and vegetarian curries. Picking over chickpeas on her plate with a fork, she turned her attention onto Colin, who was nervous in the strong light of it, mentioning his absent wife sooner than was strictly necessary. Because he seemed to want to, Kate let him believe that her parents had come as refugees from Hitler's Germany: his professional respect struck in.

—You know why we Jews play the violin so well? she explained loudly. —So that we can pack our livelihood in one small case and get out at a moment's notice. Don't I play the violin well, David?

David with his mouth full was at a disadvantage; he had been applying himself earnestly and silently to his plate. He nodded his head with obliging eagerness, putting the back of his hand over his mouth, swallowing hard.

—Although, he added, scrupulously honest, when his mouth was clear, —I don't suppose it's that easy to earn a living, playing the violin. I mean, unless one has a professional training.

—Don't be so literal, dear, said Carol. —Kate only wants you to flatter her. She isn't really calculating for a fascist takeover.

—Sorry, said David. —Of course not. She's a very good amateur player.

—Colin will have to flatter me, Kate said. —David's the truth-teller. He never will.

Colin, uneasily in thrall to her tragic past, prevaricated: said he had never heard her play. She invited him to the next concert given by her quartet; he said his wife had played the cello when she was a girl; Kate yawned. The conversation, limping, took refuge in politics, the number of women AMs in the Assembly. Carol brought out hazelnut and chocolate torte (home-made: she was good); they all eyed it embarrassingly keenly, because their minds weren't elsewhere. Only Kate refused it.

—I don't like women politicians, she said.

Angharad was steely. —That's a ridiculous statement, in the twenty-first century.

—Are we in the twenty-first century? I'm always forgetting, aren't you?

—No one's having that argument any more. Even the reactionaries are only quarrelling over the methods of achieving parity.

Kate shrugged. —I used to be a feminist, of course. Everyone goes through a phase. But now I'm glad men rule the world. Who wants to, anyway? What a bore.

—Take no notice, Carol said, cutting big slices in compensation. —She's only being provocative.

—Women are too weak, too far-seeing, too deeply drawn by emotional tides. Too pessimistic. If there were only women, we'd still be living in caves, prophesying through our genitals. Civilisation's such a foolish optimism, really: it takes men.

David laughed inappropriately.

—You are just being provocative, Angharad said, smiling as if she wasn't amused.

Carol handed cream. —You're too naughty, Kate. Don't tease. Anyway, you'd be useless in a cave. Don't forget I've slept with you inside a tent: you hated that.

—Oh, I know. Women are so duplicitous. When men make houses, we're very glad to scurry inside them, to keep warm.

When Carol retired to the kitchen to make the

required assortment of coffees and herb teas, the arrangement around the table broke up in relief; Colin and
Angharad sank into the sofa at the other end of the room
and the sounds of their mild conversation rose over its
back. Carol turned up the music (Elvis Costello still,
unbelievably, after all these years). Only Kate and David
stayed in their places, separated by the ruins of the meal:
collapsed cake, smeared plates, empty glasses.

—All those centuries of struggle, he said reproach-
fully. —Women campaigning for their rights. To vote,
for instance.

—Well, I don't vote, said Kate. —It was wasted on
me.

—You're not serious?

—Haven't ever. Never even registered. Darling Billie
does, for all she's seriously senile. God knows who she
votes for: Natural Law Party, perhaps? Or Plaid Cymru.
Something from fairyland.

—You're not serious. I'm no good, I know, at being
playful.

—It started in the old days: I was a Trotskyite then,
and no party was revolutionary enough.

—Now?

—Maybe the same thing. Or its opposite: no party is
conservative enough. No party is interesting enough,
anyway.

—Kate. It was as if he made a huge effort, although
he only leaned forward across the table. He was wearing
a dark blue shirt, unironed, with the sleeves rolled up;
she noticed the dark hair on his brown forearms. —I

wish we weren't quarrelling. I'm not really that interested in voting either.

She put down her unlit cigarette and lighter heavily on the tablecloth, still without looking in his face. —Are we quarrelling?

—I don't know. Are we? But I would always like to be frank with you.

—That's usually bad news. That's usually when people are going to say something horrible.

—Nothing horrible.

—Then it makes me feel sad. Because I'm not the sort of person people want to be frank with.

—Aren't you? Well, perhaps me neither. Don't feel sad.

Abruptly Kate stood up, scooping her things into her bag. —Actually I have to go. I promised my Billie-sitter.

David stood up too, in consternation. —But you've hardly been here an hour. Surely they'll be all right for a bit longer.

She picked up some silly kid gloves that had been part of her dressed-up look. She had found them in a drawer in Firenze and they had made her too hot on the way over. Bending over them, she struggled to do up the tiny mother-of-pearl buttons on the inside of the wrists. —I shouldn't have come out in the first place.

—I'll give you a lift.

—No, really, I'd rather walk. Carol: do you hear? I'm going. For what it's worth, she said to David, flinging her wrap over one shoulder, —I can't bear to quarrel with you either. We are good friends, aren't we?

Kate gave David her hand, snatched it back, scrabbled off the glove, and gave him her bare fingers, in token of her sincerity; he grasped them hard. Carol came out from the kitchen protesting, wiping a mug with a tea towel. No one but them would have noticed anything happening.

Nine

On the first day of the new school term, Giulia telephoned just as David came through the door from work.

—Is Suzie there? she said.

—I don't think so.

—She hasn't been in today. Do you know what's up?

—Hasn't been in?

—Hasn't even rung, all day. I mean, I know she's been going through a bit of a time recently, but I've had a whole class without their teacher, on the first day of term, with a new pupil intake and two new members of staff. I could have done without it. Is she ill? David?

The lights were all pointlessly on in the kitchen, even though it was still bright day outside. On the counters there was a mess of chocolate milk and scrapings from burned toast; the margarine tub had been ravaged, its lid was on the floor, greasy side down.

—I did speak to her last night, he said. —She wasn't here, she called: she was making sure Jamie could pick the kids up. I didn't ask where she was calling from.

—Listen, I'm sorry.

—It didn't occur to me she wouldn't be at school today.

—David, if there's anything that we can do to help. Do you mean she's actually walked out?

—She hasn't said so. But I suppose she's just done it. Giulia sighed helplessly.

—What about the other girl? David asked. —Menna?

—Oh, she's finished here. It was only a maternity leave, she finished in the summer. Do you think that's where Suzie is?

—I don't know.

—She's bound to be in touch.

—I'll let you know.

In the snug they had drawn the curtains against the daylight. The television capered weakly, the children hardly looked up as he peered in; Jamie was extended longways on the sofa, Hannah sitting under his raised knees, Joel at his head, with an arm thrown carelessly across his big brother's chest; like somnambulants they gazed at the screen. David too felt as if, in spite of the sunshine, only one small swinging lamp of his consciousness was alight in a huge inert darkness. He put sausages to cook under the grill, opened tins of baked beans, cut his hand on the sharp edge of one of them, leaked surprising thin wet blood onto the bread. There wasn't enough bread for them all, and when he looked into the freezer there wasn't any left in there either. Hannah at some point planted herself, pouting, in the kitchen doorway and asked where Mummy was.

—Not here, he said shortly.

—Doesn't she even live in this house any more or something?

—Don't ask me.

Later, he thought, he would address all this with the children properly and as his better self. Little jets of fat shot out from the sausages and blazed up under the grill.

—Only I've got bottom problems, Hannah said, —that you can't deal with.

He was wearily solicitous, putting down his fork. —I'm a doctor, remember? I'm sure I can help.

—Don't worry, she said gloomily, stumping off upstairs. —I'll be just fine.

He picked up his fork again. After a fairly long while she stumped down, and he forgot to ask if that meant her problems were over. They had their food in front of the telly; he sat with them to eat through his heavy plateful, although afterwards he couldn't remember what he'd watched; he imagined the fatty food dissolving sourly in his stomach, sending spurts of acid into his oesophagus, squeezing his heart. He piled up the dirty dishes in the kitchen. Instead of talking to the children properly, he left Jamie in charge and drove out to the place in Splott where he had dropped Suzie off earlier that summer, after Kate Flynn's party; miraculously he knew the way, didn't make a single wrong turn, as if the little cottage in its close-nestled row behind overgrown gardens had lurked waiting for him all the time beneath his conscious thoughts. Shapes were silhouetted in the dusk-light against a clear sky like an eye stretched wide just before it shut; he could see that the wildness of the gardens, which he had remembered dense with foliage as miniature forests, only consisted in fact of broken sofas, concrete, buddleia, a fallen wall, a garage sunk under its weight of ivy. The fanlight above the front door through which Suzie had disappeared shone feebly yellow, as last time.

Children still played out in the streets round here, as if they'd seen through the taming effects of PlayStation: a gang circled on bikes, shouting to one another, two boys to a bike, the front one standing to pedal, the one behind with his legs splayed wide; wheeling past they turned their heads, taking what might have been a sinister interest in him. He got out of the car and locked it behind him, scowling at the boys; then strode up the path, pushing through dense bristling shrubs that blocked his way. Of course there wasn't a straightforward front-door bell, only a sellotaped-on note that said absurdly 'Knock three times': so he hammered with his fist, then both fists. When the door yielded and Neil stood warily, holding it half open, David pushed forward across the threshold.

—I have to speak to my wife.

Neil didn't move from where he blocked the way. —She's not here.

—Suzie! David bellowed past him. —Suzanne!

A female shape moved into the shadows where a door opened at the end of the hall (which was lit only by a dim bulb in a pink shade). Too slight for Suzie; he made out the pale oval of Menna's face. —You don't have any right to come bursting in here, she enunciated in cold condemnation; the South Walian in him discriminated vindictively against her adenoidal North Wales accent. David had never been in a fight in his whole life: he knew that he wouldn't have a chance against Neil if it actually came to that. Neil was short and slim but wiry, he laboured all day out of doors, everything about him suggested the alert force of the capable male, kept decently in reserve. David pushed past him clumsily nonetheless: the little narrow hall, dreadfully wallpapered, with pinned-up shawls and posters, was just as he would have imagined it, even down to its smell of dirty landlord's carpet overlaid with incense.

—Neil, said Menna. —Let him, if he wants to. We've got nothing to hide.

—You can take our word for it, mate, said Neil, not offensively. —She isn't here. We haven't seen her for a week.

David was sure immediately that they were telling the truth. Yet in a parade of angry expectation he had to storm about, searching, slamming open all the doors of the secretive little house; he even ran noisily upstairs, blundered into a bathroom whose walls were stencilled with flowers, switched on blaring central bulbs in two little den-bedrooms made for lamplight, draped with patchwork, scarves and beads, reflected in mirrors. More dignified than he was, they didn't even follow him: Menna made a sign to Neil. Everywhere in the house was surprisingly neat, in its junk-shop way. Whatever he was looking for, it wasn't here. Eventually he came

211

to rest in their kitchen, breathing heavily, drooping, propped with his knuckles resting on the little table where they had been eating when he came pounding at their door: their soup, which looked like lentils, was getting cold in green pottery bowls (he remembered what he'd cooked for the children and felt reproached). He considered upsetting the soup bowls wildly onto the floor, but didn't do it.

—Then where is she?

—If I did know I wouldn't tell you, Menna said. —But to simplify matters, as it happens, I don't. She must have been at Ladysmith today: why don't you ask them? We haven't seen her for a week. She doesn't live here, you know: she's just a friend. We don't insist on knowing her whereabouts.

—Then is there someone else?

—Someone else? She mocked. —I don't know what you mean.

—She didn't turn up at school today.

Menna shrugged, but not without curiosity. —We're not her keepers. Clearly you imagine you are.

—I'm the father of her children, he said. —If she's gone, I only want to know it.

—If she's gone, Menna said, —I'm not surprised.

—What rubbish has she been telling you? What half-baked idea do you think you have, about our life?

The following evening Suzie rang him in the middle of the after-supper clearing-up (pasta, with sauce out of a jar).

—David, how dare you?

—How dare I what? he said dully; even passion seemed to have reduced itself to drudgery. He had an apron tied around his waist; he had had a difficult day at work, too, and would be up until after midnight with bits and pieces he had to finish on the computer.

—Go round and make a scene at my friends' house.

—Oh that. So they did know where you were.

—No, I happened to phone them, they told me you'd been there: said you crashed around the house as if I was hidden in it somewhere. They thought it was just funny, but I was embarrassed for you.

—So where are you?

—I'm at Evie's, for the moment.

—All I want to know, he said, —is what to tell the kids. We'd better start to talk to them about it. We need to meet, to put this separation on a proper footing. And you ought to talk to Giulia, unless you're throwing over your job along with everything else.

—I don't know if it's a separation. Don't talk to them yet.

—As far as I can see: you've separated from us.

—David: give me a bit more time? I'm not sure. And I have talked to Giulia. I'm going to go back to Ladysmith next week.

—The children keep asking when you will be home.

—I *know*. Don't make me feel worse.

—Why not?

—I suppose I do see that you've got no reason not to.

213

—What happened? he said. —Everything seemed to be all right. What was the matter?

Her silence was substantial. —Wait, she made audible, at the end of a long effort. —Wait, please.

After he put the phone down he returned to scraping plates and filling the dishwasher. At one point when he nudged the full rubbish bin out of his way with his foot, it tipped over, spilling out eggshells and bean tins and muck onto the floor. Then he kicked with all his weight at the door of the cupboard under the sink, so that his foot went right through its flimsy tongue-and-groove panelling, splintering it. The children and Jamie came running from the snug and stared at the hole.

Kate settled down to her translating work. She tried to imagine this as the new shape of her days, sitting down every morning at her childhood desk with her books spread around her, turning on her computer. Perhaps the time had come for her to live more quietly. She felt as if she had shut a door behind her, anyway, on all her years teaching and researching at Queen Mary; she should have left earlier, before she grew so tired of it. There was no going back inside that world. While she worked she was gathering ideas for her introduction: she wanted to write about the particular qualities of Russian nineteenth-century pastoral, suggesting significant contrasts with Mickiewicz and the Polish tradition. Perhaps she should think more about that kind of writing, for the future. It wouldn't be bad, to try and make a bit of a name for herself in some kind of literary journalism.

While she was working one day Jamie telephoned, to ask what she was doing in the afternoon.

—Impossible, I'm afraid, she said with the briskness she had adopted for all her relations with him that weren't tender or sensual: it helped her demonstrate, for her honour, that they weren't a real couple, connected in the ordinary atmosphere. —I'm taking Billie round for tea with a friend of hers.

—Then come out to the café to meet me while she's there.

—I'm working. By myself, at home.

—Come to the café, please. There's a reason.

Through Jamie's boyishness and shyness she felt his force uneasily sometimes: he would become a man who expected his suggestions to be taken up. When Kate arrived at the café he was sitting with his back to the door, chatting across the table with a bent tall woman, her long aged face naked of make-up; a grizzled rope of dyed-red hair was pinned round above her brows, defiantly stylish in disregard of fashion, like her bright and clashingly red wool poncho. It only took Kate quick moments to recognise – in spite of a twenty-year gap since they'd last met – Francesca's mother. Kate hadn't gone to Francesca's funeral, hadn't been in London at the time (dragged transatlantic by a hectic affair with a Chicago professor), hadn't known about the death even until Carol told her in a letter. Her last memory of Jane Bell was from graduation, when the gang had gone out to eat after the ceremony with parents disconcertingly along. Billie with her hair up, in her little Hardy Amies suit (older, always, than the other parents), had been a porcelain doll beside ugly flamboyant Jane, who smoked cigarillos and used the word 'fuck' loudly (not only for swearing but, more shocking, meaning sexual intercourse). Even in pink crumpled denim, hair home-cropped and dyed carrot-colour, bead earrings dangling, Jane had assumed possession of the restaurant and the waiters had deferred to her. She had taken Billie under her wing (London in those days made Billie shy), and Kate had resented Francesca for it. Francesca's flame had burned sulkily around her mother's brightness. Perhaps Billie and Jane commiserated over the times they'd had, bringing up difficult daughters.

Jane's eyes now, alert in her rather shockingly fallen face, registered Kate's entrance benignly blankly, all her focus on the loved boy opposite. Her hunched shoulders and bent back (she'd always had a tall woman's bad posture), straining forward, expressed the intensity with which she took him in. The bell above the café door clanged behind Kate and Jamie looked round anxiously, waved to her. She wouldn't forgive him for springing this occasion on her; it was like his indifference to decorum. He was regretting it already, she could tell.

—Granny, do you remember Kate?

Jane Bell stared kindly enough, but she didn't: how could she have seen that sour half-born girl, anyway, in a middle-aged woman? She put out a big loose-skinned freckled hand.

—One of Jamie's teachers?

—I would have liked to teach him, Kate said. —He's supposed to be very clever.

—He is. It's all right, you know, for me to boast about him: it's allowed to grandparents. He's done very well in his A levels.

—So I hear.

—She's Francesca's friend, Granny. And Carol's: they were all at UCL together.

—Oh, Kate Flynn! said Jane, remembering at once and not squeamish at the opening of the past. —Of course. As you came through the door some familiarity did nudge me, but at my age I'm assailed by those all the time, I've learned to take no notice.

—I wanted you to see her, Jamie said. —To see if you remembered.

—Well, I do now. His grandmother smiled, at him: she too had that mouth with its loose louche lower lip.

—We've been doing some extra reading together, Kate said.

—He's a nice boy, said Jane when he went to buy coffees.

Kate was bland. —He is.

—My heart's treasure. At first because of Francesca; but actually it's just him, we rub along, he and I. You've struck up contact through Carol, I suppose? I'm glad you've given him extra help. The college wasn't very good: I offered to pay, but David's delicate. One hates the private system, but what to do? I had the idea from Carol, though, that you were teaching in London some-where.

217

Kate explained lightly, holding as much of herself as possible back from notice. In the other woman's face, its white skin dramatically puffy and marked as if out of a grand carelessness, she saw a puzzle of adjustment: Jane could not have expected her daughter's contemporaries to have stayed twenty-six, but she was obviously disconcerted, picking up Kate's life, not to feel that it was still all ahead of her. Kate had a chilly vision of herself on the slope down from summits that had hardly happened.

—Is David all right? she asked Jane, while Jamie was paying at the counter. —Carol was worrying about him. Things seemed to be difficult at home.

—I'm not staying there. I always stay with Bryn and Betty, the dears: we took to one another, in spite of everything. I do hope nothing's wrong at David's: I thought this time he'd chosen the right girl.

—He ought to be happy.

—Yes. Though possibly happiness is not his strong suit: he's rather in earnest, isn't he?

Bringing their coffees, Jamie asked his grandmother if she had ever seen Kate's house: she didn't think so. Kate guessed he was at a loss quite what to do with his two women now he'd brought them together; he must when he planned it have wanted to test his secret, by having it touch something in his other life. Fatally, he couldn't stop himself describing the rooms of the house, so that scenes that had taken place in there seemed to float horribly between them at the table: to deflect him Kate talked about her grandparents, the migration from

218

the East, the haberdashery shops, the house built for a dynasty.

—We have a turret even. I always feel, for lookout: my grandfather couldn't believe he'd really got away.

—Did you know your grandparents?

Kate shook her head. —We're hardly a family at all. We've heard distant rumours of one another. I've seen photographs. My father died young, so I never knew him. There's only Billie and me: not enough to count, really. We're just two individuals powerfully attached. What about your family?

—God, they procreate, they're a tribe: awful in its own way. I have seven grandchildren. But you should go back, visit Vilnius. Such an interesting place.

—Oh: have you been there? I'm not sure there would be much left for me to connect with.

—She's been everywhere, Jamie said.

—I think Jamie ought to travel, Jane said. —Don't you? Only now mysteriously he wants to stay on here. I know he's busy writing something.

—There's a lot going for Cardiff, Kate said in a hurry. —Asian immigration mixing with the descendants of the coal miners. You can walk out to a concert. Everywhere, living in these provincial cities, you meet people you know; there's one good café in town everybody goes to. In the suburbs, the last vestiges of the old tranquillised routine.

—Not provincial strictly, Jamie said. —It's a capital.

—Time for a change is all I meant, said Jane.

They walked afterwards through the park, because

219

Jane suggested it, to see Kate's house from the outside. Kate didn't know what desperate defence she might have mounted, if Jane had proposed coming in; but really Jane wanted her grandson to herself for the time she had left, and pretended to consult regretfully the big man's watch, on an expandable metal bracelet, that she kept in her jeans. Jamie didn't walk between them, carried ahead by his irrepressible young stride, looking back, walking backwards sometimes, hands in pockets, uneasy now he'd brought them together, until they were apart again. Faced with Firenze – looking in the soft late-summer light reflected off the water more like a clumsy memory of Venice – Jane seemed struck enough, after all, to want to linger for last minutes. She suggested ice cream; after a moment's flicker when Jamie, knowing Kate too well, expected her to refuse (on the grounds of whale-oil), he went obligingly off to wait in the queue at the van. Jane and Kate side by side at the railings looked out over the lake to the dreamy blue prospect: two men in a flat boat were busy forking up into heaps, off the surface of the water, the algae that grew in grotesque abundance now because of the phosphates in washing powder (Jamie had told Kate this). A miniature rattling conveyor belt carried the green heaps to the other end of the boat where the stuff was piled high.

Jane turned to look at her. —He's rather smitten with you, she said. —I think it's you he's staying for.

Kate in one second's plummeting dismay under her scrutiny had time to calculate that Jane hadn't guessed everything.

She smiled back. —It makes me feel ancient. If flattered.

—I wondered if you'd noticed.

—Noticing is what one's supposed to be good at, by forty-three. Of course it all makes me rather wish I was eighteen again.

—And what will you do?

—Do? Nothing. I mean, I'll encourage him if you like to go away, to travel or to go to university or something. That's what should happen: but it's not my business.

—We mustn't hurry him, into whatever it is he's going to be. I trust him, don't you? That it will be something good.

—I don't want to interfere.

—You don't want him to know that you've noticed. But be kind, anyway, letting him down. I think you've been good for him. His father and Suzie are kind people, but I wonder if they recognise what they've got.

—I'll be very careful. Don't worry. He really is a special boy. And I'm very fond of his father. We've known one another since we were children.

—Here he comes, warned Jane. —I suppose we'll have to eat these horrible things.

—She liked you, reassured Jamie later, in the evening of that same day.

Billie was at the piano: her Schubert Impromptus covered his talk with Kate, where they stood stiffly opposed, sideways on to their reflections in the tall

mirror over the black marble fireplace, as if in an uneasy
crowd. The sweetness of the music, though, made Kate
furious; she had grown careless recently over what her
mother witnessed, thinking it made no difference. She
wanted to shake Jamie, except that she wouldn't touch
him; her voice was intimately incensed.

—I've only allowed you to come in because I am so
angry with you. It's for the last time. This is over.
You've gone too far. What did you think you were up
to?

She saw what a difference she had made to him already,
in their few weeks; he didn't flinch, he resisted like a
rock under her onslaught, casting his eyes down to lick
the rim of his cigarette paper (he could roll up between
his fingers, with no surface to lean on: she'd loved boys
for less than that, when she was eighteen).

—It didn't matter, he said steadily. —She wasn't going
to guess: but even if she had. She's broad-minded, she's
open to all sorts of things.

—Broad-minded! Do you have any idea? If you'd
been a man, if she'd been your wife, I'd have faced it
out: but your grandmother!

—She's not a grandmother, really. She's somebody.

—Worse! And, she did guess half of it: only your
stupid infatuation, thank God.

—You're being quite conventional. I thought you
weren't afraid of anything.

—What kind of idiot do you take me for?

He cast around for a lighter.

—Jamie! To force his attention she slapped him hard,

smartly, on the cheek, knocking him off balance; Billie at the piano faltered. She raised her arm to smack him again harder, so he caught her by both wrists, frowning, hurting her slightly; her red handprint dawned on his skin.

—Carry on playing, Mummy! Jamie's going in a minute anyway.

Creakily, Schubert restarted.

—Don't, don't, he encouraged Kate tenderly in an undertone, close to her ear, coaxing her, talking round a child in a tantrum. —Don't fight. Don't let's fight. I'm sorry, if I was wrong.

When he surrounded her she couldn't see him whole, and the music after all, with her eyes hidden, imposed itself: its pleasures intricate as honeycomb.

—I rolled this one for you, he softly said.

She yielded but lit it – the lighter turned up in his pocket – drawing off and staring away from him nonetheless, in case he thought he'd won. He rolled up for himself, too, and smoked: they watched each other's reflections smoking in the mirror.

—And what is this writing she says you're doing? What kind of writing?

He hesitated for the first time. —I wished she hadn't mentioned that.

—You see? What trouble we're in? Where anything ordinary we do is dangerous. You can't write about this, I forbid you to. Is it a novel?

—No. At least, I don't think so. Do you want to read it? I don't know whether I'm ready to show you.

—Absolutely not. Never. I want you to destroy it, because I'm so afraid someone will find it. What if you died, say? Anyway it will be the most awful rubbish, you know, when you come back to look at it later.

That last idea was too much for him, he deeply inhaled. —Was that the real kind of never, or the other kind?

—I don't ever read anything, as it happens, written after 1930.

He took that in as well. —Well, I won't be like you. —God forbid.

—Let me stay, he said, subtly, so that Billie couldn't hear.

—No. You're joking. I said it's finished between us.

In the lamplight his completed adult face – long full cheeks under hard knots of bone, luxuriant mouth, eyes hooded – could seem sealed powerfully over his childhood; she had to be careful not to show how he impressed her, how relieved she was when his naivety spilled out, making his features mobile with feeling again.

—Billie, anyway, is going to be awake all night; she slept for hours this afternoon, on my bed.

—I'll wait all night. I don't care however long.

—Not tonight. Come on Friday, perhaps.

—Friday? he sighed. —That's too far off.

—Friday, perhaps.

David gathered himself in a great effort of concentration upon the children, his younger children. Suzie in those weeks came and went: she wouldn't talk to him beyond practicalities, and wasn't very interested in those.

She slept, when she slept at home, downstairs. He thought sometimes she seemed intoxicated: short of breath, incoherent, hectic, looking at the children as if she couldn't see them; he couldn't tell if this effect was psychological, or whether her new friends were plying her with magic mushrooms or cactus or pills. She seemed to manage, most days, Ladysmith; he presumed that she talked for long hours with Giulia afterwards because when he met Giulia he felt her pregnant with sympathetic knowledge of him, which he held off. What happened to Suzie only touched him remotely now; it had begun to seem improbable that they had lived close together for all those years. He judged her coldly. Their arrangement, living apart in the same house, ought to have felt eccentric; robustly they adapted and got used to it.

One evening, leaving Jamie to babysit, they drove over together to walk in the nearby parkland, open to the public; David had said they ought to discuss things. The old house had burned down in a fire years ago, there was nothing left of it but a shell with blind windows, but the rhododendrons flowered every spring, frogs and fish bred in a weedy pond. David and Suzie sat side by side on the grass at the top of a long sloping field where at the weekend families picnicked and played cricket and flew kites; midweek, they had it to themselves. David kept an eye on his watch, afraid they would miss the locking of the gates. Even as he worried about this, he was carried away by a rage that seemed to blow into him from nowhere across the open space. He began

225

shouting loudly at Suzie, that what made him angry about what had happened was that she was making a stupid person's mistake, confusing some silly sex fantasy or whatever it was, for a real thing. He wouldn't have minded if she had fallen in love, or was going through any sort of crisis: but only if she could talk about it to him, like a grown-up. Like intelligent people do. This came out so clearly formulated that David realised he must have been working it all out to himself at home, over and over. His whole body shook with passion as the words flooded out of him. Suzie lay back on the grass.

—You hate me, she said. —You really hate me. Underneath it all. How can you say those things? 'You wouldn't have minded'. Is that what you really mean? It's you who's stupid. You don't understand anything. You're suffocating me.

—You're the one who's caused all of this mess, showing off, making a fool of yourself. How dare you blame me?

She rolled over so that her face was buried against the ground and her voice was muffled.

—You don't know what it's like, she said. —You don't know what I feel.

She was wearing some kind of thin print skirt: he could see through it to her curved buttocks and brief knickers. Without knowing he was going to do it, he lifted her skirt and smacked her hard with the full weight of his hand across the back of her thighs; astonished, she scrambled to her knees and pounded with her fists

226

at his shoulders and chest. For a few strange minutes they scuffled together viciously: at one point she tangled her fingers in his hair as tightly as she could and tugged hard at it; he slapped her again, on the face this time, she scratched his neck. A dog-walker emerged from the trees at the bottom of the field and looked up towards them, then retreated; he might have thought they were making love, but in fact their fighting instinct for those minutes seemed pure and unsexual. As soon as David realised Suzie was crying he stopped in dismay. They got to their feet and brushed themselves off shame-facedly; she found a tissue in her bag for both their tears. On the way back to the car Suzie hugged her arms round herself, clenching her shoulders tightly; once or twice he touched her on the elbow to steer her onto the right path. Afterwards, because they never talked about it, he found it hard to believe that this scene had actually taken place. It didn't seem to make any difference to the way they lived together.

David tried firmly to re-establish the children's routines: mealtimes, Hannah's piano lessons, Joel's pottery on Saturday mornings, bedtimes, baths, tooth brushing. Joel didn't like his new Year Two class teacher. Hannah feuded, sprouted hot tears, crossed out and rewrote names on the list she actually kept, in a note-book, of her best friends; then ousted friends joined forces against her, cruelties proliferated, and she wilted, overcome by what she'd started. David even had to nego-tiate truces with the mothers of the other girls, at collec-tion time in the playground. He took for granted that all these difficulties were both real and also manifestations of their distress over the situation at home. Because Suzie had asked him not to, he didn't say anything to them about a separation: he told them their mother was overtired, that she had problems at work. Jamie was invaluable; guiltily David postponed worrying about him. His eighteenth birthday came and went without anyone suggesting any celebration, though Suzie bought him a card, and they gave him money: his grandmother came down to see him, bringing him books. Jamie had even begun cooking tea sometimes for the children when he picked them up from school, washing up after them, putting their clothes in the machine.

One weekend Suzie took the children away to the chalet in the Gower peninsula; Evie and her daughter Cara were going too (David didn't ask who else). When they'd gone he climbed into his car in the morning sunshine to get out some work papers from the back seat, and then felt that he couldn't bear to go back inside the empty house (Jamie comatose in his attic, having come in at God knows what time, didn't count). He drove off; went up the Wye valley, stopped at Ross, filled the car with petrol, walked around the little town without seeing it. He wouldn't even have known afterwards that he had bought coffee somewhere, except that he could taste it at the back of his mouth, brown and bitter, something to focus on. Eventually, as if it was where he had been meaning to go all along, he drove in the early afternoon back into Cardiff and to Kate Flynn's house. Standing waiting at the door he heard music; he was afraid she might not let him in if she was rehearsing with her quartet. At last there were footsteps crossing the empty hall, and Billie came slowly to peer at him through the queerly distorting coloured panes.

—Oh, it's you, she said, with her capaciously accepting smile, when she opened the door; he wondered whom she thought she recognised. She seemed a pressed flower, faded and weightless, lilac colour in ivory cheeks; but her hand grabbing his arm for her return journey bore heavily down on him, claw-like, a real old lady's. He thought she looked less well than when he'd first seen her in the winter.

The gas fire burned hotly in the drawing room, blotting out the mild weather outside; the curtains were half drawn against the slanting sunlight. Kate, standing with a blonde woman he didn't recognise, poised to play, signalled with her bow for him to sit out of the way on the sofa opposite.

—From thirty-two? She collected the others in a glance, the viola player turned her pages back, Billie resumed at the piano stool; then Kate dropped her head decisively, starting them. They were playing Haydn's 'Gypsy Rondo' Trio. Kate was wearing extraordinary shoes, impossibly high, pink with black suede flowers: they made her almost tall, swaying in her dark-rose-coloured dress which was cut somehow so that it fitted tight around her breasts and tiny waist and hips, flared out and swung around her knees. David shut his eyes to listen, judged their playing pleasantly adequate, heard them stumble and restart once or twice (usually Billie with cold fingers), knew they

229

flaked out in the finale, had to stop and go at half speed. For all their clumsiness, even mysteriously because of it, he seemed to penetrate deeper and deeper into the truth of the elusive enchantment.

Then Kate stood over him; he was looking up at the underside of her black tea tray. —How flattering. You fell asleep. I've made you coffee.

—The music was in my dreams, he apologised, and it was true: they had been illuminated by an idea of the eighteenth century, glass and rococo gold, stone nymphs in garden recesses.

—Best dreamed, said the viola player (Ann, he'd heard Kate call her), compact, neat jaw jutting just enough to make whatever she said sound resolute. —We're crap at the finale.

—I'm not sleeping well at night, he said, wondering how crumpled he was, whether he'd dribbled onto the sofa cushions. —Then I fatally relaxed. Also it's hot in here.

—It's all right, Ann said. —We forgive you.

He gave in to remaining slumped down in the sofa corner under their scrutiny: after a moment he even shut his eyes again.

—Who is he? Ann asked.

—He's David Roberts: Carol's brother.

She was doubtful. —He doesn't look like her.

—More like his mother. He felt Kate's fingers rest for an instant coolly at his temple, recognising them by the hard bristle of her rings: as if she was demonstrating some trick of his appearance, to which Ann guardedly assented.

—Do you have a lot of men calling in to fall asleep here?

—He's unique.

—Does he really want coffee?

—We'll let him sleep.

David, though, struggled repentantly upright.

—Things are hard at home, he spilled out, to his own surprise. —Hence the tiredness.

—Really? Ann was mildly interested. —What kind of things?

—My wife I think is leaving me.

—You *do* collect them, Ann said to Kate.

She was pouring coffee. —Meaning?

—Ben. Cello Ben.

—Well, I've certainly never collected Ben. David, do you like sugar? Cream?

—Do you have whisky? Ann said, looking about. — If it's really cream, we could make Irish coffees: you know, the kind where you pour it in over the back of a spoon.

—In that cupboard: but I don't know how to.

—I'll do it!

Ann stirred sugar and whisky in the coffee, then, concentrating, made the cream float on top; intently they watched. —Would Billie like one? Where's she gone?

—She likes everything sweet. Do one for me, too.

David remembered he hadn't eaten anything since he got up.

—It'll be nourishing, Ann reassured him.

—Is Suzie really leaving you? Kate asked.

—I think so.

—Aren't the coffees delicious? Ann was triumphant.

—So, do you blame yourself?

The cream left moustaches on their upper lips: David's probably made him ridiculous as he turned to answer her, dutiful as if he was under oath.

—I expect she thinks I'm too careful. Dull. I haven't lived: I've never taken any risks.

—Risks! Kate was wildly disparaging. —Anyone can take those! And anyway, what about Francesca, to begin with? Didn't you take a risk with her?

He was scrupulous. —I suppose strictly speaking Francesca took me, and not the other way round. There wasn't much volition on my part: I was just chosen. Strange as that may seem.

—She didn't deserve you.

—So which is his wife? Suzie or Francesca?

—That will be a question at the resurrection, Kate said.

—Both, said David, and was about to explain when Billie came absorbedly into the room from wherever she'd wandered, perhaps to find cake.

—Oh Kate. She held out her forearm for them to see: on the loose pale flesh inside, a long red weal.

—You've burned yourself! Kate started up, pushing her coffee cup clatteringly on the tray, slopping coffee. —For God's sake! What on?

—We need to put it in cold water right away. David was practical.

—I'm so silly. I thought I had to light the grill for

something, then I tried to put it out and burned myself.

—Perhaps we ought to check the gas, he said.

Ann ran.

They hurried Billie to the downstairs cloakroom and David, supporting her, held her arm awkwardly under the tap in the small basin, cupping the water in his hand to bathe the injury.

—I'm making a bit of a mess in here.

There was water all over the floor; they jostled together in the cramped space, Kate pressed up behind him, peering over his shoulder —Is it bad? Casualty?

—No, I don't think so. But the trick is to go on cooling it even after it feels all right.

Billie complained the cold water hurt, and tried to pull her arm away.

—Just a little longer, Mummy. He knows what he's doing.

—Do you have cling film? That's good for putting on a burn.

—I don't keep it.

—Then a clean soft cloth will do. Don't worry if it blisters. But perhaps I ought to come back and see how it is in the morning.

He could feel, even as he concentrated on Billie's arm, the forceful pressure of Kate's body against him, through her dress and his clothes. The sensation was unexpectedly fiery; he had thought that she would be cold, underneath all her layers. He turned his head to look in her face, so close at his shoulder that he could taste the coffee on her breath.

—Should I call by in the morning? It would be no trouble.

Agitatedly she stared back at him, as if she was recognising something.

—Oh: no, she said. —Thank you. There's no need, you'd better not. She'll be all right. Actually, I'll ask our doctor to pop in: he's been our family doctor for years, such a nice chap, he always tells me he'll come out for Billie for the least thing, he doesn't mind. He's got a bit of a thing about you, hasn't he, Mummy?

David felt rebuffed. —Would you try to find a couple of dry towels? Nothing fluffy, preferably, which could stick: something smooth like linen would be best.

Kate went gratefully to look.

She gave Jamie a ring for his birthday present, fishing it out for him from an old shirt box full of bits of the apparatus men once used: cufflinks and collar studs and tiepins, a buttonhook, a shoehorn, a gold pocket watch, a cut-throat razor, a hairbrush with yellowed bristles.

—We've been burgled once or twice – not recently – but they only took stupid things, toasters and television sets, money. They looked for jewellery, but not thoroughly enough: there's a secret panel, would you believe, in one of the drawers in the wardrobe. Perfectly obvious, I'd have thought, to anyone not out of their mind on drugs. I don't even know: were these things my father's or my grandfather's? They look too antique for my father. I suppose Billie put them away in here, because she couldn't bear to throw them out. She nursed the three of them, you know. She's not such a delicate flower, really.

—The three of who?

—My grandparents, then my father. One heart (I think my grandmother didn't come downstairs for years), one cancer (my grandfather, who went first), one tuberculosis of the spine. They did have servants, of course. For my father, she paid a nurse: she told me, the woman used to tiptoe down into the kitchen at night to eat. Billie used to try to feed her more at mealtimes, she pretended not to want it, left stuff on her plate like a fine lady. Here, have this to remember me by.

Warily he looked at the plain gold band.

—Should I take it?

—Of course you're not to wear it, not on your finger. No one must see.

—Then what should I do with it?

—Haven't you any romance? Wear it on a chain around your neck, next to your heart. Sell it, if you like, and drink the proceeds. Anyway, I expect my grandfather had hands like bear paws: the ring would never fit.

In fact, it fitted Jamie's fourth finger perfectly: Kate would have to adjust her idea of Sam Lebowicz.

—I don't want to remember you, Jamie said, putting the ring away in his pocket. —I mean, I want to have you now, in the present.

After the day when David fell asleep on her sofa, Kate clung to his son with more ferocity. All the time she

235

was telling him that they had to stop, they couldn't go on like this; she told him that he would never have any idea what she had given up for him.

—What kind of thing? he asked miserably.

—Possibilities.

She accused him of boasting about his conquest to his friends. He was pale with dismay that she could imagine such a thing was true; she knew he wasn't capable of it, but couldn't stop the flow of her fury. Physically, at the same time, her surrender to him was extravagant, complete. Pictures and the aftershock of sensations from their love-making intruded all the time into her thoughts while he wasn't there. He was set impenetrably apart from her by his youth, however close they came. She wondered if this was how men felt, making love to very beautiful women: like pressing up against a simulacrum of the desired object, battering at a trick of flesh in desperation for it to yield possession. Thwarted, she hunted shame-lessly in Jamie for signs of his father, the taut cords in the neck, the delicate ears, the fine flickering purple of eyelids; who knew, perhaps the swirls of body hair too, perhaps his long feet, the taste of sweat on his stomach? Sometimes his youth was tedious and she punished it.

—There are so many things I can't tell you, she said.

—Go on. I'd rather hear them.

—I don't mean I mustn't tell you, or I shouldn't. I mean, even if I said them in words you couldn't hear them, they can't pass through the distance between us.

He stared intently. —You can tell me. Try. It's what I want to know.

236

—There's no point.

She wouldn't make love to him anywhere but in the master bedroom; he liked her own room with her things around them, but she couldn't let it happen there. One night when they were together in the big bed, the door opened; no doubt they had forgotten to bite down their noise. They scrabbled for the bedclothes to pull over their nakedness, and Kate struggled up; Jamie hid his face in the pillows. Billie in her nightdress stood against the light from the landing behind, her silvery hair spread on her shoulders.

—Go away, Kate yelled. —What are you doing in here?

—Mama?

Billie took uncertain steps towards them, unsteady, blinking. She never came into this room, she was afraid of it.

—Leave us alone, Billie! Go back to sleep!

—Mutti? Tremulously, not able to believe her eyes, she peered at them. She spoke in Yiddish, which she always pretended not to understand. —Are you here? Is it you?

Ten

Carol had a phone call from Kate.

—You were right, she said. —I am finding Billie difficult. I think she's getting worse. She follows me round all over the place. She talks about the marks I got for my O levels. Sometimes I think it's me that's losing my mind: I begin to wonder which century exactly I'm in, I start to think I've come back from the dead. I'd like to be alone, just for a day or two.

—Do you really want to be alone? Carol said.

—To collect my thoughts.

—I know somewhere you could go.

In the end it was arranged: Carol would move in with Billie for a few days while Kate went down to the Parrog in Pembrokeshire. Betty and Bryn were pleased to have the place warmed up and aired. Betty sent her love, she knew how hard it was, she had thought Kate was so brave, moving in to live with her mother, she was happy to do anything she could to help. There were clean sheets in the airing cupboard; Carol, who would drive her down, could show her how the Rayburn worked. (Carol worried, but to herself, over whether Kate would manage the temperamental stove.)

Kate stared through the windscreen and gave nothing away. Spats of autumnal rain forced Carol to put the wipers on and they squeaked awfully, so that it was impossible to talk; she always had old cars, and never bothered to fix the bits and pieces that went wrong. When it wasn't raining Carol spoke about work, about pressure the Housing Association was under to sell off valuable property in Cardiff city centre and build cheaply further out. The trees were still thickly leaved but at their tips they were turning colour; long grass at the side of the motorway was bleached silvery beige, lying in swathes where it had been blown. They drove through the bruised industrial aftermath along the South Wales coast: once-blighted bare brown hillsides, pressing close down on Port Talbot, were austerely resurgent; on the flat coastal plain there was still enough business for smoking chimneys, desolate proliferations of pipes, functional yards bleakly unpeopled. Sun flashed briefly, wetly, on the windows of the decent houses on the hillside that had been the steelworkers' (the pay hadn't been bad, in the last decades); now you couldn't get any kind of a price for them. Kate snuggled deeper into her black-and-white checked coat, not because she hated it but because it didn't interest her. Carol had always felt differently. She had suffered as a child, conscientiously, when they wound up the car windows against the smell, driving through here to the Parrog for family holidays. She had been taken once, aged eight or nine, to the steelworks in Cardiff her grandfather had part-owned and managed; the molten fire tipping, the sweating intent dirty men, had impressed themselves with indelible power, a high mark of importance life might never reach again.

They struck off north and climbed into green hills: there was a lull in the need for the wipers. Kate, looking about her more curiously, said she hadn't been to the countryside for years, and that it was just what she needed; she was looking forward to dedicating herself to her work. —Such a simplification: this clean space with nothing in it.

—There isn't nothing in it, Kate. It's a little seaside town: a mix of locals, with their austere old codes, and incoming spiritual types. Sacred sites and all that are clustered pretty thickly round about. The two species cross paths at the butcher's, who's very good, Welsh-speaking: organic meat. Our house is at the edge of town, on the quay.

—I shan't be going to the butcher, anyway.

—You haven't turned vegetarian? You don't eat enough as it is.

—Just queasy: I've gone off it. My life at home is such a mess, I think it's made me sick: no wonder I can't get down to anything. Here, I will be able to pretend I'm in old Russia, Russia before Napoleon.

—It's not quite that archaic down here, you know.

—I'm working on a part where he describes the old landowner's rages. He's a lovable good-hearted old man, but when he's angry with one of his daughters he beats them all with a stick, pulls his wife across the floor by her hair, they have to run out into the woods and stay there in the cold overnight.

—Doesn't sound all that lovable.

—*Autres temps, autres moeurs.*

—You can telephone me any time you've had enough and need rescuing.

—I only long, you know, to be pulled round by my hair.

By the time they drew up outside the house, conversation had been swamped again with the shriek of the infernal wipers: through veils of rain it looked uncompromisingly a square stone box. For some time, climbing down to the west coast, having driven up from the south and cut off the corner of Wales, they'd had their sight of the sea: for Carol the first glimpse always commanded a reflex of childish worship. Today it was grey and crawled dirtily with white-capped waves. When the engine had died and Carol had wrestled with her recalcitrant handbrake, they unbent themselves stiffly into the downpour. The front door swung open on an unwelcoming cold, as if the place slipped out of possession between visits. They dripped in the hall.

—You mustn't be disappointed. In a minute, when I've got the stove lit and the kettle on, you'll see.

Kate shivered and stood uselessly while Carol busied round, making the place come to life, slipping naturally inside her mother's routines. When they drank tea Kate was still in her coat, she wouldn't take it off.

—I would write at this table, Carol suggested. —If I were you. It's the warmest place. I used to do my school work on it.

The wood of the big table was worn to velvety whiteness with scrubbing and bleaching.

—I remember you coming here, in your holidays.

—Every holiday. Or if not, we pined. Our grandparents, Mum's parents, were still alive then. We thrived on it: in fact it was a kind of passion with us. And now there are David's children.

—Show me round. Tell me what you do in all the different rooms: where everyone sleeps.

Carol had not expected Kate to be so interested in the beloved old place, but took her willingly up and down stairs, the pink roses almost faded from her grandmother's grey carpet, into the bare high rooms with their disproportionately generous windows. It was like a dolls' house in its spare symmetry; you half expected the whole front to swing away on hinges. In her own bedroom at the back – it had been Betty's when she was a girl, and looked out onto a little ferny black cliff – she noticed, looking freshly through Kate's eyes, the picture she had made thirty years ago, out of shells from the seashore pressed into Polyfilla.

—Billie had no idea, Kate commented, —what to do for family holidays. Do you remember that she used to take me to Nice? Because her own parents had taken her there. We stayed in a hotel, up until I was fourteen, fifteen: the other guests were ancient, mummified with wealth. I used to read myself into a stupor. I never met

242

any other children; not that I would have wanted to.

—Your going there seemed to me glamorously strange, at the time.

—Strange, it was.

They crossed the landing to the front of the house.

—Mum and Dad sleep in here if they come: or Suzie and David.

Rain obliterated light at the window, pictures were pits of deeper darkness on the pale walls, the double bed loomed; the room's emptiness was filled with the rushing noise of water, cocooning them inside. —Imagine being married, Kate said.

—Married? That's an old-fashioned thought.

—Without it though, won't we be insubstantial?

—Speak for yourself. *With* it, anyone could be, anyway. And you've been a couple, over and over: Max and Tommy and Fergus and what's-his-name, in Chicago. It's me that ought to be insubstantial. Look at me! Substance!

—But being a couple over and over isn't the same thing. I'd like to have been broken up and remade, by something bigger than me. An institution, not a person. Changed out of what I am.

—That's rubbish. You'd have hated it.

—Anyway, now it's too late.

—Kate: you talk as if we're a hundred! Who knows what could happen?

—Too late for me. I can imagine you in one of those enlightened marriages of middle age, taking up t'ai chi together, barge holidays in the Norfolk Broads.

243

Carol, used to her, hardly flinched, was only mildly reproachful. —How did you manage to make that sound so dreary? For all you know it might be the height of what I long for.

Kate wrote by hand in a notebook, in her gloves, sitting in the living room at the desk where Carol said Betty's mother had paid her bills and written letters to her old school friends. Betty's father had been an auctioneer and a farm agent. Kate wrapped herself in her coat and in blankets; she made hot-water bottles for her feet. She had forgotten to put coke in the Rayburn the first night, after Carol left: it went out while she was asleep and in the morning she couldn't relight it. She brought the electric heaters downstairs from the bedrooms and put them all on. At night – she slept in Carol's room – she made more hot-water bottles and wore all her clothes; she heaped up duvets borrowed from the other beds. She couldn't take a bath; she boiled water in the kettle for her wash in the morning. The cold did strange things to her mind, sharpening it sometimes almost to the point of delirium, so that she seemed to be able to see through the Russian words to the writer on the other side, as if the page was only a glass between them; sensuously she disinterred lanky, jointed English sentences from out of the compacted density of Russian.

Every day when it wasn't raining she made huge efforts and went out to walk: she knew you were supposed to walk in the country. She hadn't any shoes suitable for the muddy paths, but in a musty cloakroom by the back door generations of coats and sticks and boots were piled up, along with the leads of departed dogs, and trophies of driftwood and bird skulls from the beach. Kate sorted out a pair of icy and dank wellingtons (most were vast: perhaps these were David's daughter's, or Betty's?) and borrowed walking socks she found discarded there. She discovered a little walk along the quay and up the path along the edge of the low cliff, exulting at the bleak sea with its resolving, emptying crash of waves, and the smashed beach, the pounded broken rocks; then back across stubble fields to the little town, where she bought food and cigarettes. She felt mildly ill all the time, but made herself eat. In the evenings she telephoned home to talk to Billie: there weren't many evenings in her life she hadn't done this. As a first-year student in London she had called every night from a red public telephone box in a sinister street, and had once seen a knife fight outside and been afraid to come out, pretending to go on talking into the receiver long after Billie had hung up.

Jamie called her. She hadn't told him where she was going: he'd found out from Carol.

—What are you doing there? he said. —It's strange to imagine you. I used to love that place when I was a kid. Which room are you sleeping in?

—I'm working hard all day. In the evenings I'm reading everything on the shelves here: I take it all to bed with me. Refutations of communism; denunciations of the death sentence. Books about the agricultural year, merrily advocating the use of the new pesticides. Novels by Howard Spring, Joyce Cary; the *Reader's Digest Book of Laughter*. I can't read the things in Welsh. Or the Dylan Thomas, on principle.

—Can't I come down? I could hitch. Nobody would know. We could really be alone together.

—If you came down, I'd have to leave. We can't be here together. In fact we can't be anywhere together. That's the whole problem. It's time we faced it.

He was simply silent, whenever she named their impossibility: he made her weaker to resist him than if he'd tried for words. Putting down the receiver, Kate caught herself reflected: there weren't many mirrors in the house, but a narrow one with distorting bevelled edges on the hallstand must have been meant once for checking respectability before leaving home. She switched on the hall light, contemplated the thin slice of herself unforgivingly, peering close up at her face pinched with cold, flesh drooping – yes, surely, it was beginning to droop? – under her jaw; she was a schoolteacher-witch in her glasses, sliding away at the mirror's rim into fairground grotesque. What would Betty's mother have thought of her coupled with beautiful youth?

On her third day, most extraordinarily, in the butcher's shop (in her resolution to look after herself properly, she had decided after all to queue there for protein), someone touched her arm from behind.

—Kate? It must be you.

She turned to see Suzie Roberts.

—What are you doing here? she said: her first impulse was defensive, as if Suzie must have pursued her, found her out. There was an expression in Suzie's face – tanned, exposed, her hair wind-blown and bleached – making a more intimate claim than the acquaintance they were supposed to have.

—I'm here for the weekend, camping at Mwnt with friends. We came to see the dolphins.

—Are there dolphins?

—Every day at teatime. They're marvellous. Haven't you seen them ever? I mean, it's only the fins and backs, curving up out of the water.

—But why didn't you bring your friends to stay at the Parrog? I hope my staying there hasn't spoiled any plans of yours?

Suzie's hand was still on Kate's arm, arresting or claiming her; she coloured. —They're not those kind of friends. I couldn't have asked Bryn and Betty for the house. I don't suppose they know I'm over here. I don't think even David does.

At this point Kate reached the front of the queue, and had had no time to think what she wanted. —What should I buy? she asked, panicking.

—Oh: lamb chops? Sausages? I think it's very good here. I only came in because I saw you: my friends are vegetarian.

Kate bought both; at the door of the shop the two women stood hesitating as if they were reluctant to part, although Kate knew she ought to get rid of Suzie. Next door to the butcher's there was a café, closed out of season like so many of the shops: they peered into its windows.

—I'd ask you back for coffee, only it's very cold in the house.

—Oh, are you having trouble with the Rayburn? I could sort it out for you. I'm good with it, although Betty never believes me.

—What about your friends?

—They're not the sort who would worry. I could go off anywhere.

If she was plaintive, it was the merest hint. —I've got the car. Let's drive. Have you finished shopping? It's funny to see you in wellingtons.

Kate had thought of Suzie as one of those flatteners who clamp down complex feeling. Today though she jumped with nerves, driving with quick jerky changes of gear; she had surely lost weight, she was angular under her thick ragged jumper and skein of coloured scarves, the skin was pale around her eyes, behind her fading summer freckles. Leading the way into the house, she was proprietorial and intruder-like at once. Kate could imagine how solidly the place must seem to belong to her family-in-law: this was Suzie's chance to surprise and dominate it. She laughed at the little nest of Kate's books and blankets, holding her shape where she'd stepped out of them, in the front room.

—You've been frozen! Weren't you awfully bored, here by yourself?

Kate, on her dignity, denied it.

Swiftly Suzie cleared out the Rayburn and lit it, then squatted on her heels to watch, her hands black with coke, a smear of coke dust on her cheek, altering the draught adjustor as the flames took hold. Kate made coffee with the electric kettle; Suzie, hunting for drink, found an old bottle of sherry among the cooking things.

—We'll buy more and top it up, so Betty won't know.

Kate sat pressed up against the metal of the stove as it heated. Warmth crept into the kitchen languorously: she realised how her muscles had knotted in resistance to the cold. The sherry went straight to their heads, and it was only two in the afternoon.

—I've always wanted to ask you, Suzie said, nursing her coffee mug at the table. —Did you really not see me that day?

—Which day?

—An accident on the motorway: we were both standing on the hard shoulder. I thought you recognised me but you didn't say anything.

—Oh, you mean when that swan came down? You looked as if you didn't want me to.

—So you did see. Suzie appeared gratified. —I've often thought about you since then. It was odd when we met in the supermarket: I felt as if, because you'd seen that happen, you knew something about me. You'll think I'm stupid – David does – but it's always seemed to me more than just an accident, that swan falling onto my car, not anybody else's.

—It had to fall on someone's.

—But it seemed to have a message for me.

—What kind of message?

—I don't know. I wanted to ask you.

—Me? How absurd. I don't believe in messages.

Suzie poured them both more sherry. —May I tell you what I thought I saw? You won't be outraged at me desecrating sacred old memories or anything?

—I don't have sacred old memories.

—David couldn't bear me to talk about it. He thought I was just dabbling, you know: making games out of serious things. I believed it was Francesca when it fell. I hadn't been thinking about her or anything: I really didn't think about her much. Of course I've always known about her, but I hadn't ever seriously tried to imagine what she did. You were a friend of hers, weren't you? Then out of the blue – only it wasn't blue, was it? it was horrible weather – this body came hurtling down onto my car. It was so heavy, the whole car leaped under the blow. It shook me out of my skin. Without giving it a second thought, I understood that it was her.

—Free association. Perfectly natural. You probably thought about her more than you realised you did.

—But ever since then I've been possessed.

Kate looked for a flare of madness in the wholesome face: perhaps these earthbound types were more suscep- tible to the freaks and fumes of delusion, having no resistance when once they stumbled in.

—Really, as if something jumped inside me that I haven't been able to shake off in all this time since. First, I couldn't let David touch me. I'd think every time he came near me: it's in his hands. Death or something. Don't imagine I don't know how unfair that is.

—You didn't think for one minute David 'drove her to it', did you? That only happens in films. With

Francesca he was the most considerate, the gentlest, the most decent . . .

—Oh don't! said Suzie sharply. —I know!

—She'd moved out from their home anyway, with the baby. With Jamie. She was filthy to David. I'd seen them, during that time before she moved out; although I'd gone to the States by the time she died. The poor girl was ill, she was depressive, she'd overdosed once already, I believe, when she was a teenager. She was a bore with it all. Forgive me speaking rudely of the dead.

—A bore! No one's ever said that to me before.

—It might be a useful thing for you to know.

Suzie shuddered: perhaps melodramatically. —Since the thing with the swan, I've been behaving so badly. As if its message was: make a mess of everything you've got.

—You funny creature, said Kate. —How old are you?

—Thirty-five, said Suzie gloomily. —I've made such a fool of myself.

—With these friends of yours? I hope you've had a good time doing it.

—I couldn't tell you what I've done, I'm too ashamed. She laughed and covered her face with her big hands, the skin around her fingernails torn and sore. —I've got a bad streak in me. I knew it would come out. Blame my misspent youth.

Calmly Kate asked if she was going to make up with David.

—That's what I wanted you to tell me. Should I go back? Are we right together? You're his friend.

—No, said Kate. —I mean: no, I won't tell you.

Suzie peeped between her fingers. —Do you want him for yourself? He likes you, doesn't he?

—I don't know what you're talking about.

—I rather thought you liked him.

When, late in the afternoon, faint sunshine touched the stones in the garden, Suzie said she wanted to swim. Kate – who told her she would die if she did, especially after drinking alcohol (they had finished the bottle) – stood watching, swaddled in coat and scarves and gloves and hat, while Suzie, shivering, stripped on the beach. The low blurred chilly sun was reflected in the rocking water, a silver path from the horizon. Suzie had her black swimming costume on under her clothes; she stepped long-legged, lean-thighed, across the shingle, laughing and grimacing, balancing with her arms held out.

—You're mad, Kate called. —I really think you're mad. You'd better come back. I've no idea how to cook those lamb chops.

Suzie only waved, stepped in, tottered at the shock of cold, forged on up to her knees, then with a shriek plunged, and swam crawl with strong strokes into the glittering path. Kate watched the black shape of her head bobbing, disappearing and reappearing against the dazzle; she was wrapped in the sensation of absence, the gulls crying and circling, the crash and drag of the waves, the freezing wind slicing underneath her clothes. After a while she worried that Suzie must be going much too far, there would be currents out there, the sea was treacherous; she was seized with the idea that she would be left alone on the shore for ever like this, holding the towels. How absurd: she was entirely alone, all the houses on the quay were probably holiday lets, there was no one to call for rescue; what would she do if suddenly she couldn't see Suzie, and there was only the emptiness of the ocean left, meaning nothing? Accidents really happened: it really had been foolhardy to swim in this cold, after all that alcohol. For a moment the stupid girl with her raw ragged life seemed as mysterious as if she was lost. Kate imagined having to tell David. Then she caught sight of the black bobbing dot of a head again: grateful, she saw it turn and head back towards the beach. She clutched the towels against her chest inside her coat, to warm them.

David woke when it was very early, perhaps just after dawn. He was filled with joy, from a dream he'd had; even as he came to complete consciousness the joy didn't dissipate but persisted, as if it was something he must act upon. Mostly these days his dreams were an idiotic mishmash of petty anxieties, repressed resentments, sexual pressures, and he took no notice of them; but aesthetically this one satisfied him. He had been standing with Kate Flynn in a room that had seemed to belong in his own house; now he only thought he remembered it from other dreams. There were high windows on all sides of the room, as though from outside you could have seen right through it; the space was full of air and light; in fact gusts of birds darted past them as if blown out of trees around, although both of them knew this wasn't normal, indoors. Kate had stepped back giddily, with a little laugh, from the swooping birds, and he had steadied her against his arm; then he reached with his other hand inside her clothes, where it was intensely warm, and took out something. They bent together over the little brown bird that sat hot and still in his palm, too frightened to fly, its whole body beating with its fear.

—It's a wren, he said. He was pleased to recognise its tininess, its wood-brown spotty breast, its pert uptipped tail.

—What a lovely metaphor, said Kate.

He thought in the dream that that insight was typical of her, typically clever, that he would never have understood by himself what the bird meant, or known the word to use. But when he woke he realised that of course it was he who had understood, because everything that was in the dream was his.

—In truth, he thought with absolute clarity in his waking self, —she's the one I want.

He was afraid of staying in bed, dwelling on his dream, in case he consigned it to becoming only a sex fantasy among others; he dressed quickly and went downstairs. There was no sound from the kids; Suzie was here, asleep in the study; Jamie was home too, his bike was in the hall, the attic steps were down. David picked up his car keys and went out. Suzie for once could get the kids to school; he didn't care if she heard him drive away.

Outside in the muffling greyness, yellow light beamed out from windows in one or two of the other houses, promising and homely as lanterns; his steps scrunched on the gravel drive damp with dew. When he was a child he had loved listening from his bed to the sounds of cars starting up in the early morning, then droning away from him through the sleeping streets; now he felt himself inside the kind of significant adventure he had attributed to those adults then. He wasn't sure yet whether he was going to go to work today or not. The streets he drove through were mostly empty; he imagined a comradely connection with the few cars that passed him, lit up as he was, obscurely purposeful like him.

By the time he drew up on the road opposite Firenze, the dark had lifted enough for him to see through the railings into the locked-up park: each bush, still thickly leaved but wintry-numb, was doused in its own cap of grey mist; it lay three-foot deep like dirty wool along the grass and on the lake, the tall trees standing disdainfully out of it. Unpeopled, the park seemed alive to itself. He mustn't wake them in Firenze just yet; he had an idea they didn't get up early. Kate was home from west Wales, David knew, because Suzie had told him how they had met down at the Parrog, and how she had driven Kate back to Cardiff to save Carol a trip. He hadn't liked the idea of the two of them hobnobbing together (they had drunk his mother's sherry, Suzie said), or Suzie's air of suppressed excitement, telling him how she had swum and Kate had watched.

If he hadn't been such an idiot he would have understood from the beginning why he had always wanted to have Kate to himself, dreading dissipating their relationship by introducing her inside his family life. Sitting in

255

the car, feeling the cold creep up from his feet once the engine died, he could remember again how it had felt in his dream to reach inside Kate's clothes, his fingers closing in that warm dark around a fluttering live thing. Was it a metaphor or a simile? He tried to remember from school English lessons. And was it a metaphor for sex or for love? Flooded with revelation at how these twisted together, he was too restless to sit. He left the car and took a walk around the lake – only the promenade across the bottom end was locked – rousing the Canada and barnacle geese still huddled, holding back from the shrouded water, on the trodden bank dark with droppings. Honking, they bustled and shifted. Swans sublimely turned their heads to look at him. Last year's young ones, though they were fully white, still had necks ungainly stiff, not bent yet to adult sensual poise.

He met runners breasting the mist, absorbed in their own panting, and an early dog-walker, averting her eyes from her half-visible dog squatting to make hot urine in the early cold. Then the grey fume began to thin and they were all beached in the ordinary eye of the day; visibility unspectacularly gathered, delivering the familiar city. The islands that seemed from the promenade to belong to a dream distance weren't really far; sooner than he expected David was crossing behind them, at the end of the lake, through a scrubby little patch of wood in a crescent of suburban houses, some showing signs of morning awakening, lights on, steam billowing from gas water-heaters, a murmur of radio. David's joy was not susceptible to these deflations. I could wake her

256

now, he thought. Other people are about. It would not be ridiculous to wake Kate now

He made his way down the other side of the lake and then around the far side of the park to where it was partitioned by a road, and he could cut back. Traffic was busying and had lost its glamour. He imagined the locked park, circling it, as if it contained his fate. Inside there, unknowable yet, was what was going to happen next; in the time that ticked away on his watch the park would be opened up, a difference might be made to everything through his act, whatever it was going to be. Of course Kate might not answer the door. He could still imagine having to get into his car and drive to work as if nothing had changed. As he made his way back up along the last stretch to Firenze, an ambulance passed him, not using its siren in the momentarily empty road; it turned into Kate's street. It didn't occur to David at first that it could have anything to do with him. When he himself turned that corner away from the park-side road, he saw that the ambulance was stopped where the Firenze drive began between its two brick gateposts, one with its polished red stone knob missing: the black gates were permanently pushed back, grown into the grass and weeds. Two ambulance men stood at Firenze's front door; David broke into a run. 'Not Kate, not Kate,' he bargained as he ran. 'Not yet.'

Of course it wasn't for Kate. As the ambulance men turned to watch him approach he saw through the glass windows of the porch that she also came running: the door swung open. She had pulled on some skirt and sweater that didn't match, her hair was scraped back in an elastic band, she was wearing her glasses: he knew the look of an emergency. She flung one bewildered glance at him past the ambulance men.

—Yes, come inside, come in, she's upstairs. She's awake, she's looking at me, but she can't talk. What does that mean? Is she concussed? She's hit her head, blood everywhere. I thought I shouldn't move her. David's all right, he belongs here: he's a doctor, anyway.

In her panic Kate was clumsily assertive, fell back upon the hauteur of her upbringing. He could imagine how she might not be liked: it made him protective. Tactfully he explained himself to the ambulance men. They were professionally steadying and charming, their solid tread in the hall and on the stairs filled up the wild private space of disaster. David had never been upstairs in this house before: at the top of the flight was a stained-glass window, girls carrying water jugs in some Old Testament scene, suspended oblivious above crude hurrying intrusion. Kate's story, tumbling out, hadn't settled yet into the pattern it would acquire by the time she'd repeated it over and over: she had woken, heard a crash, found her mother on the bathroom floor.

There was a step down into the bathroom, and the old lady was lying, diminutive as a child, on her side on the lino: her face was drained and yellow, her hair was soaked in blood. Probably she had managed somehow to hit her head as she fell on the side of the ancient claw-foot bath. Kate had covered her with a blanket: she was alive, her eyes were open and conveyed somehow apology for her indignity, as well as fearful confusion. She seemed to see Kate, who crouched down again beside her where she must have sat waiting for the ambulance to arrive. Kate told her mother everything would be all right now, help had come. The men bent over Billie; David held back, they knew what they were doing. One of them was a talker, with a small tight face like a jockey and soothing hands; as he had been trained he explained everything he was doing to the old lady, whether or not she could hear him. There was nothing, he seemed to tell her, bringing the unknown out of the dark, that he and his companion hadn't seen. Once he called her 'Billie darling'. David was alert for any condescension, or signs of the tedium of routine, but he couldn't fault them.

While they manipulated Billie onto the stretcher Kate stood out of the way and grabbed at David for support. He put his arm round her, held her tight, felt how she quaked. She remembered to puzzle at him: —How are you here, anyway?

—I was coming to see you.

—But it's the crack of dawn.

—I walked round the park, so as not to wake you too early. Now I wish I hadn't. I could have been here.

—What's going to happen?

—They'll take her into A & E, do lots of tests, find out if she's broken anything, why she fell. Shall I come with you?

—But you'll need to be at work.

—I'll phone in.

—All right. Come in the ambulance with me. I'm terrified of that. I'll tell them you're my brother.

—I'll follow in the car, he said. —I don't want to be your brother.

It turned out, as David had expected from the moment he saw her, that Billie had had a stroke. Probably that had caused her fall rather than the other way around; in the fall she had fractured her hip. The cut on her temple was only minor, although she had some nasty bruising. David saw she was admitted under the neurosurgeon he most trusted; she was put in intensive care, sedated, given an anti-clotting agent, monitored. They explained to Kate that what mattered for Billie's prognosis was what happened in the next twenty-four hours; she needed to be prepared for the possibility of a second stroke. David sat with Kate. In the afternoon he drove to Firenze to pick up a few necessary items; Kate said that if Billie came round she would want to be surrounded by her own possessions.

It was strange to be in that house on his own. With clumsy hands he fumbled shyly through the drawers of Billie's night-things, not good at deciding which were suitable; Kate had warned he'd find improbable quantities of clothes. The cat came complaining around his feet and he fed it. Consulting Kate's list, he took pleasure in her bold spiky black italic writing. Also while he was there he ran hot water and found bleach and cleaned up the blood in the bathroom as best he could. He was mysteriously happy while he did all this. He was sorry for the old lady, and for the troubled days he knew lay ahead for Kate, but he also felt, among Kate's things here, that she came close in a new intimacy. He took in the old house as he never properly did when she was home, peeking into the absurd vast pompous bedroom at the front, probably not changed since the place was built, murky because all its blinds were down. Not wanting to pry inside, he stood in the doorway to Kate's own room and took in her desk with its computer and open books, the scatter of her shoes and clothes, the paintings stacked against the walls, the piles of papers and journals everywhere, the duvet in its brilliant red-and-gold cover thrown back where Kate had leaped out of bed: all the mess and drama and colour of her life.

He rang home to tell them what had happened, warn that he would be late.

—But how were you there? asked Jamie. —How did you know? What time was this?

—I was passing. I saw the ambulance. Is Suzie back?

—D'you want to speak to her?

—No. Just to know.

Of course there would be so many complications: he hadn't begun to think of the consequences, if Kate would have him, for his children. No doubt at first there would be all their suspicion and resentment to contend with; but he was not afraid.

Eleven

illie didn't have another stroke within twenty-four hours, but she never spoke again; she lived for three weeks in the hospital. Kate spent most of every day there (although Carol tried to persuade her to let her take turns) so that it became her world: its routines were her element, the nurses were her allies or her enemies, even her dreams at home in Firenze were suffused with its noises and smells, its clattering trolley-pharmacopoeia. Billie's transfers from ward to ward, each with its own culture and atmosphere to be learned, were convulsions. Kate brought in books, old books from her childhood and youth that she'd read over and over; she sat beside Billie's bed absorbed in them, lost, rousing with a shudder when she had to return to the burden of moving and speaking and being herself. The hospital was both a visionary space – from the upper floors at night a vast ship, lit up, sailing out into black-ness – and a real place she walked about in, knowing her way, heels tapping loud in the bright labyrinthine corridors. She had never felt herself so taken up inside the common machinery of living and dying, its momentum like a hum from great engines below.

Billie in those three weeks after the first stroke had some movement on her left side: convulsively sometimes she gripped Kate's hand, sometimes she seemed to be rehearsing fingerings on the bed sheet. She could swallow, although she could only drink with help from a cup with a spout, and had to be fed liquidised foods with a spoon. She didn't want anything. She lay on her back, slipping between sleep and waking; her immobility, her high prow of a nose, seemed carved out of some ancient denser material than flesh, yellowed and smoothed with wear. She dribbled and groaned while she slept, and once or twice, awake, she made effortful noises; Kate, encouraging her, saw a familiar convulsion of distaste twitch the still mask of her mother's face. The whole thing was too awfully ugly: Billie repudiated it, she hated ugly things. Girls with paper sheets of drawings – a cup of tea, a sad face, a happy face, a toothbrush – came and sat at her bedside, encouraging her to point, to communicate: only Billie's eyes were eloquent. She was such a good patient, she made no trouble, she lay in her pretty nightdresses among her flowers and cards with her angel-hair combed and plaited (Kate plaited it). She wasn't, for example, like one dreadful old woman who cried and fought and shouted for her mother and at night for hours on end rubbed her feet fiercely noisily together; whose visitors – meek husband and daughter of no doubt once-meek wife – dropped their eyes in shame. Nor like Kate, who, when she wasn't sunk

263

in her book, sometimes complained, protested that the nurses condescended to Billie, questioned whether the doctors were doing enough.

One afternoon Kate went for a coffee downstairs in the hospital foyer, and while she drank it Billie died. She tried to recall afterwards what she had been thinking about while she drank her coffee. The foyer had been refurbished in the last few years. It had been once an austere antechamber to terrors, painted in institutional colours, smelling of disinfectant; bandaged and disfigured patients, in her memory, were wheeled to the WRVS counter by their visitors for tea and sandwiches. Now it was like a mall, with a bookshop, shops for flowers and gifts, an outlet of one of the coffee chains. Kate thought it was more ghoulish. No doubt there were statistics to prove that the sick were more likely to recover if they were encouraged by well-known brand names. She had bought a *Times Literary Supplement*, astonishingly available, and had read an article in it reviewing a book on Milosz; she had thought about the late Pope, whom Milosz had lunched with, and about a film she had seen of the Pope losing his temper with demonstrators protesting against the persecution of radical priests in El Salvador. Then she went back up to the ward, and when she got there the curtains were drawn around Billie's bed: no big fuss, only the one nurse, Sarah, was standing inside at Billie's pillow, and Kate knew Billie must be gone because Sarah wasn't holding her hand but just standing there.

—I'm sorry, Sarah said. —Sometimes it seems as if

they just wait for the relatives to leave, wanting to slip away by themselves.

Sarah was one of the nurses Kate liked, half-Turkish, dark-haired, soft-bodied, with a crisp quick mind and intolerant politics: she hugged Kate against her large elastic breasts and Kate yielded to the embrace, although she didn't cry. She felt bereft – not quite of Billie, yet, but of these weeks of her illness, the medical ceremonial, its importance. An hour later she was leaving the hospital. She said she would come back the next day for her mother's things. It was dusk, and windless: the fountain outside was still turned on. In an area laid out with benches and trees, and a reedy pond with ducks, shadowy figures were moving and speaking, smoking; she couldn't hear what they were saying. Briskly staff and visitors passed one another, moving up and down the covered walkway from the car park: through windows they could see into a lit-up swimming pool where someone in goggles and a swimming cap strove effortfully through blue water reflected choppily against white tiles.

Sarah had asked Kate if she was all right, if she had someone to go to; impatiently she had said it didn't matter. Now she stopped short before the crossing to the car park, and had no idea where her car was, or which floor she'd left it on. Day after day she'd driven here, paying a fortune in tickets: now all the days were one day and she had no picture whatsoever of an arrival. She imagined herself searching for her little Citroën on floor after floor of the monstrous building, unpeopled, hollow, stinking of oil, only resonant with the roar of engines, its darkness criss-crossed with headlights descending round and round the ramps. Something appalling surely lay in wait in there. Then she couldn't remember what colour the Citroën was anyway. She thought, not figuratively: I am in hell. She also realised that she hadn't ought to drive anyway, in this state. In her bag she found the mobile David Roberts had given to her on that first day when Billie was admitted, showing her how to use it, telling her to call him any time of day or night she needed him. She hadn't called him; in the evenings he had rung her at home for news. But in the evenings she had had so many calls.

She stopped someone passing, a young man in a boxy grey coat with a scarf wrapped over his mouth. Perhaps it was cold: Kate hadn't noticed. She gave him the phone and asked him to help her dial the number written on a crumpled piece of paper she fished from her pocket; David had put his number into the phone but he had also written it down for her, guessing she might not know how to access it. It occurred to her that Jamie might well answer the phone, or Suzie: but they didn't.

—Wait there, David said. —Just wait exactly where you are.

It seemed as if she waited for an hour beside the crossing while people passed, some looking curiously at her; the road was only an internal road running round inside the hospital, but it was busy at this time of the evening. She watched groups of pedestrians accumulate at the red crossing sign, then spill over when it turned green and the cars stopped: she forgot that all these individuals were separately purposeful and imagined them only as a flow moved along by the changes of lights. Eventually she forgot what she was waiting for: when David did come (he said he had only taken fifteen minutes), he had to leave his car at the kerb, indicators flashing, and cross to where she stood, collect her, lead her over, see her into the passenger seat of his big warm comfortable car (she only knew then how cold she'd been before).

—I can't go home, she said, as soon as he pulled out into the flow of traffic. —I can't go back to the house, not tonight.

—Of course not, he said. —Come to my place.

—I don't know. Who will be there?

—No one. I have it all to myself. Suzie's taken the kids away for the weekend.

—Oh, is it the weekend? What about Jamie?

Probably he was surprised she even remembered the name of his older son.

—At his grandmother's: Francesca's mother's. Her seventy-fifth.

—I don't know.

She closed her eyes. Nothing mattered.

Kate had never been to David's home. They came to where the city dissolved at its edges into the surrounding dark; when they got out of the car she heard the drone of traffic on a fast road nearby, hurrying elsewhere. The house was a box among others just the same, arranged around a little curving cul-de-sac in a pretence of organic accumulation, the raw new gardens hardly grown. David steered her indoors, kicking aside with his foot children's junk littered everywhere – trainers, school bags, toys: he didn't want to frighten her off, she thought, didn't want her to take in the thickness of his life apart from her, his belonging to these others. The place was a mess: even she, who was not domesticated, could recognise it. It was strange to be seeing his taste for the first time (or if not his taste, then at least what he was satisfied to live with): pink carpet, blowsy flowered faux-Victorian wall-paper, gold-framed school photographs. Kate felt her own discrimination humbled, she was stricken with envy of a life so innocent of style.

—I really just need to sleep, she said. Solicitously he eased her free of her heavy coat. —I'm so tired. I haven't slept properly for weeks.

—Won't you let me make you a drink? A hot drink? Or an alcoholic one? Brandy? It might do you good.

—No, really. I think I'd just be sick.

She accepted his offer of sleeping tablets though; then he took her upstairs to his own room – it must be his, his clothes were lying about everywhere, a drying rail hung with his socks was against a radiator. He turned on a wall-light over the double bed; to close the curtains across the window he had to undo tie-backs, then pull a cord (how touchingly well trained he was).

—I'll find you something to put on, he said. —Suzie's got pyjamas somewhere.

—No: I'll be fine like this, if I take off my shoes, take out my contact lenses. I haven't even got the strength to get undressed. I'll just lie in my clothes under the duvet. It is a duvet?

—This sort of cover thing we take off first; and those top pillows are only ornamental. Give them to me, I'll put them on the chair.

—Ornamental pillows!

—Are they horrible? he wondered.

—Not horrible. Only I am.

Kate with fumbling fingers couldn't undo the tiny buckle on the strap of her shoes; he crouched with concentration and did it for her, and she imagined him helping his daughter put on her shoes for school in the morning.

—I don't know if it's the right moment, he said. —I hope it's not clumsy of me: but I wanted to say that there was no chance really that Billie would ever have got back to what she was before. You won't feel it now, but really this probably was the best thing. That's a brute of a doctor's opinion.

Kate nodded. —I know it. Of course I know it.

—Of course you do.

—And that, this way, I'm free.

—You are free.

She lay down under the duvet and closed her eyes.

—Would you like the light out?

—No, leave it on please. I feel too afraid of the dark.

She knew through her closed lids that, lingering, he stared down; taking in the surprise of her there, between his sheets.

—Will you stay with me? she asked. —I don't want to be alone.

Perceptibly he hesitated over what she meant, then

sat heavily down, not wanting to mistake, on her side of the bed. —Of course I will. When she put her hand out to him, he took it eagerly in both of his; she lost herself in the cool hollow of his grip. He brushed the bristle of her rings with his blunt finger-ends, as if he was reading Braille.

—Don't you want to take these off? Aren't they too heavy?

When she didn't answer he pulled at the rings one by one, twisting them off, dropping them with a chink on the glass top of the bedside cabinet, until her hand was naked inside his (apart from one old silver ring that was too tight, from her teenage years). For a few long minutes – before the sleeping tablets and her exhaustion and shock kicked in, obliterating everything – longing for him surged in her, as if her spirit craned out of her body towards his. But she didn't make a move. Neither of them, under the circumstances, made a move.

When she woke it was morning. She couldn't remember the last time she had slept all through the night. David, also in his clothes – he had at least taken off his jacket – was under the duvet beside her, with his back turned. As soon as she started to get out of bed to find the bathroom, he sat up anxiously.

—So, she said, —we finally slept together.

He wasn't the type to find that funny, and blinked at her, bemused, creases from his pillow pressed into his cheek; roused if not out of sleep then out of some deep trance of reverie.

270

—Did you mind? I didn't want to leave you alone, but it got cold, I kept nodding off

—Don't be silly. It's your bed anyway.

His hair was stuck up comically behind one ear: he had let it grow rather long recently, so that it was less stiff and neat. Kate used the en suite bathroom, closing the door discreetly. She washed her face, borrowed a toothbrush, smoothed at her crumpled clothes, stared at herself short-sightedly – horrible, probably – in the mirror where Suzie his wife must have looked a thousand times. She used Suzie's soap too, and noted her shower gel. It was strange, not to have to go to the hospital. The shape bereavement would take was unknown to her as yet, she felt she only circled it in trepidation; it waited like a new place for her to move inside. This morning she had a sense of the completed arc of her mother's whole life that was almost visionary and exulting, relieved: but no doubt that would not be the last of it.

David had put on his shoes, sitting on the side of his bed, though he hadn't flattened his hair; when she came out from the bathroom he stood up urgently. Putting on her rings, fastening her watch, she held him at bay, never looking quite at him: without her lenses he was blurred anyway.

—I've got a busy day ahead, she said. —What time is it? Strangely, now it's over, there are all sorts of things I have to do. I think I'll leave my car in the hospital car park for ever: I can't afford to pay the ticket. You know, Billie and I never talked – isn't that awful? – about whether she wanted a Jewish funeral or not. Well, we talked, but she never decided. They were so beastly to her, you know, when she married my father. What shall I do? I'd better ask her friends. I said to her that I did want a Jewish one, for the drama, the rending of the garments: remember that, won't you, if I go first? There's no one else to remember for me now. Or, if that lot won't have me, then at least the resurrection and the life and so on. No humanist namby-pamby, please: everyone choosing the wrong poems and reading out bits of their own creative writing. How grim would that be?

She picked up her shoes and swung them by the straps, looking round for somewhere to sit and put them on; seizing her by the arms, he tried to look into her face.

—Kate, I have to tell you what I feel. I know there couldn't be a worse time.

—Oh no: don't tell me, please, not now! Not today.

—You can see my marriage has fallen apart. You were going to say to the ambulance men that day that I was your brother. Is that what you really want?

She rocked on her stockinged feet in her distress, pulling away from him: it was almost a scuffle. —I don't want you to make me decide this.

—Isn't it possible, he persisted doggedly, —that I could be something else?

—I don't know.

—After last night I feel it, I feel that it's possible.

—Anything's *possible*. Aren't we the generation that decided nothing – nothing of this sort – was impossible?

—So what's that you're saying? I'm stupid, I know, but I have to be very clear. Yes or no?

—I don't know. Wait. Yes, maybe.

—All right, he said, subsiding, unsatisfied, not trying – as she half expected, half wanted him to do – to kiss her. —That'll do for the moment.

—All right, she said. —Wait. Yes, maybe. We'll see. Why not?

And he let her go.

Days later – how many, she couldn't count – Kate met Jamie in a pub one afternoon. She arrived wearing dark glasses, a dark scarf wrapped round her hair: outward signs of the state she was in. Her mother's funeral (Jewish after all) had been unexpectedly terrifying; she felt panic and a cold excitement at her liberation, her future as unknowable as if it was a blank. All through Billie's illness and since she'd died, Kate had forbidden Jamie to come near her: when he had turned up once at the door she had not let him in. His father, instead, had spent a couple of evenings at Firenze when Suzie was home with the children, helping Kate sort practicalities, mostly to do with Billie's money. ('I don't suppose you ever paid tax,' he had said with concern, 'on all these large sums she made over to you?')

David was the model of restraint, he held off as she had made him understand he must, waiting for her word. She did not let him see the noisy grief she gave in to a few times because it seemed disproportionate to the quiet fact of Billie's death, he might have thought she was putting it on. At work David was helping to oversee the preparations for vaccine development, in case of an influenza pandemic.

—There isn't a vaccine yet, of course, because there isn't a virus. But there are things we can do to be ready to make it.

—Will we all die? Kate asked with curiosity.

—Don't be silly. We don't even know for sure if it will happen, although it probably will. If it does, there will be some increased mortality.

—'Some increased mortality'. The way you say that. We will be in your hands.

—Not just mine, luckily.

All the time David was in her house Kate had known that Jamie might turn up; meeting him at the pub, she almost invited discovery (it was a place that she knew Carol liked, for instance). That was her bargain with hope, in exchange for what she'd done: she wouldn't confess, but she wouldn't make any effort to conceal it either. The pub at two o'clock bled coloured light from its windows into the windy corner where two long terraces, blowing with litter, bleakly met. Jamie was already halfway down his pint because she was late; she was probably late enough for it to be his second one. Pausing at the pub door – dramatically, wound in her black scarf: people stared – she took him in before he saw her. If she hadn't known different things about him, he might have been a boy among the others in here, rowdy and joshing at their table, drinking to get drunk, comradely competitive. As he waited, for all his visibly anxious expectancy, he even cast an eye up at the sport (rugby?) showing on a big screen high on the wall. Seeing her, he rose responsibly to his feet: tall, intent, hair pushed behind his ears, straight nose skewed poignantly off-centre. She wound between the backs crowded round tables laden with glasses and bottles, towards where he'd kept a seat for her in a corner.

He loomed over her clumsily; forbidden to touch her, he didn't know what to do with his hands. —I've really wanted to see you.

—Will you buy me a drink, now I'm here? Have you got money?

He jangled coins in the pocket of his crumpled khaki zip-up jacket, setting off for the bar, forgetting at first to ask her what she wanted.

—You really have to sort out, she said when he brought her whisky, —what subject you want to do at university. You have to get your applications in, for next year.

He wondered. —That was what you wanted to talk about?

—After the awful mess I've made, I owe you one useful thing at least: some good career advice.

He stared into his beer. —That's all?

—That's the mistake I made at your age – thinking that all that really mattered was the personal stuff. If you're not careful, you build your life around smoke.

—It's the rest that's smoke.

—Anyway, this – between us – doesn't even count as personal life. It was just an accident that happened. Talking of smoke, I've given up. At the hospital I couldn't, and since, I haven't wanted to. Isn't that incredible, after all these years?

—You've brought me here to get rid of me, he said.
—I knew I shouldn't come. I wanted to meet you at the house, not in this crowd.

—It couldn't make any difference wherever we met.

He gulped at his beer and grew visibly drunker, his focus thickening. —I know you better than you think I do.

—You know one of the worst things about me that there is to know.

Dents of embittered concentration appeared in his cheeks. —Is that what you think it was? Didn't you like it at all, then?

—If you're fishing for me to tell you how good you are, that women will love you . . .

—I don't want other women.

—You just don't know yet that you do.

—You don't know how I feel.

—Well, that's true. Because of our age difference, do you think, or because I haven't tried? Would you like more beer?

—No. This is my fourth. If you're interested, I have decided on a course to apply to. In Edinburgh.

—Edinburgh! That's a good idea. I can imagine you acquiring the necessary northern sceptical rigour.

—To do Classics, with Arabic.

Kate had to think about it. —You see: you are exceptional. Of course that's the right thing, a brilliant mix. You can go into the Foreign Office. You'll be an ambassador.

—Don't exaggerate, he said.

—Think how you'd have grown to hate my exaggerating, over time.

—I can't.

Kate hadn't touched her whisky: she dipped the edges of the beer mats in little pools of spilled beer. They were both leaning with their chins in their hands, elbows on the table, heads close together, the conversation an intimate rumble kept from everyone around. She imagined people thinking she was an aunt with her nephew.

—I want it to be as if this thing hadn't happened, she said. —That's what I came to ask you for. Not as a figure of speech, but actually: I want it to disappear.

—What are you talking about?

—It's possible, trust me. I used to think what you probably think: that everything we do endures, has consequences. But really, bits can disappear. We decide what happened and what didn't. Whole pieces of our selves float off, they aren't kept anywhere.

—No.

—There are reasons for me asking you this, complications. I will tell you what they are. Also, by the way, you have to promise me not to do anything silly.

He was uncomprehending for a moment. —You mean, that I won't kill myself?

—But I think you're more like your grandmother than your mother. She's an endurer.

—She did find some of my mother's poems, I meant to tell you. She had them all cut out, in a scrapbook.

—Oh: are they any good?

—I don't know. Yellowed: clipped out on pieces of yellowed newspaper.

—Poems do yellow.

—I haven't found a way of getting into them yet. It's like a code: I don't know what anything stands for.

—Will you try, acting just as if all this hadn't happened?

Blearily, he rubbed his face. —It's not possible. But I'll think about it, on one condition.

—What's that?

—That you let me come back to the house, now.

—Come back to the house? Is that a euphemism? Because I just couldn't.

—Just for another half an hour, to talk to you. Not with all these people watching. Then I'll do what you ask. I'll try.

—All right. We'll go back to the house. An hour. Can you walk straight? It's windy outside.

—It'll sober me up. You haven't drunk your whisky.

—I don't want it.

David watched a young silver birch, still with its full skirt of yellow leaves, blown sideways by the wind outside his office window. The sky was mostly heavily grey, but the straining dancing leaves and long whips of twigs were dazzlingly black against a swell of light. With every strong burst of wind the leaves were dragged inside out, clouds of them were carried off. Joanne of the administrative staff sat with her back to the window, but turned nervously around every so often to look; she was collating for David the results of a questionnaire sent round to health authorities. She confided that she hated the wind; she didn't mind the rain, but if it was windy at night she could never sleep. David, though, was exhilarated by the contrast between the purposeful peace within, the steady light and subdued thudding of their keyboards, and the ecstatic scene outside: impossible to know if it was assault or pleasuring. At four, an hour before he had meant to finish, he got up from his desk. It was time to insist, with Kate. The violence of his feelings reassured him: he had never been so forceful in love before. He was pleased to surprise Joanne, uncharacteristically leaving their work unfinished.

He drove the route that was beginning to be familiar as his own, up to Firenze; Kate wasn't expecting him, he hadn't said he'd call. The trees in the park were rowdy, the wind blew dark gusts of birds and leaves indistinguishably into the road in the last light. When he parked in the side street opposite the gate, then crossed to the house, David was surprised to see the front door standing a few inches open. He hesitated, pushed at it and went inside: the wind's ceasing in his ears was like a drop into a different element. He breathed the musty air of the porch; no one had put the lights on in the house, but he thought he heard voices somewhere. In the dark he blundered, stepping into the hall, but not noisily; he opened his mouth to call, but couldn't bring himself to break the hush, and closed his mouth again. A note sounded on the piano, and then a different one: not as if someone was going to play, but as if they touched the keys with their thoughts elsewhere, punctuating a conversation. Under David's feet little squares of black and white tile stirred where they had come loose from the floor.

The murmuring voices didn't resolve, as he drew nearer, into chat: he had thought it might be his sister visiting. Perhaps it was consolation of a mourning daughter that he listened to, straining his attention, stricken with dismay at himself (he had never eavesdropped in his life). Or could these be intruders, leaving the door so sinisterly open behind them; ought he to surprise them and chase them off? He had said to Kate that she was careless, that she needed mortise locks on the doors, if not an alarm. But the exchange was too soulful for thieves, the voices were too rich with feeling, they ran in his mind like a score, he followed their rise and fall, their rests. There was no doubt, as he grew used to them: some male voice mingled with Kate's. And if anything, it was she who was consoling, the other who complained and pleaded. David knew he had no right to be here. Then out of the not-quite-decipherable music a phrase detached itself with emphasis, as if whoever spoke it drew at that point further off from Kate. He also struck another, lower, note on the piano.

—I know who it is, the voice said. —Don't think I don't know who it is.

Kate didn't answer, but she must have moved because David heard her heels loud on the parquet, and then a lamp clicked on inside the room. The configuration of everything loomed out of the darkness, and David was appalled to find himself half crouched near the open drawing-room door. He fled, knocking into something on his way: an umbrella stand. Who these days had an umbrella stand? Idiotically, he had time for the thought that there were probably umbrellas in it that hadn't been opened in the rain for thirty years. He heard Kate's voice then distinctly, raised to a new sharpness out of its murmuring.

—Who was that?

Someone replied, but he didn't wait to hear.

He waited outside in the car: he couldn't have said how long he waited, nor what he was waiting for. But by the time Firenze's front door banged shut – out of sight, behind the turn in the drive where the house was hidden by the monkey-puzzle tree – he knew who he was expecting to come out. He thought he might have seen, when the light in the drawing room came on, a crumpled khaki jacket thrown untidily down, sleeves half inside out as usual, onto the oak chest in Kate's hall: its familiarity so unconsidered that at first it had hardly seemed to mean anything. Anyway, hadn't he heard the voice?

It was dark: but Jamie, exiting between the brick gateposts, the jacket slung over one shoulder, saw him waiting in the light from the street lamp. He hesitated, but not as if the sight of his father was a surprise; then he crossed over to the car. David stayed sitting in the driver's seat; Jamie came close and leaned against the car heavily on his side – one arm tensed against the car bonnet, the other against its roof, as if he wanted to push it over – staring down through the windscreen. If

Jamie had made any gesture for him to do it, David would have wound the window down: instead they contemplated one another through the glass. The boy was distressed: David didn't know what emotion he showed himself, he had an idea that they reflected one another, that whatever he saw on Jamie's face was his own feeling – only Jamie's hair was blown about by the wind whereas inside the car everything was stale and still. Then Jamie pulled himself upright away from the car and walked off.

David went on sitting there. He knew as if he could see it that Kate waited for him inside the house: she walked around between the rooms, she put all the lights on. One by one windows sprang into brilliance behind the thrashing trees, first downstairs, then upstairs: stained glass flickered like cartoon jewels through agitated foliage. He fantasised that he heard snatches of Kate's violin. Once he had an idea that she came to the front door and looked out for him; even took steps down the drive to where she could see him, stood there hugging her arms in something wrapped round her shoulders, thin dress blowing. But the garden was dark and he couldn't be sure. He heard the wind groaning along the lake, and then at some point an eruption of honking geese, wings cracking like shots, splashing noisily into the invisible water: as if this was David's signal, he started the engine.

On his way home something happened. Naturally he wasn't attending as conscientiously as usual to his

282

driving. There was traffic, it was the winter evening rush hour. The streets were strung already with Christmas lights, and bright shopfronts swam in a blur of the rain that began to be spattered in angry fistfuls across the windscreen. For minutes he peered stupidly, forgetting that he could turn on his wipers. It took him half an hour to get through the thick crawl of cars, woven with crossing pedestrians, on the main roads: released at last into residential streets, he perhaps pressed down his foot too hard on the accelerator, leaping forwards. At the same moment, in a sudden squall of the weather, a white shape in violent movement broke out in front of him from nowhere, or from between two parked cars. He stamped on his brake and swerved, and the car slewed screeching sideways; but surely too late. He must have struck something: the blow seemed to resonate in the bodywork, his heart thumped out of his chest as if he'd been hit himself. He had, in an immense effort, not been thinking of anything: into that willed blankness had burst his fate. He seemed to recognise it, as he threw himself out of the car door to see what he had done, ready for the worst: his fate, that had waited for him in hiding, but whose familiar form he at once knew.

He found nothing. Only an empty street panted, reeled, recovered, closed over what it had shown him. Whatever had seemed white and alive, did not exist; perhaps the sheet of sodden filthy newspaper under his wheels had been his phantom, inflated by the wind into a moment's lifelikeness. He felt so sick that he had to pull in at the side of the road and rest his head against his arms on the steering wheel. For some time he couldn't drive on.

When at last he let himself in at the side door, his children were sitting painting at the kitchen table. Their tranquillity seemed uncanny after the storm outside: their absorbed breathing, the stroke of their marks on big sheets of sugar paper, the chink of their brushes in jamjars of clouding water. The tip of Hannah's tongue stuck out in concentration; unnoticing, Joel sucked his brush, so that his lips were blue. Gazing, to take it truly in, at the china dish piled with tangerines – Suzie must have put it out for them to paint – they seemed themselves deliberate as a composition.

—Is Mummy here?

They blinked at him, surfacing reluctantly.

—Having a shower, Joel frowned.

He took the stairs two at a time. Suzie had begun to tidy up; the mess that had waited on the landing to be sorted into different bedrooms had been put away. She was not showering: she had run herself a bath perfumed with something, she was floating in it by candlelight, her body showing vaguely pink through the foamy water, her knees an island. Little candles on saucers were burning at intervals all round the edges of the tub and on the windowsill. David put down the lid of the toilet seat, for somewhere to sit; Suzie hardly stirred the water, only turning her head to look at him.

—Are you going to be cross?

—Cross?

284

—About the candles. Aren't they dangerous?

He sighed. —Am I so dreary?

—That wasn't what I meant. I'm sure they really are dangerous, only I'm being very careful. But I just wanted to relax. I want to have a nice weekend at home, with you and the kids. David? Are you all right?

—Is Jamie back?

—Back, and gone again, with a bag. He said he was going to Granny Bell's. I didn't know they had anything arranged. You two haven't had a row? David, you're not all right, are you?

He felt himself unreal, as if there were no words for what had happened to him. —I nearly crashed the car on the way home: I thought I saw something.

Suzie stood up in the bath then, water sluicing off her breasts and her thighs; they were still pointed plump girl-breasts, even after two children. She pulled a towel off the heated rail and stepped out; rubbing at her hair to dry it she stood carelessly naked in front of him.

—I'm not really all right, he said.

—I knew another woman had been in the bathroom, said Suzie. —Not in this one, in the en suite. I could smell her perfume: and she'd used my soap. But it's OK. I don't want you to tell me anything about it. We'll leave it like that, shall we? I won't tell you anything either, about me. We won't tell. It'll be better for us, really.

She bent down over him where he sat, wrapping the towel round both of them for a moment, squeezing him in tightly, printing her heated body wetly against his clothes.

285

Twelve

limbing the zigzag path from the road beside the lake, Carol paused at the top not because she was out of breath – she could still tramp twenty miles in the Beacons without noticing it – but to take the place in, because it might be for a last time. In the wintry gardens and the park beyond, the vitality of shrubs and trees was sunk to the root; stiff twigs were silvered, dark clods of earth veneered, in cold sunlight. Footsteps – schoolchildren not dawdling home, the walkers of dogs in little dog-coats – rang iron-hard on the pavements. They had been promised a hard winter; now something in the collective mood, Carol imagined, embraced its austerities. Kate was selling Firenze; she had had an offer already and although it was well below the asking price – the estate agents urged her to wait until after Christmas when the market would improve – she seemed in an unholy hurry to close the deal and be rid of it. Carol was burdened with strong attachments to places as well as people. Robustly pragmatic in her working life, she quailed at the idea of the loss of this fantastical silly house. The purchaser would of course – whatever else to do with it? – convert it into luxury flats: that had happened already to other big houses nearby. (In her professional self, she ought to have wanted to move in several homeless families.) The precious past slipped away in solidities: individual deaths were less visible than the disappearances of fringed blinds at windows, of evening glimpses into rooms where paintings were hung from a picture rail, of summer striped awnings to protect front doors. Firenze had been a last link, not only to her own past.

Kate was supposed to be clearing out, but when Carol came round to help, nothing ever seemed to have moved on: there were a few boxes in the hall, but those were mostly the things Kate had brought down from London anyway, a year ago. Sometimes Carol found her in one of the rooms they hadn't used for decades: the breakfast room, or the room Billie had always called the office, or one of the spare bedrooms. These were dismal with neglect, even if Buckets and Mops had occasionally dusted: in damp corners, papers rotted; woodworm had eaten out of the furniture into the floorboards; carpets smelled where the roof had leaked upstairs. Kate pulled things out from cupboards and drawers, she lost herself in them – roused with a shudder at Carol's arrival, once, from a cache of her parents' letters – then recoiled or grew bored, and left everything heaped on a bed or in the middle of the floor: china tea-sets, tarnished silver cutlery and a menorah, armfuls of damp sheet music,

tomes in Hebrew with pages tissue-paper thin and fron-
tispiece lithographs of venerable rabbinical scholars,
certificates from the 1920's thanking Kate's grandmother
for her donations to Zionist causes, white damask table-
cloths spotted with rust, her father's violin with all its
gut strings snapped and waving.

—It's a treasure trove, said Carol. —You need to have
it all valued; you need an antique dealer to give you an
idea what it's worth. You need to sort out the things
you want for yourself, to keep.

—I know, Kate said. —You're so sensible. But I can't
be bothered.

—The folk museum might be interested in the haberdashery stuff. If you didn't want to sell it.

The rooms in the turret had been locked since Kate
could remember: a pantomime-sized key that had hung
for ever on a hook in the kitchen, labelled mysteriously
'store', had fitted the lock when Carol tried it. Inside, in
two circular rooms joined by a spiral stair, ill-lit through
tiny windows whose frames were so rusted they wouldn't
open, was all the overflow of Sam Lebowicz's business:
in good condition, compared with most of the contents
of the house, perhaps because the rooms had been shut
up so airlessly tight. There were piles of flat boxes of
sample stockings in cotton lisle and silk, one of each kind,
all shades of brown and beige, folded weightlessly between
sheets of tissuepaper: there were also two pink plaster feet
for modelling them, pointing toes fused together. There
were busts, too, their blank faces painted and over-painted
in the styles of different decades; and suspender belts,

knickers, corsets, brassieres, camisoles, liberty bodices, knitting patterns, brown-paper packs of balls of wool, a flutter of invoices. It all smelled of old lavender. For a couple of hours Kate had wondered over all this, exclaiming with delight at the workmanship, the virgin appeal of items untouched, the seductive feminine idea behind this underwear in baby pinks and creams and satins and with tiny buttons, threaded ribbons: in such contrast, surely, to the flawed and bloodied bodies to be stuffed inside them? She lifted up wisps of embroidered silk nightdresses, petticoats: who bought these things? When you thought of what the miners earned, in those days. Dreaming betrothed girls, perhaps; spinster schoolteachers. Then she lost interest and locked the door on it all again.

Carol this time found her dozing on the sofa in the drawing room, wrapped in an eiderdown, with the gas fire full on as well as the central heating. Books – contemporary paperbacks, not old books – were opened face down all around her on the floor.

—How many, Kate? I'm only clever enough to read one book at a time.

—Nothing written now has enough in it. I have to swap about, as soon as I get the hang of what they're up to; they're only ever up to one thing at a time.

—You're full of prejudice. I've read some brilliant new novels recently. Carol, unwinding from her scarf, fighting out of a jumper, pressed notes on the piano. She sighed. —I can't believe Billie isn't going to play it ever again. Without her, the piano's dead too. It used to have such sweet songs in it.

289

—I miss her body heat, Kate admitted. —Even her old body helped: the two of us kept warmer together than I can get by myself now.

—It's sweltering in here. There must be something wrong with you.

—Everything's wrong with me.

Hot-faced, quelling impulses to fling windows open, Carol frowned down at her. —You don't get enough exercise. It's a good thing that you're leaving here, you know.

—You're so unfeeling. You want to be rid of me.

—It breaks my heart, in fact: you'll never know what this place – the two of you in it – has meant for me. I've so loved having you at home this year. But it isn't good for you. I'm glad you're getting out, now there's nothing to keep you. Only I wish I felt confident that you knew what you were going back to in London. Will they give you your old job again? Those people are still in your flat, aren't they?

—There's always Max's. Kate was vague.

—You are joking? You can't go and live at Max's! Not with Sherie there.

—Or there's America.

—America? said Carol. —That's new. Which probably means it's serious. Oh, Kate: America's a long way off!

—Is it? Kate said doubtfully. —I wonder if it's far enough.

—Do you still have your old friends there?

—You mean my lovesick professor? We haven't

spoken in fifteen years: but I may look him up again. Perhaps I've found myself thinking yearningly of him, recently. I might get in touch.

—But wasn't he nuts? Hadn't he taken too much LSD?

Kate's look was sententious. —Time's a great healer.

—Not of blasted synapses. Anyway, he'll be ancient now, he'll be worrying about his pension. If he can still add up.

—Me too, I'm worrying about mine. I ought to settle down, really.

—I suppose you might, sometime. Why do I always expect you to surprise me with the next thing?

—I can't keep the surprises up, you know, just for your entertainment.

—And what will you do with Sim?

—I wanted to ask you about that.

David only saw Kate Flynn once more before she left Cardiff. He knew that she was selling Firenze and leaving, because Carol told him so. When he came with his mother to see *The Marriage of Figaro* at the Millennium Centre he did wonder if Kate would be there: he wouldn't have bought tickets, just in case, but Betty bought them, and then he thought, it's a huge place, the odds are against Kate's coming, but even if she does, we'll miss one another. He tried not to think about Kate at all: it was as if he kept a heavy door shut against what he knew, against what had happened. Whatever he had imagined, sitting outside Firenze that night in his car, he must keep at bay. It was the kind of mess that women like Kate made: better not to know too much, better that the boy had gone to his grandmother's for a while. Apparently Jane was helping him make his university applications. Probably Jamie had had a crush on Kate; they must have met through Carol. David was lucky to have got out of such a tangle. He remembered sitting there in the car, and Kate coming out into the garden, in the dark, in the wind, to look for him; and he had been determined not to make a move, not if she wouldn't come over to him, to explain, to make everything all right again. He tried not to see it all, what an idiot he must have looked, what a puritan, stuck like a dummy in the driver's seat, weltering in his judgement against her. But he couldn't change what he was. He was lucky, really, that it had all come to nothing. His life with Suzie had resumed, they were companionable again, she had moved back into their double bed; he was relieved and grateful.

Betty loved going to the opera with her son. (Bryn couldn't manage opera: too highbrow for him, he said, made him fidgety.) She was dressed up in a new green silk dress, with her best Welsh wool stole; at the first interval they met people they knew and chatted, exchanged Christmas plans. How could his mother actually sound excited about Christmas after so many repetitions, getting the decorations down from the upstairs cupboard, putting them away again? She had her little line about *The Marriage of Figaro*, how pleased she was that they were doing it in proper eighteenth-century costumes; she knew she was old-fashioned, but she hated it when they messed around with the clothes. David went to look for the interval drinks he'd ordered. As he claimed their tray, he looked down over the balcony, behind the great front of the building with its carved-out lines of poetry, to the level below, and saw Kate with a gang of friends, all laughing and noisily declamatory. He recognised the blond American he'd seen at Kate's party, and Ann the viola player. None of them looked up to see him.

David was shocked: he'd somehow pictured Kate as left behind, sad and alone in the old house, mourning. When he'd worried about bumping into her at the opera, he'd imagined her here by herself; instead, she was sitting while the others stood round her, as if she was holding court; she threw back her head at someone's joke and clasped her hands round her knee where her legs were crossed in some kind of dramatic silver-and-black skirt. Light flashed off her angular modern jewellery, her bony shoulders were bare. They were all drinking beer from bottles; relaxed, they made the place their party, so that everyone outside it seemed stiffly polite. One of the crowd sang: exuberantly, badly. Kate sang back; more laughter; then the blond man demonstrated something musical, marking great swoops and patting tiny tensions in the air with his hands. If they irritated David, he couldn't tell himself it was because they were uncultured, or too self-admiringly fashionable; if anything, from his angle on the balcony above, they were collectively interestingly ugly. Kate had had her hair cut, she'd had something else done to it that David didn't like, although he could see that it worked, it was striking: more streaks were added among the dark hairs to her authentic white ones, so that their effect was lost, or multiplied.

This must all do him good, David thought. He had been deluded, imagining he could have ever had any place in this life of Kate's. Her friends were the clever, stylish kind of people he couldn't possibly have kept up with, didn't even like. Fortified, he carried back his mother's sherry and his orange juice (he was driving) to where Betty, queen in her own circle, had meanwhile beckoned across an old friend of his father's, a retired gynae consultant who'd worked for years up at the Heath. David and he stood talking shop until the bell went. These men of his father's generation had so recently ridden the great system under their planted feet, breasting hospital corridors as if waves parted for them: now they were out of the thick of things and all their perspectives had slipped off the point. Their prevailing note, retired, needless to say, was triumphant gloom at every change. (Also: 'public health is nobody's favourite', the consultant said jocularly.) Protective of the man's dignity, David conceded concerns as far as he could without telling any untruth; he was glad when he could subside again beside Betty into the expectancy of the tuning up. He thought the story of *The Marriage of Figaro* was silly, an inferior pretext for the sublime music; often he shut his eyes while he was listening. As soon as he shut them, images of Kate and her friends intruded.

The set for the last act was the least elaborate. Swathes

and swags of fabric, dimly green-lit, were the night-time garden; there was a bench, there was a door, presumably into some grotto or summer house, through which the Count was trying to coax the veiled woman he believed was Susanna. David opened his eyes: he could bear this lightness and vagueness of suggestion better. For the last act, they were right, there must be concentration, the enchantment narrowing to the tiny indefinite space between the lovers. On the bench Figaro and the woman who seemed to be the Countess kissed and cuddled, driving the Count into a frenzy. David found himself drawn in, despite himself, to the familiar twists and turns of misapprehension; the secrets, concealments, longings, devices, trickery, notes fastened with a pin; the promise of joys. Where else did the music come from? The women in their disguises flitted with rustling skirts between the bemused men, their masters. When it was over and the characters hurried away out of the back of the set, hand in hand in pairs as if they escaped into the unseen dark garden, he was bereft. Coming back to take the applause, they were only singers and actors. David's throat was constricted so painfully with sorrow that he couldn't swallow, feeling himself shut out and left behind.

Kate wasn't left with nothing. It was more complicated than that.

One morning, a few days after her last talk with Jamie, when she was still hoping David might ring her, she woke up in all the mess of the unsorted house and knew something she had been trying not to know for weeks.

She had been vomiting in the mornings, she had felt horribly ill, her periods had stopped, her breasts had swollen, she had not wanted to smoke; she had refused to connect these things, or she had told herself they were her signs of shock, at Billie's death, at all the turmoil in her life. But it had begun before Billie's illness, before her stay at the Parrog: how many months, then? It seemed such a stupid accident. Apart from anything else, she was too old, wasn't she, for this? She lay in her bed, in rumpled stale sheets, listening to the cat prowling hungrily in and out of the empty rooms, batting doors open with a disdainful paw. The central heating rumbled into action at the time appointed, then shut down again hours later. The phone didn't ring.

This was her punishment, for living as if life was a playtime, to be made up as you go along. This was sent to smite her, she was smitten – in the Old Testament sense, not the courtship one – by a low blow: to the body of course, where one was always, always weak. She thought of her mother, finding out she was pregnant when she, too, was over forty and must not have expected it: her husband much younger and already sick, fighting her in his rages, drinking, staying out with other women until he could hardly drag himself home to be nursed. Among all the detritus in the house, Kate had never found anything to do with babies: wasn't that odd? Two had been born here – and her grandmother was supposed to have had all those miscarriages and still-births before Billie – but there were no cots or prams or baby clothes, though everything else had been kept, the bikes and school exercise books and tennis racquets from their childhoods. It was as if the babies in this house had been born walking and talking.

Of course, there was no reason for Kate to go through with this (although, how many months was it, already?). She didn't really think she would go through with it. She didn't move, though, from her bed, to telephone her doctor in London who would have been so understanding (he had been understanding once before). Late, late in the afternoon she got up, when the room was dark enough for her to dress without having to catch anything but the palest scrap of her body reflected in the mirrors; scrambling out of her too-skimpy nightdress (she had taken one of the pink silk ones from Sam's store), the night intruding through the window was like gooseflesh on her shoulders. Bent over with cramps and nausea she crept to the shop ten minutes' walk away, tucked in a little sixties brick row out of sight of the dignity of the lake, and bought food for herself: fruit and milk and wholemeal bread and a tin of sardines (when she got home she couldn't bring herself to eat the sardines, so she gave them to Sim). Probably, anyway, this wouldn't last: she hadn't looked after herself, her body wouldn't hold on with any tenacity to what was planted in it, this wasn't the sort of thing she was good at. Something would go wrong. Every time she used the bathroom she expected to find blood.

Max came to stay, to help her pack the place up: although he wasn't all that much use, yielding too easily to the stories in everything, marvelling excitedly, pulling out more and more boxes and bundles from the backs of cupboards. Kate at first stood over him impatiently; then left him to it, went to read her book. She could imagine him spilling out to friends with his charming boy's eagerness, over dinner cooked by Sherie, the story of the fantastic old place: untouched, full of the hoarded treasures of lost lives. She thought of how strenuously David would have cleared out everything for her, wordless, relieved to see the back of the old rot: but that thought winded her like a blow. Mostly she was good, she was good, she didn't allow herself to think of David. She mustn't think of how he hated her, she mustn't open the lid on all that. Blind, she made herself stare at the words of her novel.

Max phoned people he knew who were collectors and dealers, and piled up in the porch a few particular things to take away – some Clarice Cliff, an old pearwood knife box that might have come from Lithuania, that horror of a brass light fitting that had always hung from the hall ceiling, other bits and pieces. Kate knew she would be scrupulously paid for these – overpaid, for anything Max kept for himself – although she didn't care. She swore she didn't want any of it, she would be glad to be rid of it all; even the knife box, which he had thought she might feel tender for, in case it came out of her family's deep past. The volume of belongings left behind didn't seem in the least diminished by what Max had taken out: they wandered round the rooms together, demoralised.

—It reproduces itself when I'm not looking. Like gold into straw. It's like one of those houses in fairy tales where there's always more food on the table, however much you eat. I think I'll just have to start sticking all this into black bags.

—Black bags! You'd need a landfill site.

—Or house clearance. Just let them have the lot.

—You're brave, Katie. Are you sure? There's a whole history intact here. You won't regret letting it go, later?

—Later! Later, I'll be dead.

Kate tried to hide herself from Max; she went before he came to Vidal Sassoon, she used her brightest lipstick, she chose dresses and skirts that hung concealingly across the slight convexity that might be there (that shape was fashionable, luckily: flaring slightly under the bust, falling loose over the waist). Sometimes she thought she was deluding herself; other times her stomach seemed hard and round under her hand, swollen like a nut, not soft as she had expected. She was beginning to feel less ill. She hadn't seen anyone about her problem yet, pretending to herself that if she didn't take any steps in either direction, she was safe: whatever that meant. She hadn't even done a pregnancy test. She and Max went to the opera – Ann had tickets, someone had dropped out from her party – and to the cinema; apparently Sherie had given him leave, for three days he was Kate's. Kate kept up until the end of the last night a performance of her most volubly and outrageously sociable self. They talked about Billie and she was weepy, serene, reconciled. Max's intimate observation of her prickled on her skin (who else knew her so well?); he was almost but not entirely convinced that everything was, miraculously, all right. Tactful, he didn't ask after her amours.

Home from the Arts Centre after the film, he drew the curtains at the windows in the library and asked Kate – crouching over the new-lit gas fire, rubbing at her knuckles yellow with cold – if she wanted coffee. Not coffee, no. She meant to sound lightly considering, not crabbed and nauseous. Max stopped on his way to the door – freshly fair, eager and long, his big camel overcoat hanging open, Paul Smith lilac-and-yellow scarf dangling – to take her in: she looked no doubt witch-like, she knew how her skin was showing her moods transparently. Max might marvel over the thickness of history in this old dark den of hers, but he couldn't have lived in it; wherever Max went he couldn't help shining his tasteful civilising light. She forced herself to her feet, trying to deflect him by smiling, ferociously. Just hot water, perhaps. She'd found herself lately enjoying a cup of hot water at this time of night. Just one of the little cups he'd find on the draining board, with rosebuds and a gold rim. It didn't taste good out of anything else.

—Katie! he exclaimed. —My God! You're pregnant!

Illuminated, he was all wondering generosity, bounding over to scrutinise more closely. —I knew there was something: against the light of the fire, it showed. All along, I've sensed a difference: but this, I'll admit, didn't occur to me. Aren't you? Last night at the opera – it's funny – I kept noticing your breasts in that gorgeous dress you were wearing, but didn't think to wonder why.

He put out his hand to touch: palm curved ready to fit in homage over the little mound that pushed out – she glanced and saw it – through the loose but clingy silk of her top. She pounced – like a rat, she imagined – and seized him by the wrist, holding him off.

—Don't dare, Max! Don't you dare touch me.

—But aren't I right?

—You're talking shit as usual, she said.

He twisted his wrist forgivingly out of her grip. —I am right. It's OK. Don't be mad at me. No one else would have noticed in a million years: it's almost nothing.

—It's nothing.

—No it's not. Don't you think I know you? Is it bad news? Are you sorry?

—Whatever you think you saw, you saw nothing.

She gripped his upper arms tightly in both her hands, pressing her nails in, standing up tensed on her toes in her effort to hurt him as much as he could; he persisted in smiling, as if he couldn't help thinking of happy events.

—Does anyone else know? Have you told your nice doctor man about it yet? I suppose it's his.

She pushed him away hard and caught him off balance so that he stumbled back against the black marble fireplace, slipped, hit his shoulder and cursed, nursing it tenderly; then she subsided again in front of the fire. Max jackknifed his long length down onto the hearthrug beside her, hugging his knees.

—I'm sorry, she said.

—No, I'm sorry. It isn't any of my business.

—Isn't it implausible, though? Me, of all people.

Cautiously, he expressed the feeling he said he'd always had, that pregnant she'd be splendid.

—But whatever you think you know, dear Max, please promise me, for my sake, for ever and ever, that you know nothing.

He was impressed. —Of course I promise. Didn't you think that I could be trusted?

She nodded contritely, patted his knee-top.

—So what are you going to do, then?

It became more definite for Kate as she explained. — I'm going to have it in America. It's going to have an American father.

Max considered that (he might once have hoped to be her baby's American father); in his clear-skinned face his feelings showed in nervous tiny movements of muscle. —That's why, in the future, I mustn't have known that you were pregnant now.

—You see? If I really am, anyway. Because you know, I haven't seen anyone about it.

—Are you happy, Katie?

—Oh: how can you think it? Quite apart from Billie – who to my surprise I miss every minute of every hour – if you knew half the mess I was in . . . But I won't tell you, so don't ask.

—I wish you would.

—It's so odd having to make plans. I'm used to thinking of my life as metaphor: now, this intrusion of real things, schemes and dates and months and concealments.

302

The march of facts, from which I can't extract myself:
contingency.

—It has a kind of grandeur.

—Grandeur? You smooth-talking copywriter. Oh
well, I'll try to cling to grandeur in bad moments, from
now on.

She never got around to cancelling Buckets and Mops,
so from time to time they showed up just when she'd
forgotten to expect them. Kate liked Alison. Faced with
the mythical scale of the mess in Firenze she had never
panicked or abdicated; all the time she'd been coming
(from long before Kate moved home), the rooms they
lived in, at least, had seemed to shine almost as they
must have done in the days when there were maids, even
if behind those surfaces chaos waited. She was Kate's
age and had four children, the youngest fourteen; she
cleaned one day a week to help eke out her student loan
while she finished her degree course in occupational
therapy (she also did bags of other people's ironing).
Her hair was black and wirily curled, her skin was cold
milky coffee with pale freckles; her mother was from
the valleys and her father was from the docks, her grandfather a sailor from Sierra Leone.

When Alison arrived one day, in those last weeks,
Kate had just unearthed from the wardrobe in the master
bedroom a chocolate box heavy with whatever was
inside, held shut with rubber bands so perished that they
shrivelled into dry strings as Kate touched them. The
picture on the top was of a woman in high heels and a

white robe edged in fur, popping into her mouth a chocolate from another box just the same. She looked across it at Alison beseechingly.

—Photographs, Alison said. —That's what people keep in chocolate boxes.

—I won't know anyone. We're not that sort of family. I wish I hadn't found it. I was always relieved there weren't any.

—Go on, it'll be interesting. Won't there be pictures of you and Billie?

—I don't know. Those are all in albums somewhere. Sit with me, will you, please, while I open it? It makes me nervous.

Kate made them both tea then couldn't drink hers; it steamed on the kitchen table while she tugged at the box lid. The box was crammed with photographs; when the lid came unstuck they cascaded out over the table and onto the floor. Rescuing them, Alison marvelled.

—Look, here's Billie! Isn't it? Just a girl – doesn't she look lovely? Look at that outfit! And the hat!

Bracing herself, Kate squinted at it warily from a distance. —And my grandparents. I never knew them. I have seen pictures of them, of course: although not these.

—They're so elegant!

—That's probably the same hotel in Nice where Billie took me when I was a teenager. It really might be: the palms, that stone pineapple thing at the bottom of the steps. If I imagine purgatory, there's always a string trio playing light classics.

The photos came in no order: Billie was a girl, dreamily poignant in a profile portrait (her nose slightly modified?); then a suspicious child in a garden (Firenze?), white-blonde, holding a toy monkey by the ear; then a laughing young woman in Pierrette costume in a crowd of others – gypsies, pirates, clowns – one with a guitar. Billie opened herself eagerly to the camera; her melancholy mother, stoutish, with little gold-rimmed glasses, bore it patiently. On a few occasions Sam Lebowicz, ironic, allowed his likeness to be captured: showing not a sign of his barrow-boy origins, zestfully well dressed as his womenfolk, with a clean-shaven lean face and the high-knuckled cheekbones that you might have attributed to a violinist or a doctor; he only betrayed his business preoccupations (what mess would his people manage to get into, while he submitted to this leisure?) in a right foot, crossed suavely over his other knee, blurred where he quivered it too restlessly. One photograph was of Firenze: disappointing as somehow old photographs of buildings always are, looking hardly different to how it was now except for the lake road empty of cars; the house bleached and withdrawn under shallow light as if it was just a facade. A flag was flying from Sam's turret: what flag, for goodness' sake? No matter how closely they peered, they couldn't make it out.

Under that layer of familiar faces, the box was full of strangers: muddled together, studio portraits from before the first war and snapshots of picnics and parties from the twenties and thirties. A woman with her hair bobbed and little white teeth showing in her smile posed at an upright piano; a boy with a freckled snub-nose had his face licked by a dog, its paws on his shoulders; a middle-aged couple in fur collars strode towards the camera down some broad tree-lined street, in a sunshine that sprang strong shadows. Alison puzzled out the photographer's address, embossed in the bottom right-hand corner, for an unsmiling family group, eight children gazing forwards with huge eyes in mouse-sharp faces, the flashbulb making their parents look staggered, at how excessively they had brought forth and multiplied.

—Sierakowski Street? Alison suggested. —Wilenska Street, this other one. Poland?

—Vilnius, perhaps. In Lithuania, where my grandparents came from. This could be my grandmother in this one, as a girl. But then, so could this one. I suppose they brought some pictures over with them; the others must have been sent afterwards, in letters. They'll be my grandmother's family, not my grandfather's: he made his way up, he came from nowhere, he had nobody.

—You must know who some of these are.

—They all died. Jews, in the war. So I never did know.

—Oh, I see.

—I'm exaggerating slightly. A great-uncle and -aunt, my grandmother's brother and sister, did go to South Africa in the twenties. I believe there are still some of us there. Also, sons of Billie's first cousin went to America, for what was meant to be a short trip, just before war broke out. They stayed; she kept in touch with them for years. I don't know which ones they are, the ones that got away. Billie never showed me these, she didn't like talking about all this. As if she was ashamed.

Alison picked up a few of the photographs and looked at them again, with a different attentiveness. Then, reverently, carefully, she pushed them into a heap in the middle of the table. —What will you do with them?

—I don't know, Kate said. —Shall I take them with me? Do they belong to me?

—I don't know.

Kate walked through the park on her way home from seeing her solicitor. Its first section was unfenced, a long grassed recreation ground marked out in white lines, and with goalposts; a path and a little tamed brook followed along its far edge, beside the road. In the city's lapse, the sky was hugely empty: looking across, big houses on the opposite side (more dilapidated, over there) seemed remote and flat as toys. The path's tarmac was hillocked and cracked by the roots of a long row of towering beeches, planted between the path and the open space; magpies on too-thin dipping twigs did balancing acts with their tails; the cold was a grey-white miasma, although it was not mist, everything was starkly visible. Intermittent between the trees to her left, she was aware of groups of boys, or young men, playing something – rugby? football? – informally in the frozen mud, scratch sides, not in strip, not even full complement. How could they? At the very idea Kate shuddered, drew deeper in under the cashmere stole wrapped up to her nose, so that she breathed her own warm exhalation. Their shouts nonetheless, blunted by the cold, were poetry in the attenuated afternoon; the pounding of their boots on resonant turf reached her as vibrations coming up through the path; they seemed to thud willingly into one another, perhaps for warmth, subsiding in winded grunts (rugby, then): she felt herself by contrast cocooned in cold inside her warm clothes, separate.

In her black-and-white coat, she must have flickered distinctively between the trees, if anyone was watching. A gang of boys in tracksuit bottoms and T-shirts were playing football; they weren't very good, mucking about and joking, their language blue. You knew this was a whim and not a practice. One figure detached itself to stare at her: she didn't stop, but he must have seen her turn her head, looking back at him. For long seconds he stared; of course anyone knowing her would recognise her, in that coat. His friends noticed, glanced over, weren't interested (too old! – even at this distance), and cursed: get on the fucking ball! Kate carried on without faltering; she had to look back at the path so that she didn't trip over the tree roots. It did seem possible that it was Jamie. He must have played football sometimes, in another life, with other boys.

When she looked back, she wasn't even sure which one had stared; they were all running again now. Two of them were in black T-shirts; both, from this distance, had Jamie's young grace and long hair. It could have been either of them. She hurried, looking at her watch (the park gates closed soon) into the second section of the park, with howling green and tennis courts, the brook meandering under a mossy bridge like a stage set from an old operetta; she dropped onto one of the benches in memory of somebody or other who had loved this place. An intimate stirring and ticking sounded from all around and seemed like a subtle sign, a message for her, before she understood what it was: the first warning raindrops falling on shrubby evergreen groundcover. She ought to go. Could that really have been Jamie? She might have only imagined it. She could have begun to think she had imagined the whole thing, everything that had happened to her here, if it hadn't been for the child planted inside her. The reality of the child was vivid for the first time, distinct as a ghost from the future approaching on the path, scrutinising her frowningly out of unknown eyes. It would be a girl, surely. She was bound to have a daughter.

And then the rain came down in earnest. Kate put up her umbrella and hurried on through winter suburban streets where the water ran noisily, purging and cleansing, rousing a perfume from the compost and the tarmac, gurgling into drains, backing up into pools behind block-ages of dead leaves and pine needles, soaking her feet through her unsuitable shoes.

Acknowledgements

Thanks to Shelagh Weeks, Richard Francis, Richard Kerridge and Sara Hayes, who read drafts of this novel, and whose advice was not only invaluable but also taken. And thanks to Dan Franklin and Caroline Dawnay, for everything.